Georgiana Darcy, Matchmaker

A Pride and Prejudice Alternative

by

Bronwen Chisholm

HARVESTDALE
PRESS

Some passages in this novel are paraphrased from the works of Jane Austen.

Cover art by Richenda Janeen (Klepper) Hershey, Artist/Illustrator/Graphic Designer.

ACKNOWLEDGEMENTS AND DEDICATION

As always, I must begin by acknowledging the muse herself, Jane Austen. The characters she created have touched so many over the years. I humbly offer my attempt in the hopes that it brings some joy.

Thank you to my beta reader, MK Baxley, and the devoted readers at BeyondAusten.com and AustenUnderground.com. Your assistance, as always, is indispensable.

The idea for this story began after listening to my 13-year-old daughter, Julianna, discussing her friends' relationships, and how she put a finger in here and there to get them on the right path. Georgiana's attitude, insecurities, and childlike spirit were inspired by the beautiful changes I see in Julianna as she grows and matures faster than her father and I would want. As much as she is determined to rebel and not like anything Jane Austen, this one is for her.

Chapter One

Netherfield Park
Hertfordshire

My Dearest Georgie,
I cannot tell you how pleased I was to receive your letter. It appears Mrs. Annesley is very devoted to your improvement of both mind and spirits. I believe I shall be quite satisfied with her practices.

Forgive me, my dearest, but Miss Bingley is insistent that I express her desire to see you again. I am certain she will continue to eject comments throughout, but I beg you would understand the reasons behind her requests and excuse me from further bowing to them.

My time with Bingley has been quite productive. I believe his knowledge of estate affairs is increasing sufficiently that I might be able to rejoin you in London sooner than originally anticipated. I only fear leaving him alone amongst the local gentry.

As we have discussed in the past, Bingley is apt to fall in love hastily wherever he goes, and Hertfordshire is no different. The lady in question is the eldest daughter of a landed gentleman. The ladies, there are five sisters in all, are lovely; but they have few connections and relatives in trade.

Of course, you are aware of my intentions to only marry for true affection; having seen first-hand how unfulfilling a marriage of convenience can be in the matches of our parents and other relations. Therefore, I would wish the same for my friend. My fear is this particular young lady's heart remains unaffected. Certainly her look and manners are open, cheerful and engaging, but without any symptom of peculiar regard. She behaves as any young lady of breeding should, but

Forgive me again, my Precious. You must understand that Miss Bennet, the young lady to whom Bingley is showing such attention, took ill in his home this Tuesday past and her sister has come to care for her. Where Miss Bennet is all that is proper, her sister is a bit more spirited than is fashionable. Miss Bingley has deemed her unworthy, perhaps due to a misguided comment I made regarding her fine eyes. Be that as it may, Miss Elizabeth Bennet and Bingley began a discussion based on one of his sister's many compliments to my person, and I was forced to respond. I am now completely unaware of what I meant to say before I was interrupted.

I have never met such a person as Miss Elizabeth. She is both enticing and irritating. Though we appear to begin well enough, it seems every conversation devolves into an insult or attack. I fear I come away feeling quite out of sorts, yet desirous to engage her quick wit once more.

I believe it is best that I return to London at the earliest available date. Once Bingley is secure, I will notify you of my anticipated arrival. Until that time I remain,
Your Affectionate Brother,
Fitzwilliam Darcy

Absent-mindedly I tapped my finger against the edge of the fine stationery as I looked unseeingly about the room. My companion noticed my distraction and cleared her throat discreetly. My gaze returned to the older woman at my side in time to see her smile.

"Forgive me, Mrs. Annesley, I was contemplating my brother's latest letter." I gently bit my lower lip as my thoughts wandered once more.

"Is there cause for concern?" she asked.

I am certain she noticed I was behaving unusually. Normally when I receive a letter from my

6

brother I am exceedingly pleased and read it aloud. Not so today; he had given me too much to consider.

"I do not believe so, but I fear my brother may make an error in judgement." I turned toward Mrs. Annesley, having made a decision and imperturbably asked, "Have we any engagements in the next week?"

"We are to attend tea with your aunt, the Countess of Matlock, on Thursday, and we had discussed visiting the museum but had not set a definite day." Mrs. Annesley set down her needlework and studied me closely.

"Then if we were to decide to visit my brother in Hertfordshire, we need only send word to Lady Matlock that we shall be unable to attend tea."

"Is Mr. Darcy not visiting Mr. Bingley? It is highly questionable to invite yourself to another's home." Her brow arched as she awaited my response.

"Oh, but Mr. Bingley did invite me."

"You are certain?"

I began to wonder just how high Mrs. Annesley was capable of raising her brow as it continued its accent. "I was in the room when Mr. Bingley invited Fitzwilliam and he included me. Fitzwilliam stated I had other engagements, as he knows Miss Bingley can be quite overbearing. We discussed it after Mr. Bingley left and I agreed there would be little for me to do in Hertfordshire, therefore I remained in London."

Mrs. Annesley peered suspiciously over her spectacles as she pursed her lips. "Your opinion has now changed?"

"Yes, I believe it has." I took up the letter and perused it once more. "Indeed, I believe it best that we leave as soon as possible. Might we be ready to depart tomorrow before midday?"

"So soon? I must ask again, is there cause for concern?"

With a great sigh, I reluctantly read the letter aloud before concluding, "I fear Fitzwilliam is running away, and I have never known him to do so. I wish to meet this Miss Elizabeth Bennet for myself. You must see that if he returns to London, I may never have the opportunity."

"Do you believe Mr. Darcy would approve of your travelling to Hertfordshire? Might he not be displeased?" Mrs. Annesley asked, though the way her eyes narrowed made me hope she was contemplating what need be done for us to leave so quickly.

"He shall certainly be surprised." I felt the corners of my lips turn upward mischievously as I considered Fitzwilliam's reaction when he saw me in his friend's home. "I believe he will enjoy a respite from Miss Bingley's attentions."

"Well then, I suppose we must speak with Mr. Barnes to determine if arrangements can be made immediately."

Overjoyed, I hugged her before nearly skipping to the bell pull to summon the butler. If my suspicions were correct, I may very well be travelling to meet my future sister.

I had longed for this day for quite some time. My only fear was that Miss Elizabeth Bennet would not like me. From Fitzwilliam's letter, it was clear the lady was nothing like the Miss Bingleys of the *ton*. I always knew my brother would not take interest in any of the pompous members of the first circles. He seemed determined to find someone who would meet our family's expectations, but also touch his heart. I had begun to doubt such a person existed.

Mrs. Annesley and I had left the door open after we entered the front parlour, and Mr. Barnes now stepped into the room and bowed. "How may I be of service, Miss Darcy?"

"Mr. Barnes, I have decided to join my brother in Hertfordshire. Could you make the appropriate arrangements?"

The older butler eyed me suspiciously. "I believe that can be arranged, Miss. When would you like to depart?"

"Tomorrow, if possible?" My previous confidence began to wane and I twisted my fingers at my waist. I had never been comfortable asking for things, and my experiences of the last summer had made me realize how immature I truly was. I often felt the servants knew it.

"I see. Yes, I believe all could be readied by then." He hesitated and glanced toward Mrs. Annesley; but she, angel that she is, maintained a serene expression. He returned his gaze to me. "Forgive me, Miss Darcy, but is anything amiss?"

"No, Mr. Barnes, I simply wish to see my brother." I attempted a nonchalant air, but fairly quivered with suppressed excitement. I simply had to travel to Hertfordshire as soon as possible.

"Very well, Miss Darcy. I shall speak to the driver and have everything readied." Barnes bowed and left the room as I released the breath I had been holding.

Mrs. Annesley tied off her thread and put her needlework into her basket. "I suppose we should see to having our things packed. Have you decided how long we will be staying in Hertfordshire?"

This I had not considered, and a sudden feeling of unease passed over me. "I had not, only of getting there as quickly as possible." I tried to remember how long my brother was staying. "I believe Fitzwilliam originally intended on remaining there through the end of November; he mentioned returning in time to travel to Pemberley for the holidays. I suppose we could prepare to do the same?" I looked questioningly at my companion.

Happily, Mrs. Annesley smiled as she stood and crossed to my side. Her comforting arm slipped about my shoulders as she nodded. "That is a very wise decision, Miss Darcy. I am certain there will be house parties to attend, consequently, you must pack accordingly. As you are not yet out, you will not be expected to participate in all the activities Mr. Bingley and your brother may choose."

We climbed the stairs to our rooms, both of us lost in our thoughts; I of what awaited us in Hertfordshire, my companion, I know not what. My unease regarding Elizabeth Bennet's opinion crept over me once more. As I entered my room, I shook myself in an attempt to dispel the thought and smiled brightly at Mrs. Annesley.

"I believe this is a good decision, do you not? It would be unwise of my brother to leave if this lady is …," I faltered, suddenly unable to find the proper words to complete my thought.

Mrs. Annesley smiled and patted my hand. "Your brother will be pleased to see you, and it is good for you to make new friends. I have a suspicion the Bennet ladies are unlike the women you have met thus far in your life. For Miss Elizabeth to have your brother unsettled, leads me to believe our time will be entertaining, if nothing more." She paused, giving me a wicked grin. "I believe it may be beneficial for you to see your brother in such a state. As you love him dearly, you see him without fault. I fear no man, or woman for that matter, is such."

"Fitzwilliam is not without fault, I know; but he is a wonderful brother and I believe he will be an affectionate husband someday. I only want him to find someone who will love him for the man that he is, not his rank in society or the proposition of being the Mistress of Pemberley." A sigh escaped me and I squeezed her hand. "I have brought him such distress. If I can see him happy, I shall feel redeemed."

"You know he does not ---"

"I know what you are about to say. I was a foolish child. Fitzwilliam and I have discussed it and he has taken the blame upon himself. He decided I was too sheltered and therefore easily led astray." I suddenly felt very weary, unable to hold my rigid posture, and I slipped into the closest chair.

"Your brother was wise, if uncommon, in deciding to share more with you after your experiences at Ramsgate."

Nodding, I slowly began to smile. "I am certain he tells me things now he would never have shared before. I believe he might have mentioned Miss Elizabeth, but he would not have expressed his opinion of her as he has." Determinedly, I sat a bit straighter. "I must show him I have improved and am able to be of assistance to him." Feeling a bit impish, my smile grew. "After all, men can also be led astray; they do not consider their emotions as thoroughly as women do."

Mrs. Annesley nodded as she turned to leave the room. "You are correct, of course. Shall we dine early this evening?"

"Yes, I believe that would be best." I stood and crossed to the dressing room where I could hear Hannah, my maid, moving about. Clearly word had already spread through the staff regarding our impending journey. My earlier excitement returned and I entered to choose which items would accompany me.

Chapter Two

As the Darcy carriage entered the town of Meryton, I leaned excitedly toward the window. When we stopped an hour prior, the driver had told me the next town was the last before reaching Netherfield Park.

"This must be it; this must be Meryton." I grinned at Mrs. Annesley.

"Yes, I believe you are correct," she replied as she nodded toward a sign reading Meryton Inn and exchanged a knowing glance with Hannah who sat to her left.

I was unable to suppress my giggles and watched the pedestrians wandering about the town. "It appears the Army is in residence. I have never seen so many officers in the streets of such a small town." Turning, I glanced out the other side of the coach and gasped. "Look! It is Fitzwilliam!"

My brother had obviously not seen the coach as he was focused on a group of people standing upon the boardwalk. I was about to call for the carriage to stop when I noticed him stiffen and saw a grimace flash across his countenance. Just as the carriage was moving out of sight of him, I saw him begin to move away from the group.

"That was odd," I murmured.

"Shall we stop the carriage?" Mrs. Annesley asked, obviously unaware of what I had seen.

"I do not believe we should." Fitzwilliam's reactions were so out of character.

As the thought crossed my mind, the carriage did indeed draw to a halt and the door opened suddenly.

"Georgie? What the devil are you doing here?" My brother appeared concerned and displeased. His voice was louder than normal and there was a hint of annoyance I had never heard before.

"I wished to surprise you," I mumbled, casting my eyes down to my lap in an attempt to avoid witnessing his anger.

From the corner of my eye, I could see him shift slightly, and I thought he might be looking behind him. Tilting my head somewhat, I determined he was looking back toward the group he had just left and I wondered who they might be.

"Bingley, I will be riding in the carriage to Netherfield." Fitzwilliam stepped away from the door to tie his horse to the carriage, before returning and climbing inside, closing the door behind him.

I slid over to make room for him beside me as he began lowering the shades on the windows. "I thought you would be pleased to see me," I whispered, choking back tears. Suddenly my newfound confidence slipped away and I was once more his younger nuisance of a sister.

He sighed. "Forgive me, my dearest. Any other time, I am certain I would be extraordinarily pleased to see you." He took a deep breath as he placed a hand over mine. "I have just this moment learned Mr. Wickham is here in Meryton."

"Here?" My voice squeaked as I forced the word out. Swallowing, I raised my eyes to his and attempted again, hoping to hide the surprise and concern from him. "Why ever would Mr. Wickham be in Meryton?"

Fitzwilliam's lips formed a thin line before he spoke. "I do not know, but I am determined to learn his reasons. Until then, I believe it best if you return to London as soon as possible."

"No."

"I beg your pardon?" Fitzwilliam turned his entire body toward me.

Taking a deep breath, I glanced across at Mrs. Annesley. She smiled and gave a slight nod, giving me the added encouragement I required to address my brother. Turning back to him, I met his incredulous gaze.

"I have reason for my journey, and I shall not return to London until I am satisfied."

The corner of Fitzwilliam's lips twitched ever so slightly as he also looked toward my companion. From the corner of my eye, I could see Mrs. Annesley had returned to her reading and Hannah had become preoccupied with her needlework. I waited patiently for my brother to question me.

"Precisely what are your reasons, Georgiana?" he asked, a bit of humour evident in his tone.

Forcing myself not to waver, I lifted my chin and spoke as forcefully as I could. "I believe you are about to make a most disastrous error and I wish to stop you."

The startled expression upon his countenance nearly undid me. Biting gently upon my lower lip, I fought the urge to smile.

"And what exactly is the 'error' that I am about to make?"

"In your last letter, you announced your intentions to leave Netherfield at the earliest date in order to avoid ..." suddenly I realized it would not be proper to discuss this in front of Hannah or Mrs. Annesley. I glanced their way and back to my brother before deciding upon the correct way to broach the topic. "A certain young lady. It appears to me this will only add to your unease regarding her."

Watching his growing incredulity caused my nerves to begin to overwhelm me and I looked down at my gloves in an attempt to steady myself. "I believe it would be best if you learned all you could regarding this lady so you may make an intelligent decision regarding your future and not ... oh what is it Richard says? Ah, turn tail and run."

"I ... I ..." Unable to find the response for which he searched, my brother turned forward in his seat, refusing to look at me. I could tell he was attempting to regain some semblance of equanimity, but was not certain how successful he would be. Finally, he released a huff and turned back toward me.

"Firstly, I did not say I was leaving Netherfield to avoid ..." he too glanced toward the servants and back, "the lady."

"Perhaps not, but the reasoning was clear."

"Secondly," he said a bit louder, clearly beginning to lose his temper, "I do not feel this is any concern of yours."

"Your choice of wife is not my concern?" I stared at him, aghast.

"Choice of wife? Whatever are you saying? I have no intentions of proposing to Miss Elizabeth Bennet," he sputtered, clearly having completely forgotten the others' presence for a moment.

Remembering himself, Fitzwilliam turned his full attention upon Mrs. Annesley. "Madam, perhaps you might be able to enlighten me regarding my sister's unfounded remarks. I was under the impression you were employed to give her a sense of veracity, not add to her fantasies."

Before she could respond, I leapt to her defense. "That is unfair, Fitzwilliam, and unkind. Mrs. Annesley has been perfection. It was my decision to come to Netherfield to meet Miss Bennet and her family, based upon the letter *you* wrote. I have noticed a change in your writing since you came here and I believe she is the reason. Now," I looked forward and sat perfectly straight, "if we are not allowed to remain at Netherfield, we shall simply take rooms at the Meryton Inn."

Fitzwilliam cursed softly under his breath. "You shall do no such thing; however, Georgiana, we are not finished with this discussion." I looked at him in time to see a smirk cross his lips. "I am certain Miss Bingley will be overjoyed to see you and monopolize your time for the remainder of the day. Shall we meet before dinner in your rooms to relieve any of your concerns regarding my future happiness?"

"That will be acceptable," I replied coldly.

The carriage slowed and stopped. We all sat in an awkward silence, waiting for the door to be opened and the steps lowered. Fitzwilliam left the carriage first. I gathered my things and moved closer to the door, but waited while he appeared to take in the surroundings. Finally, he turned back and offered his hand to assist me from the equipage.

His silence continued as we walked together into the house; Mrs. Annesley followed closely behind us having been assisted by the footman. Anyone looking upon us would recognize the tensions; any, that is, but our hostess.

Miss Bingley glided out of the drawing room, exclaiming her joy over us, her guests. "Why Miss Darcy, what a wonderful surprise. I only just received your express alerting me of your impending arrival. Your rooms are not yet ready. Please," she took Fitzwilliam's other arm, "join me in the drawing room for a cup of tea while you wait."

In the most polite manner possible, Fitzwilliam extricated his arm from her grasp and bowed to us. "Forgive me, Miss Bingley, but I have business to which I must attend." He turned coldly toward me. "We shall speak before dinner?"

I nodded. "Of course, Brother."

Fitzwilliam replied with a single nod and walked away from the group.

"Well, that is very unlike him." Miss Bingley startled, possibly realizing she had spoken the words aloud. She appeared to recover quickly. "I fear your brother has not been himself since our arrival in Hertfordshire. I believe it would be best if we all returned to town, but Charles is insistent that we must remain."

She linked arms with me and, without acknowledging Mrs. Annesley, turned toward the drawing room. "I ordered tea a few moments before you arrived so it should be brought in at any time. While we wait you can tell us all we have missed since we came away from London."

I took a breath to speak, but apparently she was not quite finished.

"Louisa and I have been so terribly miserable in this backwater country. The local gentry are simply intolerable. There is no style, no taste, no beauty. Their families are positively wild! How I long to return to town." Miss Bingley turned toward me and smiled; a false, ingratiating smile which turned my stomach. "I am so pleased you have chosen to join us. Mr. Darcy and Charles have been besieged by ladies hoping to increase their standing in society by vying for our association, as if we would condescend to a connection with them. It is simply disgraceful how they behave. With your presence, we shall be much less likely to attend social gatherings, and perhaps we will be able to persuade Charles to return to more sophisticated society."

"I fear I must disappoint you, Miss Bingley." I held myself stiffly, making no attempt to hide my displeasure. "I purposely left London to meet a few of the individuals my brother has mentioned in his letters. I believe I shall quite enjoy my time in Hertfordshire." Donning my sweetest smile, all the while knowing it appeared contrived, I continued. "Oh, but you must have forgotten, Pemberley is in the country, and my brother and I quite prefer it to town."

Miss Bingley's false laughter rang in the air. "Of course, I am aware Pemberley is in the country; but that is Derbyshire. The views are so majestic, and Pemberley is without rival. I understand your preference completely." Her smile slipped slightly, and she turned toward her sister, Mrs. Louisa Hurst. "Louisa and I were just talking of Pemberley and expressing how we long to visit there again. We are quite distracted by the thought of it as we are reasonably certain it is lovely in December."

I am well accustomed to individuals attempting to garner invitations to my home from my years of schooling. I also understand the best way to address the attempts is by ignoring them or changing the subject. "Yes, I believe it is my favourite time of year. Though in summer I am certain I would say that was my favourite. I suppose Fitzwilliam and I would simply *always* prefer to be in the country." I turned to take Mrs. Annesley's arm and moved toward a settee just big enough for the two of us.

Miss Bingley frowned before taking a seat nearby. "Oh, I am certain you exaggerate. Though I suppose it may be because you are not yet out. Once you are able to fully enjoy society, you may never wish to leave London."

"I sincerely doubt it. Neither Fitzwilliam nor I are comfortable amongst crowds of people. We prefer smaller settings, intelligent discussions, and quiet, peaceful moments. We find gossip despicable." Feeling a smile tug at my lips, I turned once more toward my companion. "Though Mrs. Annesley and I have taken advantage of our time in London to visit several exhibits."

Miss Bingley opened her mouth as though to respond, but her sister quickly interrupted her. "You must tell us all about them. Hopefully we will be able to attend a few if we return to London in time."

"Oh, I am certain several will be in residence into the Season." I went on to speak of my time in London, focusing mostly upon Mrs. Annesley, but including Mrs. Hurst and, when unable to avoid it, Miss Bingley.

It is not that I thoroughly dislike Caroline Bingley. Indeed, the woman can be entertaining, if she did not think so highly of herself and were she to relinquish her expectations of marrying my brother. As she has not yet done so, and in fact it appears to fill her every waking hour, it is obvious she sees me as a means to an end and nothing more; something else schooling has taught me to expect.

Mrs. Louisa Hurst, on the other hand, is married and holds no expectations of my family. Though she is a bit empty-headed and fidgety, always playing with her bracelets, at least she is not apt to praise me repeatedly for little purpose. She is simply content to accompany her brother in visits to Pemberley in order to brag of it to her friends.

Eventually the tea arrived and discussion returned to the neighbourhood. Miss Bingley was determined to think ill of all she saw, but Mrs. Hurst did allow there were a few intriguing individuals in the surrounding area. She spoke mostly of welcoming hostesses or fine figured men, making me smile as I thought of the lady's rather expansive husband.

Finally, the housekeeper, Mrs. Nicholls, entered and announced our rooms had been prepared and we could refresh ourselves. Mrs. Annesley and I both stood, eager to be away from the sisters.

"Miss Bingley, if you would excuse us? I believe we would prefer to rest until dinner."

"Of course." Miss Bingley stood and curtseyed properly, irritation written upon her face.

We followed the housekeeper from the room, but were only a few steps from the door when we heard Miss Bingley express dismay regarding the changes which had overcome me and her assumption the cause must be placed at the feet of my loathsome companion. Mrs. Nicholls was clearly embarrassed by her mistress, and increased the speed of her steps so we would be out of hearing before more could be said.

I, for one, was not surprised, and instead found Miss Bingley a bit amusing. Her earlier comments regarding socially ambitious ladies had nearly caused me to choke upon my tea as I was certain her words were more descriptive of her own actions than any she had observed in others.

We reached our rooms and parted ways. I requested the housekeeper notify my brother I was available whenever he was ready to speak with me before entering my dressing room to find Hannah busily unpacking my trunks. After changing, I took a seat by the window and stared out at the beauty of the countryside, impatiently waiting for him to arrive.

Chapter Three

"Georgiana, you must realize the danger of your remaining in this neighbourhood."

I doubt I had ever seen my brother as frustrated with me as he was now; even this past summer.

As if reading my mind, he continued, "If Mr. Wickham learns you are here, he might speak of what occurred at Ramsgate."

"It was my understanding, Brother, you made it abundantly clear to him that any mention of the incident would be unfavourable to him alone. Why do you believe he would reveal it now?" I sat calmly, my hands folded properly in my lap, and prayed my rigid posture hid my unease.

"Mr. Wickham is unpredictable at best; I prefer we have no contact with him. I fear the damage he could do." Fitzwilliam paced the length of the sitting area and returned.

"Have you learned why he is here?" I asked, looking down at my hands, in an attempt to hide my insecurity.

"No." He knelt at my feet and took my hands in his, running his thumbs over the backs of them. "You understand my concern?"

I drew a long, deep breath and raised my eyes to his. "Perhaps he has joined the army. There appears to be a regiment in the area."

"It is the militia. I know not how he could have afforded it and he was not in uniform." Fitzwilliam shook his head, obviously convinced the man could only mean us harm.

"I do not wish to leave." I heard the whine which entered my voice and thrust out my chin in defiance. "Not until I meet the Bennets."

Fitzwilliam released an exasperated sigh. "I do not understand your fascination with them. I swear to you there is nothing between Miss Elizabeth Bennet and myself." Releasing my hands, he pushed up from the floor and turned toward the window, twisting his signet ring, something he always did when unsettled. I knew my brother well. I was close to the mark.

"I do not believe you." I knew it was childish, but I continued to pout. He was being so unreasonable and obtuse.

His jaw dropped open in amazement as he turned about to look at me. "You do not believe *me*? I am your brother; have I ever deceived you?"

The heat rose in my cheeks, as I was suddenly ashamed for speaking to him in this manner. He was nearly a father to me and I owed him my respect. "No," I whispered as I lowered my eyes once more.

"Georgie, I fear I must be insistent on this matter. I do not want you anywhere near Mr. Wickham."

"Will you warn the people of Meryton regarding his ways?" I asked, still unable to meet his gaze.

Fitzwilliam hesitated causing me to finally lift my eyes to see the reason for his delay; then he shook his head. "I fear it would only draw attention to your situation, my dearest."

The small hairs on the back of my neck stood on end as I stared at him. "How? If you spoke of his past indebtedness or gambling, especially in Lambton, how could that lead anyone to know of my indiscretion at Ramsgate?"

"Mr. Wickham may speak of it in retribution for my demeaning his character." His voice held a hint of defeat that I had not heard before. I was seeing so much more of my brother than I had ever seen in the past.

I considered his words and found merit in them. "But you will speak of him to the Bennets?"

His brow drew together and he frowned. "The Bennets? Whatever for?"

"Why to warn them, of course. Would you allow Miss Elizabeth Bennet and her family to be seduced by his words as I was?" I looked incredulously at him, shocked he would allow Mr. Wickham such liberty. "You must protect them, Brother. You know you must!"

Fitzwilliam's frown transitioned into a scowl. "I dislike revealing our personal interests to strangers."

"Well if you are unwilling, then I shall do it." I sat taller, determined not to concede.

"You shall do no such thing! I forbid it!"

"Fitzwilliam, I shall not return to London until I have met Miss Elizabeth Bennet, determined your intentions toward her, and made certain Mr. Wickham is unable to harm her or her family." Thrusting my chin outward in a manner that I knew mimicked his own, I crossed my arms and waited for his response.

I watched as my brother's frustration increased. He opened his mouth to speak once or twice, but shook his head repeatedly instead. Finally, he stood directly in front of me and met my gaze with something just short of vexation.

"Once you meet Miss Elizabeth Bennet you will return to London?"

Surprised he had relented so quickly, I simply nodded my agreement.

"Very well." He glanced at his timepiece before returning it to his pocket. "Miss Elizabeth Bennet is a most enthusiastic walker. During her stay at Netherfield I noted she walked every morning. I believe we may encounter her if we were to ride out tomorrow morning. Early."

"How early?" I asked reluctantly as a sense of dread filled my stomach.

A wicked grin crossed his lips. "Miss Elizabeth and I appear well suited in regards to our morning habits; we are both early risers. To speak truth, I believe she has broken her fast before me on several occasions."

I could not suppress my moan, but refused to relent. "What time must I be ready to leave?"

"I shall escort you to breakfast at half past seven."

He stood before me in a smug manner and waited for my response, clearly hoping I might decline, but I was resolved not to give him the satisfaction. "Very well. I shall have Hannah press my riding habit." Rising from my chair, a thought struck me and I paused. "Does Miss Elizabeth not ride?"

"No, I am uncertain if it is due to a lack of available horses or because she prefers to walk. Her sister rode to Netherfield the day she took ill, but Elizabeth walked the following day." His eyes had taken on a glazed appearance while he spoke, as though he were remembering something, and I was certain he was unaware of his slip in using her Christian name.

I turned away quickly in order to hide my smile. I was now completely convinced; my brother was in love with Miss Elizabeth Bennet. Perhaps she would be able to convince him that I should stay.

****

Suppressing another yawn, I looked out over the fields of Netherfield. Only the prospect of meeting Miss Elizabeth Bennet was sufficient to draw me from my bed on a brisk autumn morning, or any morning for that matter; but I was determined to appear in good spirits. I would not allow my brother to witness my lethargy. "Mr. Bingley has found a lovely bit of land."

"It will do nicely, for now."

Confused, I glanced back at him. "For now? Do you believe he will not remain here?"

A blush covered Fitzwilliam's countenance. "Georgie, Bingley may eventually find the society less than he originally imagined."

"But I thought you said he was quite taken with Miss Bennet. You made me promise not to disclose our destination this morning for fear Mr. Bingley would wish to accompany us. Why would he change his mind?"

I could see his unease, but refused to release his gaze. He would answer me or I would simply continue to ask.

Fitzwilliam sighed as he turned, showing a sudden interest in the fields. "Mr. Bingley may yet be persuaded Miss Bennet is unsuitable."

Once more I was filled with surprise and a bit of displeasure toward my brother. "And who might wish to persuade him of such a thing?" Before he could respond, I answered the question hoping I was correct. "Oh, his sisters would not be pleased to have Miss Bennet as a relation, I am certain. I was shocked by the way they spoke of their neighbours last evening. I thought Mr. Bingley would censor them."

"Mrs. Hurst is older than he, and I doubt Miss Bingley has ever taken anyone's counsel, including their parents." Fitzwilliam spurred his horse forward, clearly in an attempt to avoid the subject. I followed.

"But he is the head of their family."

"Quite so, and he must assert his authority at some time."

"And would his choice of bride not be a sensible opportunity? You must advise him to do so, Brother." I was about to push my horse into a canter when I noticed his hesitation. "Fitzwilliam, you do not agree with Mr. Bingley's sisters, do you?

He turned away from me and pointed toward a group of trees. "I believe we may have the best opportunity to meet Miss Bennet in that wooded area."

"Fitzwilliam?" I coaxed my horse before him and drew to a halt. "Are you ignoring my question?" He turned and reluctantly met my eye. "You are, because you do agree with them." I felt my jaw drop as my incredulity grew.

"Georgie, I have told you of their connections …"

"Yes, but Mr. Bingley's father was in trade, and Miss Bennet is a gentleman's daughter. I do not understand how that is an unsuitable match. Please, explain it to me." I crossed my arms and waited.

Fitzwilliam sighed and looked longingly toward the trees. "If Bingley is to have any hope of advancing in society, he must marry from the first circles."

Tossing my head back, I urged my mount forward. "I have never thought that to be Mr. Bingley's objective. Truly, Fitzwilliam, in your letter you stated you want only your friend's happiness, but when it is before him, you are ready to discourage it. I do not understand, unless it is due to your own feelings for Miss Elizabeth Bennet. Brother, do you think her unsuitable for you because her father is a county gentleman?" I paused and watched him closely as he said nothing, and then I pressed my point. "Our father was merely a country gentleman when he married Mother.""

"Georgie," his voice held a warning. "I will say once more; I do not have feelings for Miss Elizabeth. You must release these misguided ideas."

A motion in the woods drew my attention and I spurred my horse faster. As we reached the wall separating properties, I took position to jump and sailed over it easily.

"Georgiana Darcy! You know not where you are going, I insist you wait for me!"

I watched as my brother followed me over the wall, turning in time to see a small feminine figure just as he landed. The surprise which suffused his features was enough to draw my laughter. The woman's shocked response was equally amusing.

"Miss Bennet," Fitzwilliam attempted to rein in his horse who wished to continue on.

"Mr. Darcy." The lady curtseyed properly, though her eyes filled with merriment.

A thrill ran through me. The lady before me was exactly what I had pictured. Elizabeth Bennet was not as tall as me, and most likely would not be considered beautiful by the *ton*. Her dress and pelisse were not of the current fashion, and she had removed her bonnet during her walk so the curls, which had escaped their pins, bounced wildly about her. No, I could understand why Fitzwilliam was adamant this Bennet would not be easily accepted by our society for she was a free spirit, not polished like the ladies of the *ton*.

That being said, when I looked into the dancing, mischievous eyes of the lady before me, I knew immediately that, given the opportunity, we could be the closest of friends. Miss Elizabeth Bennet was nothing if not high-spirited. The perfect complement to my brother's staid, serious manner.

I cleared my throat to gain his attention and he startled from his thoughts. I had to wonder if he always stared at her in that unsettling manner.

"Fitzwilliam, will you not introduce me?" I urged as he appeared to be awakening from a dream.

He cleared his throat and drew himself taller in the saddle. "Forgive me. Miss Bennet, may I have the pleasure of introducing my sister, Miss Georgiana Darcy? Georgie, this is Miss Elizabeth Bennet."

The lady's eyes widened as she looked up at me and I wondered what she was thinking. "Miss Darcy, it is truly an honour to meet you. I have heard so much of you. I had not realized you were anticipated at Netherfield."

My cheeks burned and I was suddenly concerned as to what had been said and by whom. "And I have heard much of you, Miss Bennet," I responded softly, silently cursing the shyness which took control.

I had been so eager for this meeting, but now I was uncertain of what to say. I desperately wanted Miss Elizabeth Bennet to like me, and hoped to further my brother's cause; but the necessary words would not come.

The three of us stood, transfixed for a moment, until finally, Miss Bennet curtseyed once more. "If you will excuse me, I should be returning home. I was out very early this morning."

Fitzwilliam quickly dismounted and stepped forward. "If you would allow it, we would be pleased to escort you. My sister has been anxious to meet you."

"Yes," I quickly agreed, finally finding my voice. "It was the very reason for my journey to Hertfordshire."

Miss Bennet tilted her head to the side and looked at me curiously. "You heard of me in London?"

"I fear I spoke of you in the letter I was writing during your stay at Netherfield. My sister is ever anxious to meet new people, but has a tendency toward shyness. My description of you spurred her youthful curiosity." Fitzwilliam smiled as he turned to assist me from my horse.

"I wonder what you could have said which would draw her here." Miss Bennet's lips twitched in amusement. "I fear, Miss Darcy, your brother may not have drawn the most flattering picture of me."

Quietly thanking my brother, I turned quickly toward my new acquaintance. "Oh no, Miss Bennet, you are quite mistaken. It was rather the opposite."

Miss Bennet glanced from Fitzwilliam to myself before turning toward her home. "I can only imagine what was said of me. I appeared at Netherfield in quite a state from walking over the muddy fields, and I fear I have a tendency to speak my mind rather openly."

I fell into step beside her while Fitzwilliam gathered the horses' leads and walked a short distance behind us.

"Do not be alarmed, Georgie. Miss Bennet finds great enjoyment in occasionally professing opinions which in fact are not her own." My brother's jovial tone gave me cause to relax and smile. It had been some time since I had heard him tease.

Miss Bennet glanced back over her shoulder, her lips pursed as though to hide her amusement. "Your brother will give you a very pretty notion of me, and teach you not to believe a word I say. I must say, Mr. Darcy, it is very ungenerous and very impolitic, too. I may be provoked to retaliate, and such things may come out as will shock your relation to hear."

Fitzwilliam stepped closer to us as he dipped his head in a conspiratorial manner toward Miss Bennet. "I am not afraid of you."

"Miss Bennet, I have only ever known my brother to behave in the most gentlemanly like manner. Pray, tell me what he has done in my absence." I could not contain my smiles as I watched the playfulness between them.

"You shall hear then, but prepare yourself for something very dreadful. The first time of my ever seeing him was at a ball, and what do you think he did? He danced only four dances! I am sorry to pain you, but so it was. He danced only four dances, though gentlemen were scarce; and, to my certain knowledge, more than one young lady was sitting down in want of a partner. Mr. Darcy, you cannot deny the fact."

Fitzwilliam stood straighter, an odd look upon his countenance as though he were remembering something unpleasant. "I had not at that time the honour of knowing any lady in the assembly beyond my own party." Looking contrite, he continued, "Perhaps I should have judged better and sought an introduction."

"You danced only with Miss Bingley and Mrs. Hurst?" I looked at him in amazement. "But you have stated you dislike dancing in general, and most specifically with Miss Bingley."

His discomfort increased. "I fear I was obligated to dance with them, Georgie. You are not yet out; you do not understand. We shall discuss it later."

Miss Bennet turned forward once more and took my arm. I was overcome by the welcoming gesture and forgot my brother's evasiveness for the time.

"Perhaps a change in topic is in order. Are you enjoying your stay in Hertfordshire, Miss Darcy?"

"I only arrived yesterday."

"And she will be leaving in the morning." Fitzwilliam said firmly.

Another glance was thrown over her shoulder before Miss Bennet asked bitterly, "You feel your sister should be guarded from our society, sir?"

"Forgive me, no, I would be pleased for her to be often in your presence, Miss Bennet. However, there are those in the area which I fear may not be as kind as yourself."

"Mr. Darcy." Miss Bennet had stiffened. She released my arm and her countenance took on a regal appearance as her voice became haughty. "I am aware of your displeasure upon finding yourself in our community, but I can assure you there are none who would harm your sister."

"I do not doubt you, Miss Bennet; though I am concerned regarding your belief of my disliking your society."

"I am aware you find my family objectionable and myself barely tolerable."

I gasped as my brother's countenance reddened, revealing the truth of her words.

"You heard," he said softly as he lowered his eyes.

"Fitzwilliam, what have you done?" I stepped forward and laid a hand upon Miss Bennet's arm. "I can assure you, Miss Bennet, my brother holds you in the highest regard. He spoke so of you in his letters, that I felt I must meet you."

Miss Bennet looked at me suspiciously before turning cold eyes upon Fitzwilliam.

I gripped her arm tighter. "Please believe me, you are not the reason for my brother's concern. It is a Mr. Wickham who has meant me harm in the past."

"Mr. Wickham?" Miss Bennet turned toward me curiously. "I met a Mr. Wickham yesterday. Mr. Darcy came upon us as we were being introduced." She turned back to look at my brother as she spoke. "Is there anything we ought to know regarding the gentleman?"

"That he is no gentleman," Fitzwilliam said bitterly.

I looked from my brother to the lady and back before glancing about to assess our surroundings. It appeared we were in a secluded area, but I had to be certain before I spoke. "Miss Bennet, I would not wish you or your family to be importuned by Mr. Wickham. I am willing to explain our interactions, but I must be certain no one would hear of it."

"Georgie, no! I forbid it!"

"Fitzwilliam, someone must be told so he is unable to hurt another." I felt tears fill my eyes and began searching my reticule for a handkerchief. Miss Bennet offered me one before I could find my own.

Her arm slipped about my shoulders giving me comfort. "Forgive me, I do not wish to pry, but I would like to be of assistance. You need not tell me what has occurred; it is clear Mr. Wickham has injured you in some manner."

Fitzwilliam stepped forward and drew me to his side. "You are correct, Miss Bennet, he has injured my sister. For that reason, I must insist no more be said on the matter. Simply know you cannot trust the man."

His arm was strong and forceful about me and I allowed him to assist me to mount my horse. I accepted the reins and hesitantly looked toward Miss Bennet.

"Forgive my outburst, Miss Bennet. It was most pleasant to meet you." My voice was soft and insecure once more, and I grimaced in frustration over my lack of social skills. The one chance I had of meeting her and I had become a weepy-eyed child.

A shadow crossed over Miss Bennet's countenance before she raised her head and smiled. "Miss Darcy, I am sad to hear you will be leaving tomorrow. I was hoping you might come to tea. I believe you would enjoy meeting my sisters, though they can be a bit overwhelming at times." She looked hopefully toward Fitzwilliam.

"Please, Brother, may I?" I asked, opening my eyes wide as I had done when I was a small child.

Fitzwilliam took a deep breath and glanced between Miss Bennet and myself. "I suppose we could delay your departure for a day as you only just arrived yesterday. May Mr. Bingley and I accompany her?"

Miss Bennet's smile brightened all our demeanours. "Of course, you will both be welcomed, sir."

Chapter Four

"Do you intend to tell me why Miss Bennet believes you dislike her so or must I question you further?" I drew my horse up beside my brother's and matched his gait.

Fitzwilliam refused to look in my direction, instead pretending great interest in our surroundings.

"What is it she heard, Brother?" I was incapable of hiding my annoyance. When he still did not respond, I shook my head. "I fear I must write to Cousin Richard. He is quite capable of drawing information from you."

"Richard's battalion is currently on maneuvers. He is unable to leave his post." Fitzwilliam appeared pleased he was able to counter me so easily.

Frowning, I turned my attention toward the distant manor house. "Well then, I suppose I must ask Mr. Bingley of his thoughts regarding the ball you attended upon arriving in Meryton."

"Georgie …" his tone held a note of warning.

"No, Fitzwilliam. If you are unwilling to provide me the information, I shall learn of it elsewhere. Would you prefer I ask Miss Bennet tomorrow during tea?" I met him with my equivalent of his unwavering stare. It was something I had been practicing for some time, and I had been pleased when Mr. Barnes told me I resembled my brother at his most determined.

Finally, Fitzwilliam released a sigh and reined in his horse. "If you must know, Bingley was insistent I dance and offered to have the eldest Miss Bennet introduce me to her sister, Miss Elizabeth. I was adamant I had no interest in the activity, but he would not desist. Ultimately I became cross and declared Miss Elizabeth tolerable but not handsome enough to tempt me. It had the effect I desired; Bingley relented and returned to his dancing, leaving me be."

"Had you any idea she heard you?" I was able to ask, though I was thoroughly amazed by his ungentlemanly behaviour.

"She was close enough to have heard I suppose, were she eavesdropping; but I did not remain nearby. I wandered about the room and noticed her laughing with her friend a short time later." He straightened the reins in his hand as the furrow in his brow deepened. "I gave it no more thought. Never did I suppose it would colour her opinion of me."

"Yet it has. Oh, Fitzwilliam how could you think such a thing?" I shook my head once more and glanced toward the sun. "Well, we have a day to determine the best way for you to apologize and begin anew." I turned back toward my brother, afraid to ask my next question. "Is there aught I should know? You did not insult her family while she stayed at Netherfield, did you? Perhaps you injured her dog?"

Fitzwilliam looked exceedingly uncomfortable. "Really, Georgie. I believe I shall forbid Richard's visits without my supervision. You are beginning to imitate him."

"You have not answered my question, Fitzwilliam." I allowed my horse to begin walking at a slow pace and he did the same. "You stated in your letter your conversations seemed to dissolve into insults or attacks. What else could you have said to which the lady might take offense?"

Reluctantly he recounted the various conversations that had taken place while the Bennet sisters resided at Netherfield. By his telling, it appeared most of the insulting statements were made by the Bingley sisters, and then only after Miss Elizabeth had left the room. Even so, I feared more could have been read into my brother's words due to his statement at the ball.

We left our mounts at the stables and entered the house quietly, hoping to avoid our hostess. Mr. Bingley, however, had risen and we gladly joined him for a cup of tea while he broke his fast.

"Miss Darcy, I was not aware you shared your brother's habit of rising early." His joyous smile was contagious and drew me from my thoughts.

"Only this one time, Mr. Bingley. I was hoping to meet one of your neighbours and my wish was granted. We came upon Miss Elizabeth Bennet during her morning constitutional." I lifted my cup to my lips and waited for his response. He did not disappoint.

Mr. Bingley's eyes brightened and his smile grew as he spoke. "Miss Elizabeth Bennet, you say? Was her sister with her, by chance?"

"Regretfully no, but I hope to meet all the Bennet ladies tomorrow as I was invited to take tea with them."

"You will be quite taken with them, I am certain. Miss Bennet is the loveliest creature I have ever beheld. She is an angel." He sipped his coffee and looked dreamily at nothing in particular.

Hiding my smile behind my handkerchief, I glanced toward my brother. His eyes held a look of amusement laced with annoyance. I cleared my throat to gain his attention and nodded toward our host. Though Fitzwilliam clearly understood my wishes, he hesitated, as though he were considering whether he would share Miss Bennet's invitation. A wide-eyed glare on my part seemed to finally motivate him to speak.

"Miss Elizabeth granted her permission for us to accompany my sister to tea, Bingley. I hope you are able to attend." His lip twitched as he suppressed a chuckle, both of us knowing the gentleman's obvious response.

"Of course, of course! I shall be delighted!" Bingley hesitated. "Were my sisters included in the invitation?"

Fitzwilliam and I exchanged another glance, unwilling to voice our desire they not attend. "I fear they were forgotten in the moment," he responded.

"Perhaps that is best," Mr. Bingley's brow knitted together. "I wonder if we should tell them of our plans."

"I see no reason for it, though I would not lie were they to ask." Fitzwilliam's serious expression mirrored his friend's.

"Oh, honestly," I sighed. "Do you believe they would wish to attend if they knew? I thought Miss Bingley disliked the Bennets."

"She does consider the eldest Miss Bennet a friend," Mr. Bingley stated quietly.

I looked to my brother once more, an eyebrow raised questioningly. When he tentatively raised one shoulder in response, I realized his thoughts matched my own. Miss Bingley may have expressed such sentiments toward Miss Bennet, but the truth of them was doubtful.

"Well, we shall simply make our plans and address my sisters' inquiries when necessary." Mr. Bingley raised his cup in toast and we all agreed.

****

The following afternoon the Bingley carriage rolled down the drive toward Meryton as I stood in my window and watched it go. During conversations the previous evening, Mrs. Hurst voiced her desire to purchase a new set of gloves, and Mr. Bingley seized upon the moment. He mentioned hearing new items were anticipated at the shops and suggested the ladies go see for themselves the following afternoon.

Before I could respond, Fitzwilliam reminded their host I would be unable to accompany the ladies as I was to leave the day after and must prepare. He also expressed his desire to spend time with me while I was there. I quickly deduced the gentlemen had discussed this scheme at some time when we ladies were not about. I must say I was exceedingly pleased it had achieved the desired objective.

Now that the Bingley sisters had left, I abandoned my room and gathered Mrs. Annesley so we could leave for Longbourn. Though I was pleased to be seeing Miss Elizabeth again, I was timid to meet the other Bennets. Mr. Bingley spoke only of the eldest Miss Bennet; and I expected the angelic person he described would not be intimidating. It was the younger sisters, those nearer to me in age, which made me anxious. I was unable to draw much information from the gentlemen regarding these ladies. Indeed, they had exchanged nervous glances whenever I questioned them, and avoided answering me. My fear rose as the time passed.

Fitzwilliam approached me as I reached the bottom of the stairs and took my hand in his. "Shall we leave, my dearest?"

Capturing my lower lip between my teeth, I looked to the long case clock in the hall to determine the time. "I suppose we should." The shakiness in my voice did nothing to relieve my anxiety.

He patted my hand reassuringly. "Do not fear, Georgie," he whispered. "The younger Bennet sisters are not fearsome; merely overzealous. I am certain Miss Elizabeth and Miss Bennet will monitor their behaviour and protect you from their attentions. And, Bingley and I shall be there."

At this I was able to laugh, though nervously. "I doubt Mr. Bingley will notice me once he sees Miss Bennet."

My brother nodded. "You are correct, of course. Well, you shall have me, as always."

Holding my head a bit higher, I looked him in the eye. "Shall you apologize to Miss Elizabeth today?"

Fitzwilliam's colour reddened. "I know not how to mention it again without making matters worse."

"Will you allow me to give you an opportunity?" I widened my eyes in a pleading manner, hoping he would consider it.

Patting my hand once more, he turned us toward the front drawing room to gather Mr. Bingley. "If the opportunity arises, I shall seize it."

"That is all I ask." I smiled, suddenly fairly giddy with the possibility I might be able to assist him.

****

The Netherfield party was welcomed warmly at Longbourn; though I noticed Elizabeth watched us closely. As I had anticipated, Mr. Bingley took a seat by Miss Bennet and barely spoke to the rest of us for the remainder of our stay. Mrs. Bennet was very vocal regarding her appreciation of *his* attentions, and equally cool toward Fitzwilliam. Toward myself, she was the perfect hostess; becoming somewhat distressed when she learned of my orphaned state.

"I cannot imagine coming of age without a mother, and only having an older brother in which to confide." It was clear there was more she wished to say regarding Fitzwilliam, but Miss Elizabeth interrupted her.

"I am certain Miss Darcy must have an aunt or cousin who might be able to take the place of her mother. You are not solely dependent upon men; are you, Miss Darcy?" Elizabeth asked as though she already knew the answer.

"I have two aunts on my mother's side, who each have one daughter. The relatives on my father's side are quite distant; we are rarely in contact with them." I glanced toward my brother standing by the fireplace where he was cornered by the Bennet's cousin; a Mr. Collins, who was our Aunt Catherine's rector. "One of my aunts is the Lady Catherine your cousin often mentions."

Mrs. Bennet gushed, "Oh, to be related to such grandeur as our cousin has described. I am certain she must take prestigiously good care of you."

Not wishing to speak ill of my aunt, I dropped my eyes to my lap and said simply, "Lady Catherine is exceedingly attentive to every detail."

A sudden change overcame Miss Elizabeth and she moved a bit closer to me as her mother began speaking animatedly to Mrs. Annesley regarding Mr. Collins. "I imagine she could be a bit overpowering, if she is truly as magnificent as my cousin has described her to be," Miss Elizabeth whispered.

Looking up, I saw the spark of amusement in her eye and smiled, feeling relief wash over me. "Indeed, she can be. My brother and our cousin believe her daughter has been sickly most of her life in order to avoid her mother's demands." I, too, spoke softly that no one else might hear.

"Oh, if that were possible." Miss Elizabeth glanced toward her mother and back at me, but her conspiratorial amusement quickly slipped away.

I noticed her gaze lingered just behind me, and turned to see Mr. Collins' excited discourse. Looking to Fitzwilliam, I realized he had engaged his most steely Master of Pemberley countenance. This would not do if he wished to show Miss Elizabeth he was more amiable than he had previously appeared. I turned back to the lady at my side with a hopeful expression. "I believe my brother is not quite himself at the moment."

Sighing, Miss Elizabeth nodded. "Our cousin most assuredly has that effect upon people. Shall we rescue him?"

I agreed, though I was uncertain what she might have in mind.

"Mary," Elizabeth called to her sister. "Did you not have a passage of scripture you wished to discuss with Mr. Collins? What about the doctrinal passage in Fordyce's Sermons that has you perplexed. I am certain Mr. Collins would be enormously happy to assist you in its understanding."

"Yes, Mary," Mrs. Bennet shook her head as though exasperated. "Will you not put down your book and join in the conversations?" Before Mary could respond, Mrs. Bennet turned back toward her youngest daughters who were exclaiming over some bit of news they had obtained from town that morning.

The middle Bennet daughter, who had been sitting alone by the window, blinked at her older sister. When Miss Elizabeth nodded toward the gentlemen by the mantle, Miss Mary appeared to understand and laid aside her book. Taking up her tome of Fordyce's sermons, she stood and approached her cousin. A few moments later, after excessive bowing on Mr. Collins' part, she led him away and Fitzwilliam was able to return to my side.

Suspicious, I gazed at my new acquaintance. "It appears Miss Mary did indeed have questions for your cousin, Miss Elizabeth."

A light blush covered the lady's countenance. "Mary is the only one of us with the temperament to speak to our cousin for extended periods of time. She has chosen several passages to discuss with him in the event there are others who … do not find his company … overly stimulating."

As our eyes met, a shared understanding passed between us and we giggled softly.

"I am eternally thankful to your sister, Miss Elizabeth. I feared I would be forced to correct your cousin's view of my aunt." Fitzwilliam smiled warmly as he appeared to partake in our secret conversation.

"Lady Catherine is not the supreme authority on all things, sir?" Miss Elizabeth asked innocently, though I noted her manner had changed slightly when she spoke to Fitzwilliam. She appeared amused, but there was nearly a sense of challenge in the tone of her voice.

"I am certain she believes herself to be so, but I have often found fault in my aunt's reasoning." Fitzwilliam clearly had not noticed the changes in our companion and continued in his jovial manner.

I bit my lip and said not a word as I waited for Miss Elizabeth's response.

"Then you see little resemblance between you?" Once again, her manner was innocent, but her words were sharp.

This finally drew Fitzwilliam's attention and he snapped into a rigid posture. "Certainly not."

"Forgive me, sir, I meant no offense. I had simply heard you may possess a similar turn of mind as your exulted relative." This time, Miss Elizabeth's challenge was exceedingly clear.

"I fear your source may be incorrect, Miss Elizabeth," Fitzwilliam stated coldly.

"Truly? It was my understanding he had firsthand knowledge of your dealings." She smiled sweetly at me as she made a clear attempt to steer the discussion in a different direction. "Are you mostly in London, Miss Darcy?"

A heat began to rise in my chest as I realized Miss Elizabeth's 'source'. We were too late; Mr. Wickham had already poisoned the lady against us. For Miss Elizabeth to ask such a question, he must have mentioned Ramsgate. I was uncertain how to respond and felt bile rise in my throat, until my brother laid a reassuring hand upon my arm.

Taking a deep breath, I raised my chin, swallowed, and met Miss Elizabeth's gaze. "Mrs. Annesley and I reside in London most of the year so I might take advantage of the masters; though I prefer Pemberley, our home in Derbyshire. I did spend a portion of this past summer in Ramsgate with my previous companion, but she deceived us terribly and my brother was forced to discharge her."

I saw the curious expression that crossed Miss Elizabeth's countenance, as though my response surprised her. She glanced toward her mother, who remained deep in conversation with the younger Bennets and Mrs. Annesley, before she turned back to me and responded honestly. "How dreadful. I hope you came to no harm due to her shortcomings."

I smiled lovingly at my brother. "Fitzwilliam arrived before I could be led too far astray. I am forever in his debt for rescuing me from a most horrendous situation."

"You are exceedingly lucky to have such a guardian," she commented, her tone noticeably more affable.

"Oh, Fitzwilliam is the best of men." I returned my attention to Miss Elizabeth. "I fear he is not always comfortable in society, and may not make the best of impressions. If someone were to speak falsehoods against him, it may be easy for those of little acquaintance to believe them. However, my brother is nothing but honest in all his dealings."

"Georgie," my brother said softly.

I turned and met his gaze with a determination. "Tell her, Fitzwilliam."

"Tell me what?" Miss Elizabeth asked.

Fitzwilliam looked at me for what seemed a lifetime before finally clearing his throat and turning his full attention upon Miss Elizabeth. "I fear when we first met I was not the proper gentleman my sister believes me to be. I must beg your forgiveness, Miss Elizabeth, for a remark I made within your hearing." Her eyes widened and he continued quickly. "I can honestly say it was a falsehood."

I sat quietly while they stared at each other, afraid to move less I break the spell that had fallen over them. It appeared a great many things were being said without a word being spoken. A rush of joy filled me as my brother's unease diminished and Miss Elizabeth blushed.

"Well, I suppose I am not entirely innocent, sir. My grandmother always said 'Those who do not wish to hear ill of themselves should not listen in doorways.' It appears the lessons of my youth had not taken root as firmly as they should have."

Seeing Fitzwilliam about to protest, I covered his hand with my own. "I fear first impressions are not always the most accurate. Fitzwilliam sometimes appears quite proud when he is not familiar with those about him, while Mr. Wickham is always at ease. One would not know my brother was the better of the two men without knowing more about them."

Miss Elizabeth inhaled sharply. "Perhaps, if one only heard Mr. Darcy's telling of the interactions between the gentlemen, that may be true."

"Oh no, Miss Elizabeth, I am quite aware of the stories Mr. Wickham tells regarding my brother; and I have seen the proof which refutes them." I held her gaze, determined not to allow Mr. Wickham to prejudice her against us.

A thoughtful expression passed over Miss Elizabeth's eyes and the tension that had filled her shoulders eased. "I would be most relieved to learn your brother was not capable of the things of which Mr. Wickham has spoken. My dearest Jane was quite determined to find no fault in either man, but I fear from your words, that is not the case."

"Miss Elizabeth," Fitzwilliam leaned toward her and spoke softly. "I would gladly answer any questions which you might have; however, I would prefer it be done at another time. I fear we have overstayed our visit as it is."

The expression of wonder upon Miss Elizabeth's countenance as she gazed deeply into Fitzwilliam's eyes caused me to grin ridiculously. Seeing the warm response in my brother inspired me to hint for more time in Hertfordshire.

"I wish I were remaining so that I might invite you to visit me at Netherfield. I would like to know you better now that our misunderstanding has passed." I turned hopefully toward my brother.

"Mr. Darcy, do you truly believe Mr. Wickham would risk his living by speaking ill of your sister? I believe I can assure you, the opinion of my family would be with her." Miss Elizabeth took my hand in her own as she looked at my brother anxiously.

"And I am to deny such looks? I believe I have been outwitted." His eyes lit with his smile.

I excitedly turned back to my new friend, but hesitated as I observed Miss Elizabeth's look of surprise. It was obvious she had not seen Fitzwilliam smile in such a manner before. Well, I must simply find ways to make him do so more often.

Chapter Five

Caroline Bingley's eyes narrowed as she looked at me across the dinner table. "I beg your pardon, Miss Darcy? Am I to understand your plans have changed yet again and you shall not be leaving tomorrow?"

The warmth of a slow blush crept over me, but I was not certain if it was due to my discomfort at her question or a growing displeasure with her manners. "My brother has agreed to allow me to stay, Miss Bingley. I hope … that is to say, I understood it would not be an imposition were I to remain. Yesterday you were quite distressed when you heard I was leaving. I thought you desired my company." I lowered my eyes to my hands so she could not see my annoyance, and waited for her response.

"I believe you misunderstand my sister," Mrs. Hurst replied quickly, before Miss Bingley had the opportunity. "Of course, we are pleased you will remain; simply surprised as Mr. Darcy was so unyielding regarding his wishes that you should return to London."

Taking a steadying breath, I turned my head enough to see Fitzwilliam's response. He appeared to also take a deep breath before he spoke and I wondered if he were struggling as much as I to preserve a calm appearance.

When we returned to Netherfield that afternoon, we learned the Bingley sisters had not yet returned from their shopping excursion. Fitzwilliam, Mr. Bingley, and I took the opportunity to discuss how and when we would tell Miss Bingley of our impending visitors. It was decided we would begin by announcing I would not be leaving Hertfordshire after all. Thus far, our news had not been received as we anticipated and I, for one, was hesitant to mention the Bennets.

"You are correct, Mrs. Hurst. I was quite determined for Georgiana to return to our home in town." Fitzwilliam turned to catch my eye and smiled. "However, I am pleased to have her near. I have begun to realize she is no longer the little girl she once was, and I quite enjoy spending time with the young lady she is becoming." Looking back to our hostess, his smile took on a cunning appearance. "If it is an inconvenience, Miss Bingley, I am certain *we* could find accommodations elsewhere."

Miss Bingley appeared startled as she began to stammer. "Mr. Darcy, how could you ever think it would be an inconvenience to have your precious sister here at Netherfield? I was simply surprised you had changed your mind. You always appear so certain of your decisions, and determined to see them through; I feared you were being influenced." Her eyes gleamed suspiciously as she finished. "But of course, who could influence Mr. Darcy? Certainly no country chit or inconsequential members of a simple country town."

"Caroline." Mr. Bingley spoke softly, but his threatening tone was clearly heard by all.

"Come now, Charles," Miss Bingley turned her attention to her brother; the sweetness of her tone poisoned by the anger in her eyes. "Are you going to deny you were at Longbourn today?"

"Why would I deny it? The Darcys and I had a lovely time taking tea with the Bennets."

I eyed Miss Bingley suspiciously, wondering how she had learned of our visit. The Bingley sisters had returned from Meryton with several packages and announced they had taken tea at the local inn. They had not mentioned speaking to anyone.

"I am certain you did," Miss Bingley frowned. "Mrs. Philip's was telling anyone in the milliner's shop who would listen of the expectations held regarding your attachment to the eldest Bennet daughter. She said her sister, Mrs. Bennet, was so pleased you would be joining the Darcys when they came to tea today. She was surprised Louisa, Hurst, and I had not joined you."

Mr. Hurst glanced up from his plate upon the mention of his name. He briefly glanced about the table, before returning his attention to his dinner; clearly untroubled by the slight his sister-in-law had felt so dearly.

Fitzwilliam cleared his throat, drawing the lady's attention back to himself. "Forgive me, Miss Bingley. I fear this is entirely my fault. Georgiana and I encountered Miss Elizabeth Bennet during our ride yesterday and she invited us to tea. I asked if your brother might join us, knowing he is a favourite of the Bennet ladies."

"We did not include you as we were aware of your feelings toward the Bennets," I chimed in, feeling suddenly exceedingly confident. "I would not want to force anyone to endure the presence of someone they disliked."

Miss Bingley's eyes narrowed as she studied me. "That is exceedingly considerate of you, Miss Darcy; but I fear you misunderstood. I do not dislike Miss Bennet."

"Oh, I am so pleased!" I clapped my hands together in an exuberant manner, knowing I appeared much younger than my sixteen years. "Then you will not be upset with me."

"Upset?" Miss Bingley appeared confused.

"Yes, you see I invited Miss Bennet and Miss Elizabeth to tea tomorrow. Mr. Bingley said you would not disapprove, but I was so concerned. I am truly happy to hear you will welcome them to Netherfield." I smiled what I hoped was my most charming smile.

"Of course," Miss Bingley said through clenched teeth. "Since I was unable to see Miss Bennet today, I simply *must* see her tomorrow."

"And Miss Elizabeth," I added, feeling my smile turn slightly mischievous, as Miss Bingley eyed me suspiciously.

"Yes, Miss Elizabeth." Her gaze traveled to Fitzwilliam. "How simply delightful," she muttered.

****

Fitzwilliam sat on the little sofa in my room, watching me brush my hair. "Georgie, you know perfectly well of what I speak. I cannot condone such behaviour."

Sighing, I turned and looked at him. "I apologize Brother, but I could not remain silent. You and Mr. Bingley were going to appease her, and Miss Bingley would have gotten her way. She would have been the injured party, and she would have used it to her fullest advantage."

Laying down the brush, I divided my long blonde hair into three sections and deftly plaited them as I crossed the room to join him. "I fear gentlemen are so distracted by their businesses and war and such, that they are unaware of the tactics ladies employ to obtain their objectives."

Chuckling, Fitzwilliam patted the seat beside him. "I am more than aware of the arts ladies sometimes condescend to employ for captivation. I voiced my opinion regarding them to Miss Bingley not long ago."

"Truly?" I asked as I sank into the seat he had indicated. Tying a ribbon about the bottom of my braid, I looked at him expectantly, though he showed no sign of continuing. "Well? Will you not end my suspense and tell me more?"

Smiling, Fitzwilliam cradled his chin in his hand as he appeared to recollect the scene. "You might remember I mentioned a debate carried out between Miss Bingley, Miss Elizabeth and myself regarding the requirements to be considered a truly accomplished lady. It was during one of the evenings while the Bennet sisters were staying at Netherfield." His eyes took on a faraway look and his smile grew. "Miss Elizabeth held the upper hand over Miss Bingley at all times; though that lady was only barely aware of it. She may have had a suspicion, but was without understanding of how easily Miss Elizabeth worked her into contradicting almost every comment she made."

His silly look of admiration forced me to grin. "And? Was that when you discussed the arts *some* ladies employ?"

Shaking off the dreamlike state that had overcome him, he turned to me. "After Miss Elizabeth left the room to see to her sister, Miss

Bingley declared her to be one of those young ladies who seek to recommend themselves to gentlemen by undervaluing other ladies. She declared it a 'paltry device' and a 'mean art'. I stated quite clearly that there is meanness in *all* the arts ladies employ. I believe I also stated anything which bears affinity to cunning I found despicable." He chuckled. "She said little after that."

"I can well imagine," I raised my hand to my lips to suppress my laughter. "I doubt she was able to find anything to say which would not be found despicable by you."

Fitzwilliam watched me a moment before his smile fell away. "Be that as it may, I cannot allow you to speak to her as you did this evening. She is our hostess, Georgie, and you must show her the respect due her station."

Crossing my arms, I huffed out a breath. "I have already apologized, Brother. I will try not to do it again, but she is so ... she says one thing when it is clear she means something entirely different. I abhor disguise."

"As do I." He sighed and drew me into an embrace. "I am uncertain if Miss Bingley was aware of your subterfuge. You spoke to her similarly ... to the manner in which Miss Elizabeth speaks." He looked at me in amazement as his lips twitched. "Am I to assume this new Georgie has been prejudiced by her acquaintance of less than a day?"

I laughingly pushed away from him. "How silly! Of course not. I like Miss Elizabeth, and wish to know more of her, but I am not the sort to change my behaviour after such a brief acquaintance. No, Fitzwilliam, I believe my ability to speak to Miss

Bingley must have come from you. After Ramsgate, you encouraged me to speak my mind and ask questions. You gave me the strength to stand against things I see as wrong. Surely, any change in my behaviour must be laid at your feet, dear Brother." I smiled teasingly as I stood. "I wish to retire now. I must rise early tomorrow so I may complete my studies before tea."

Fitzwilliam stared at me, not moving from his seat. Shaking my head, I took his arm, tugging lightly. "Come now, Fitzwilliam, it is time for you to go."

He laughed, but allowed me to pull him from his seat and push him from the room. "Good night, Dearest," he said as I closed the door behind him.

****

I chewed lightly on the inside of my cheek. When I was younger, I would bite my nails when I was nervous, but that had ended in reprimands and my nails being covered with soap to discourage the habit. In a short time, I had switched to this less noticeable vice.

Miss Bingley sat upon a sofa near the windows, speaking quietly with Miss Bennet and Mrs. Hurst while all but ignoring Miss Elizabeth. Though Miss Elizabeth was not affected by our hostess' ill behaviour, I began to fear how things would change once the gentlemen joined us.

"Miss Darcy." Miss Elizabeth spoke softly and laid a hand upon my arm. "Are you unwell? You appear distracted."

Forcing a smile, I shook my head. "I am well; I fear my mind had simply wandered."

"Oh?" Miss Elizabeth's eyes sparkled. "Is my conversation so lacking?"

I opened my eyes wide in horror. "No, I did not mean to imply …"

""Forgive me, Miss Darcy." Miss Elizabeth patted my arm. "I was simply making sport." She glanced across the room to her older sister. "I am quite accustomed to Jane garnering most of the attention; as is only right. She is the sweetest of us all."

Frowning, I followed her gaze and lowered my voice. "I was wondering if you will be able to have a moment to speak to my brother once he returns to the room. I fear our hostess will abandon us all when he appears."

A light, ringing laugh caused me to turn back to Miss Elizabeth. "Forgive me, Miss Darcy." She leaned closer. "You must understand I am also familiar with Miss Bingley's behaviour toward your brother. There were times I nearly felt pity for him while Jane and I stayed at Netherfield."

"Nearly?"

She blushed. "Well, you must remember, I was most displeased with him at the time. Seeing his discomfort while Miss Bingley praised him endlessly was truly quite amusing."

"And has your opinion of him changed?" I asked hopefully.

Taking a deep breath, Miss Elizabeth smiled kindly. "I believe you are correct regarding initial impressions. I fear I have relied upon them much too heavily in the past and have learned an indispensable lesson."

"But what of your opinion of Fitzwilliam?" I leaned forward anxiously.

"Miss Darcy," Miss Elizabeth began cautiously. "I fear my experience with your brother thus far has been tainted by my initial opinion of him. I would prefer not to make a second opinion in haste and do him further disservice."

I considered her words carefully before nodding. "You are correct, of course. He truly has not shown himself to the best advantage, and your decision would have little to support it." I thought hard upon the matter, searching for a solution. "I suppose it remains that you must spend time getting to know each other better."

Miss Elizabeth laughed once more. "Why ever would your brother wish to spend time knowing me better? I am certain he is quite besieged by ladies of the *ton*, he could little desire the attentions of yet another of such low standings as me."

"Oh, you are wrong, Miss Elizabeth! I tell you my brother does desire to know you better, and that you know him as he truly is."

Miss Elizabeth looked uneasily toward the other ladies, but they appeared to be deep in discussion. Lowering her voice once more, she leaned toward me. "Miss Darcy, I understand your desire to see your brother settled, but I fear you are hoping for something that cannot be. I am certain Mr. Darcy and I would not suit at all. Our demeanours and connections are so far removed. I fear we would be incessantly at war with one another."

"Do you not see? That is the very thing which draws you together." I smiled beseechingly.

Shaking her head, Miss Elizabeth scoffed, "I fear Mrs. Annesley has allowed you to read one too many novels." She glanced about. "Where is the kind lady? I must speak with her regarding your wild imagination."

"She is resting in her room. She felt I would be well in your company, without her. I shall return to her once you and Miss Bennet have left."

With one brow arched and the corner of her lip turned up in amusement, Miss Elizabeth glanced once more toward our hostess. "Whereas others have a tendency to be trying upon one's disposition?"

I released the breath I had been holding. "Yes. I fear Mrs. Annesley would prefer to return to London."

"But she appeared much at ease at Longbourn. I was surprised by the amity between her and Mama. It was as though they had known each other for years. I believe your companion had a calming effect upon Mama which was exceedingly welcomed." Her eyes twinkled as I noticed they did just before she made a teasing statement. "Once you are wed, my father may decide to take on Mrs. Annesley as a companion to Mama."

"Oh, I am certain Mrs. Annesley would be exceedingly pleased to accept the position. She did quite enjoy spending time with Mrs. Bennet. She said your mother reminded her of her sister who died several years ago in childbirth. They had been very close, and Mrs. Annesley has missed her sorely."

"Dear Miss Darcy, I was in jest." I watched as Miss Elizabeth took a moment, possibly considering the proposition before shaking it away. "It is but a supposition, and it shall be several years before you will be wed. Why you are not yet out."

My cheeks burned. "No. I believe Fitzwilliam will delay my debut for several years. I am not ready to be courted."

"You are wise to realize this. I sometimes wonder if I am ready to be courted; and I know my younger sisters most certainly are not. But poor Mama fears Papa will pass while we are yet unwed, and Mr. Collins will send us from Longbourn."

Uncertain of the connection, I tilted my head and looked to her for explanation.

Miss Elizabeth glanced about once more and then spoke quietly. "It is well known in the neighbourhood that our home is entailed upon the male line. Mr. Collins is my father's heir. If we are unwed, our future existence will be dependent upon his generosity." She shuddered.

"You fear he will not see to your well-being?" I asked.

"I fear Mama has decided the most efficient manner to secure his loyalty would be for him to wed one of us."

"Oh." I considered the younger Bennet sisters. "Well at least Miss Mary is more accepting of his attentions. Perhaps she would welcome them."

Miss Elizabeth suddenly laughed aloud drawing a censuring glance from Miss Bingley. Nodding demurely at our hostess, Miss Elizabeth returned to our quiet conversation. "I fear Mama has chosen *me* as the object of my cousin's affections."

"You?" I cried out before I could think better of it.

"Miss Darcy, are you unwell?" Miss Bingley asked, eying Miss Elizabeth suspiciously.

"Yes, Miss Bingley, forgive me," I distractedly responded as I grasped Miss Elizabeth's hand. Glancing out the window just over our hostess' shoulder, I caught sight of my brother's black coat in the gardens below. "Though I believe I would like a breath of fresh air. Miss Elizabeth, would you like to walk in the garden with me?"

She looked at me oddly, but quickly agreed saying she would enjoy the exercise. The others declined, stating the temperatures were not to their liking. Taking hold of Miss Elizabeth's arm, I hurried her from the room before they could change their minds. I only hoped Fitzwilliam would remain outside until we reached him.

Chapter Six

"Mr. Collins?" I asked again in disbelief as Miss Elizabeth and I walked side by side.

Laughing, she nodded. "Mr. Collins. He is my father's heir, and marriage to him would secure a place at Longbourn for my mother and any unwed sisters."

"But surely you could wed someone else who would be willing to support your family should your father pass." I scanned the garden as I bit my cheek and wondered where Fitzwilliam had gone.

Miss Elizabeth laughed once more, but this time it held a touch of bitterness. "My dowry is not substantial as yours or Miss Bingley's. I am rarely in town, and when I am, it is in Cheapside. You must see my connections do not recommend me to gentlemen who are able to take a wife without consideration of financial or social gain." She shook her head. "No, Mama has deemed the best I can anticipate is marriage to my cousin as I do not possess Jane's beauty nor Lydia's liveliness."

"I do not agree!" I stamped my foot upon the dirt path sending up a small cloud of dust. "You *are* beautiful, and you are intelligent. A gentleman would be wise to consider marriage to you. Certainly you would be a far superior mistress than Miss Bingley. You care for those around you; you do not speak ill of them."

Miss Elizabeth laid a reassuring hand upon my arm. "I thank you for noticing my strengths, but you have ignored my weaknesses. I am outspoken and impertinent. Most gentlemen do not appreciate a woman who possesses a mind of her own." Her eyes twinkled. "Besides, I have little to fear. Papa will not force my hand. He would never allow me to marry a gentleman I could not respect."

"You are certain?" I asked hopefully.

"Oh, yes. We have spoken of it in the past." We continued our slow pace about the garden. "Papa does not always appear to be the most attentive father, but he desires only the best for us. He has simply wearied of attempting to control Mama." She glanced toward me as a blush covered her cheeks. "You must understand, she was not always so ... I suppose anxious is the best word to use."

"What changed?" I asked unguardedly, before remembering my manners. "Forgive me, I do not mean to pry."

Miss Elizabeth smiled as she patted my arm once more. "No, I began the topic, therefore I shall tell you." She took a deep breath and looked about. "Few people know I had a twin; a brother. My mother was so pleased she had given birth to an heir but, as is often the case with twins, we were both exceedingly small when we were born. I was the eldest and a bit larger. My brother was far too weak and did not survive." She swallowed hard. "You may have heard Mama call me selfish. It is something she has said all my life as she believes my brother would have lived had I not been so greedy. Had he survived, and I been the weaker twin, Mama's future would be secure."

"But it is not as though you chose ..." I sputtered over the words. "You were an infant!"

"Yes, but so she believes. I shall always be a disappointment and a constant reminder that I stole her son."

We walked on in silence for a few minutes, each lost in our own thoughts. So distracted were we, we did not hear the sound of footsteps approaching from behind.

"Good afternoon, Miss Bennet."

Startled, we turned to find Fitzwilliam bowing formally. Miss Elizabeth curtseyed in return as she greeted him, and I slipped a hand onto my brother's arm.

Fitzwilliam looked us over, his brow creased in concern. "It appears I have found you most disturbed. Has something occurred?"

Shaking my head, I forced a smile. "Miss Elizabeth and I were simply becoming better acquainted."

Clearly unsatisfied, he turned to the lady, perhaps hoping for a better explanation.

"Forgive me, sir. I was explaining the cause behind some of my family's oddities to your sister. I did not intend to depress her spirits." She smiled brightly and took my hand. "You shall find, Miss Darcy, that I was not formed for ill-humour." She raised her face to the weak November sun and closed her eyes as she inhaled deeply. "I believe autumn is my favourite time of year. There is a certain crispness in the air which hints of the chill to come, so we must enjoy this time before we are driven indoors."

I could not resist the urge to smile and turned to find my brother staring longingly at Miss Elizabeth. Uncertain that he remembered my presence, I watched as he involuntarily leaned toward my friend. I could not help but wonder what he might have done, but Miss Elizabeth opened her eyes at that moment and laughed, effectively breaking the spell she held over him.

"I fear our hostess shall be expecting our return." She began to turn back toward the house, but Fitzwilliam laid a hand upon her arm.

"Miss Bennet, I believe I promised you an explanation yesterday."

A cloud passed over her countenance as Miss Elizabeth met Fitzwilliam's gaze. I was unable to read her expression as it was no longer open and accepting.

"Of course, Mr. Darcy." She glanced about to ascertain if we were alone. "Shall we speak now?"

Fitzwilliam nodded as he laid a hand upon mine, which still lay upon his arm, and absentmindedly caressed my fingers. "As I am certain you are aware, Mr. Wickham is the son of my father's steward. Our fathers had been friends in school, and my father was George Wickham's godfather. My father supported George at school and afterward at Cambridge as the senior Mr. Wickham was incapable. You see, Mrs. Wickham was an extravagant woman, always spending beyond their means. A defect she passed on to her son."

He cleared his throat and motioned toward a wider path. The three of us began walking and he continued. "While at Cambridge, I became aware of George's … vices. I said nothing to my father, who was exceedingly fond of the Wickhams. My father tended toward melancholy after our mother passed, and George was one of the few people who could renew his spirits.

"When my father died about five years ago, he recommended it to me to promote George in the best manner that his profession might allow. He desired that, should George take orders, a valuable family living might be his as soon as it became vacant."

Miss Elizabeth nodded, as though acknowledging this had been said by Mr. Wickham himself.

"There was also a legacy of one thousand pounds which was paid to him," he said definitively.

Her eyes widened as she turned abruptly toward him. Clearly, Mr. Wickham had not revealed *this* information.

Without pause, Fitzwilliam continued. "His own father did not long survive mine, and within half a year from these events, George wrote to inform me that, having finally resolved against taking orders, he hoped I should not think it unreasonable for him to expect some more immediate pecuniary advantage, in lieu of the preferment by which he could not be benefited."

Miss Elizabeth stopped walking and turned to face him fully. I could tell by her expression Mr. Wickham had *not* revealed *this* information.

"I have seen the document, Miss Elizabeth," I said softly. "My brother gave him three thousand pounds and Mr. Wickham relinquished any claim to assistance in the church."

"But he mentioned no funds at all." Miss Elizabeth frowned.

Releasing my brother, I linked arms with her and began walking, leading Miss Elizabeth further down the path. "He made no mention to me, either, when we met at Ramsgate this past summer."

Her eyes grew larger and she glanced toward Fitzwilliam who now walked silently alongside us. We had agreed I would tell Miss Elizabeth of the events of the past summer.

"You mentioned being deceived by your previous companion while at Ramsgate." Miss Elizabeth appeared curious, yet reluctant to hear my story.

Seeing a bench on the next path, I motioned toward it and we took a seat. Fitzwilliam continued to stand, looking about to be certain none were near to overhear our conversation. His expression was grave and formidable.

"Miss Elizabeth ..."

"Please, Miss Darcy," the lady interrupted. "I fear you are about to reveal something truly horrendous. I pray you would not feel the necessity. It is clear Mr. Wickham has misguided me, and I shall not allow it to occur in the future. I do not want you to believe you must reveal all to convince me."

"Miss Bennet." Fitzwilliam knelt before us. "I believe my sister shall not find peace until she has shared her tale with you. I fear I have been a poor substitute for a father and mother to her." He took my hand in his own. "If you would, hear her out? It would put both our minds at ease to know there was an understanding young lady to whom she could speak regarding the incident."

A blush covered Miss Elizabeth's countenance and she nodded hesitantly for me to continue. Fitzwilliam stood again and moved a short distance away to give us additional privacy as he kept watch.

"Mrs. Younge; she was my companion before Mrs. Annesley. We had remained in London while my brother returned to Pemberley for the summer. I was studying with a renowned pianist who normally does not take on pupils. It was most rewarding and I was exceedingly grateful to Fitzwilliam for arranging it. The gentleman … forgive me, I promised not to reveal his name. He fears others will seek him out, and he dislikes having to refuse anyone."

Miss Elizabeth nodded her understanding and I continued. "He became ill and left town to take the waters at Bath. Mrs. Younge expressed her displeasure of remaining in town during the heat of summer and suggested we write Fitzwilliam to ask permission to visit the sea. He agreed and arranged for our travel and lodging at Ramsgate."

Swallowing hard, I lowered my gaze to my hands which I kept folded in my lap. I realized the leather of my gloves was stretched taught over my knuckles, and I forced myself to relax. "While at Ramsgate, we met with Mr. Wickham. I remembered him from when I was younger as he was often at Pemberley. He introduced himself to Mrs. Younge as a family friend. It seemed we saw him whenever we went out, no matter of the time or where we were going. Mrs. Younge told me it was not improper to spend time with him, as he had been a favourite of my father's. Indeed, she led me to believe my father would have been pleased."

As I spoke, Miss Elizabeth gradually moved closer to me, eventually slipping a reassuring arm about me. Her compassion nearly undid me and, instinctively, I leaned against her, drawing strength to go on.

"One day, Mr. Wickham asked to escort us to the promenade. Mrs. Younge accompanied us a short distance, but then claimed she had forgotten something and returned to the house. I attempted to return with her, but she insisted we continue and she would meet us before long. I knew it was improper, but she repeated that he was a family friend and no harm could come of it." Taking my handkerchief from my reticule, I wiped my eyes before taking a deep breath and pressing forward.

"Mr. Wickham proposed the moment she was out of sight. He insisted everyone we knew would be pleased. I asked him to speak to Fitzwilliam, but he explained there was no time. He had taken a position with the army and was being sent to the north. He suggested we elope, saying we could stop at Pemberley afterward, on our way to his regiment. When Mrs. Younge returned, he announced our engagement to her. She was exceedingly pleased and congratulated us. I told her of Mr. Wickham's plans, believing she would dissuade him, but she nearly swooned over the romance of it."

Glancing at my friend once more, I saw Elizabeth sadly shaking her head. I took her hand for added strength and finished my story. "It was decided we would leave the following day, and Mr. Wickham left to see to the arrangements. When Mrs. Younge and I arrived back at the house, we learned Fitzwilliam had arrived to surprise me. I shall never forget the odd expression that overcame her; she appeared quite ill and excused herself to go to her rooms. I was so pleased to see my brother and quickly shared my news, as I believed we could now obtain his blessing."

Unexpectedly, a sob escaped from me and Miss Elizabeth held me tighter. "I had never seen my brother in such a state. He was so angry. When he called for Mrs. Younge, we discovered she had fled the house. I began to realize all was not as it appeared.

"In all the times we had met with Mr. Wickham, I had not learned his address in Ramsgate. There was no way for Fitzwilliam to speak with him that day. I remained unconcerned, for I knew he would be coming to collect me the following day." I hesitated and lowered my eyes once more. "We stayed within the house the entire day, but he did not come." Fresh realization of where my mindless actions could have led me caused my countenance to turn a bright crimson and tears spilled down my cheeks.

"Oh, you poor dear." Miss Elizabeth squeezed me tightly.

I felt the open acceptance in her embrace and laid my head upon Miss Elizabeth's shoulder as the realization of how much I missed having a mother or sister in my life washed over me. We remained in this manner until I became aware of my brother standing before us. Reluctantly I drew back from my friend and looked up to meet his gaze. Nothing was said, but slowly we exchanged smiles and I was certain he knew I was well.

Turning to thank Miss Elizabeth, I caught the look of astonishment that crossed her face. From the corner of my eye, I could see Fitzwilliam's smile of gratitude that he had bestowed on the lady. *If nothing else, she does not believe he is merely tolerable.* I fought the urge to giggle, quickly covering my mouth and turning away.

Unfortunately, both of my companions misunderstood my actions and attempted to embrace me, finding ourselves unexpectedly entwined. With cheeks flaming red, Miss Elizabeth recovered first; and, laughing nervously, drew away from Fitzwilliam and myself.

"Forgive me," Fitzwilliam muttered as he turned toward me. "Georgie, are you unwell?"

I could feel the mischievous smile flit across my lips before I was able to suppress my expression and nod. "If you would excuse me, Brother, I would prefer a moment alone." I stood and quickly stepped down the path a short distance in an attempt to give *them* a moment of privacy, though I was careful to remain close enough to hear what was said.

I could feel Fitzwilliam's gaze upon me and was certain he nervously tugged at his gloves as he was want to do when anxious and unable to twist his ring. Finally he cleared his throat. "Thank you, Miss Bennet. I fear Georgiana misses having someone in whom to confide. Our cousin wed last season and has moved to Cornwall."

I turned in time to see Miss Elizabeth's brows draw together. "I understood your cousin was yet unwed."

It took a moment for clarity to strike Fitzwilliam. "My cousin, Miss Anne De Bourgh, is unwed and remains at her home in Kent. Georgiana has never been close with Anne as I do not wish to expose her to Lady Catherine. I was speaking of our other cousin, Lady Beatrice, daughter of Lord and Lady Matlock."

"Oh." Miss Elizabeth appeared as though there was more she wished to say, but instead she remained silent.

"I suppose you have heard rumours of my being engaged to my cousin, Anne."

Her cheeks flamed red again as she nodded. "Mr. Collins and Mr. Wickham both mentioned it."

Fitzwilliam shook his head, disgust written in his expression. "It is my aunt; she insists upon it being so. I visit her in Kent every Easter to look over her affairs, and she tells me repeatedly it was my mother's fondest wish we wed." He took a deep breath and released it quickly. A mysterious smile slowly crept across his lips and he turned to Elizabeth once more, conspiratorially. "What she does not know is my mother was resolute I *not* marry my cousin. She not only told me to follow my heart, but wrote me a letter prior to her death repeating her wishes."

Adjusting my position lest they realize I was listening, I stole a glance over my shoulder in time to witness the same bewildered expression cross my friend's countenance. There was a moment of silence before Miss Elizabeth appeared to revive, and her eyes lit with amusement.

"You would do best to guard that letter well, sir. You may be forced to present it one day should her Ladyship become too insistent, or should you choose to wed a lady who is not your cousin."

My brother's rich laughter filled the air. "I carry it with me whenever I visit Rosings Park for that very reason."

Once more, Miss Elizabeth appeared a bit surprised, but she recovered quickly. "But is that wise, sir? What if her Ladyship should learn of it and have it destroyed?"

"You will find, Miss Bennet," Fitzwilliam said as he leaned closer yet, "that I have the most faithful servants. They would not allow the letter to fall into her hands, as they do not desire my cousin as their mistress any more than I wish it for them."

Furtively stealing glances without bringing attention to myself, I noted the tension that had suddenly sprung up between my brother and my friend. Unwilling to interfere, I stood as still as possible and waited to see what might occur. The silence seemed to stretch painfully on until it was pierced by a most displeasing sound.

"Oh, there you are Miss Eliza!" Miss Bingley called out as she strode intently down the main garden walk. "Your carriage has been called and your sister is awaiting you inside."

Fitzwilliam took Miss Elizabeth's hand and assisted her to rise from the bench. Their gaze held as though they had not heard a word their hostess had said. "May I escort you inside?" he asked softly.

Quickly, I stepped to my brother's other side and took his arm just as Miss Bingley was about to do so. With me on one side of Fitzwilliam and Miss Elizabeth on the other, Miss Bingley huffed and turned to lead us back to the house.

"I have enjoyed my visit," Miss Elizabeth said quietly, not looking toward either Fitzwilliam or myself. "I hope to see you again soon." This time, her eyes lingered on Fitzwilliam before she turned quickly and smiled at me.

A warmth spread in my chest and I could do nothing to stop the silly grin that overcame my countenance. I looked up at my brother and noted his expression mirrored my own.

Chapter Seven

Mrs. Annesley's laughter broke through my daydream. Blinking, I turned from the carriage window to meet my companion's gaze, my eyes wide and questioning.

"You truly have not attended a word I have said." The older lady laughed again as I shook my head.

I felt the heat rise in my cheeks as I reluctantly admitted I had not been listening. "Forgive me?" I asked penitently.

"Of course, my dear. I am so pleased to see you happy as you have been during our time here in Hertfordshire. I believe the Bennet ladies are a wonderful influence upon you, particularly Miss Elizabeth." Mrs. Annesley waited patiently for me to reveal my thoughts and expectations, and I did not wish to disappoint her.

"Miss Elizabeth is wonderful, is she not? I know she would be the perfect wife for my brother, and I would love to call her sister." I bit my lower lip and turned back toward the window.

"What worries you, Child?" my companion asked as she laid a reassuring hand upon my arm.

"Fitzwilliam is not accompanying us again today; and he and Mr. Bingley were absent most of yesterday when the Bennets visited Netherfield. I thought he would wish to spend time with Miss Elizabeth, but he appears reluctant to be in her presence. However can he court her if he is never near her? I do not understand why he does not simply ask her to marry him." I dropped my head back against the cushions and frowned.

Mrs. Annesley's expression became more serious as she turned a worried gaze upon me. "Miss Darcy, we have spoken regarding courtship. Your brother is behaving as a proper gentleman should. He must consider more than simply your wishes or his own desires. The future Mrs. Darcy will have much responsibility. She must see to the well-being of the tenants at Pemberley, and she must be accepted within the first circles of high society. If she is not, it will be very difficult for you, your brother, and future generations."

"But Elizabeth would be the best wife for Fitzwilliam. When he is with her, he smiles and is no longer so morose. She cares deeply for all those about her. There are few who dislike her, and those who do are jealous of her."

"Precisely. You must realize there are many within the *ton* who have sought your brother's favour over the years. How do you suppose they would treat Miss Elizabeth should she and your brother come to an understanding?" Mrs. Annesley tipped her head to the side and waited for a response.

"Much the way Miss Bingley treats her," I muttered softly.

"Suppose they would snub Miss Elizabeth? It could affect you more than you realize." Taking a deep breath, she pressed on. "Would your aunts, Lady Catherine and Lady Matlock, accept her openly?"

"Oh, Lady Catherine would be furious!" I lifted my hand to my lips and began chewing upon a nail.

Taking my hand in her own, Mrs. Annesley lowered it back to my lap and smiled. "I believe Miss Elizabeth would not be concerned with her Ladyship's response, but your brother would not want you to be ill affected by his choices. You must give him some time to know his heart, and trust him to do what is best. The cost could be considerable."

Silently I considered the lady's words as we passed through Meryton and turned toward Longbourn. I understood them to be correct, but I began to fear Fitzwilliam would make the wrong choice. If he refused to see what was before him, then I must do something drastic to bring them together.

****

When the Darcy carriage drew to a halt before the front entrance of Longbourn, a footman stepped forward and lowered the steps, then assisted us out. As we approached the door, it opened upon a smiling Mrs. Hill, the housekeeper.

"You've been expected, Miss. The ladies are in the front parlour." Mrs. Hill took our outerwear, passing it to a young maid, before leading us down the hall.

"It is so quiet," I marvelled to my companion.

Chuckling softly, Mrs. Hill nodded her head. "The youngest Miss Bennets are in town, Miss. I expect they'll return soon and it will be much as it always is once more."

"Oh." I glanced at Mrs. Annesley who returned my smile. No matter how frequently we were at Longbourn, the informal manner of the family and servants surprised me.

My mother had died when I was young and, in many ways, I was raised by the housekeeper at Pemberley, Mrs. Reynolds. The woman was quite motherly toward me in private, but would never speak so to visitors. That being said, when the Netherfield party had attended a dinner at Longbourn a few days earlier, all was as it should be, without a hint of impropriety. It was almost as though everyone had worn a mask for that evening.

Mrs. Hill opened the parlour door and announced us. We were quickly drawn into the room and conversations began to flow easily. As had become custom, Mrs. Annesley and Mrs. Bennet sat to one side discussing whatever drew our hostess' attention while Miss Bennet, Miss Elizabeth, and I gathered on the sofa. Today Miss Mary was in attendance as well and we spoke of music.

Each of us was in such grand spirits as the discussion turned to the upcoming ball at Netherfield, that no one noted the passing of time. When finally the hall clock chimed the hour, we all were surprised at how long we had been in company.

"See, Jane?" Elizabeth winked at her eldest sister. "It is as I said. Mrs. Hill considers Miss Darcy and Mrs. Annesley family. If anyone else, other than perhaps Charlotte Lucas, had been here; she would have cleared the tea and made certain all knew it was time to leave."

My eyes widened. "She is not so informal to all who visit?"

"Gracious, no." Elizabeth laughed at the thought. "Can you imagine how Miss Bingley and Mrs. Hurst would respond were Mrs. Hill to smile at them when they arrived? No, Mrs. Hill is a good soul, but she knows who is most receptive to the well wishes of a servant."

Before I could respond, the front door banged open and a loud commotion ensued. Our group jumped to our feet, but had taken only a few steps when the door to the hall burst open and Miss Kitty, Miss Lydia, and three officers spilled into the room.

"Lord, I suspect we made it just in time!" Lydia exclaimed as she rushed toward the window. "Look! You can see the rain that was chasing us!"

Others joined her and noted the sheet of rain moving determinedly toward Longbourn.

She gushed on, "The clouds had turned so dark that Captain Carter suggested the officers escort us home. We thought we might not make it before being thoroughly drenched, but Mr. Wickham cried 'Run!' and so we did. And here we are safe and dry just in time." As if in agreeance, the rain and wind began to beat against the windows and the group moved closer to the hearth.

My heart clenched, and I stood perfectly still, unwilling to move less I draw attention to myself.

"Well Mr. Wickham, it appears you are the hero of the day," Mr. Bennet's voice was heard from the doorway. "What a grand gesture of you young men to escort my silly daughters home when you had no way of knowing how long you may be stranded here due to the storm."

"I assure you, sir, we thought only of their well-being," Mr. Denny said as he bowed to his host.

"Of course," Mr. Bennet drawled as he glanced about the room. Our eyes met for a moment before he looked toward Miss Elizabeth. A concerned expression crossed his features before he turned abruptly and left the room.

A second later, I felt Miss Elizabeth's hand upon my arm, but did not respond. I could not seem to draw my eyes from the dashing young officer in front of me. Mr. Wickham had not even acknowledged my presence. My breath caught in my chest, and I was suddenly uncertain of how I should feel.

This man had the ability of revealing my greatest indiscretion, completely ruining me; but the last time I saw him was when he left to make arrangements for our elopement. I understood that Mrs. Younge most likely had notified him of Fitzwilliam's arrival and he had left Ramsgate, but I still desired an explanation. Fitzwilliam was insistent Mr. Wickham had felt nothing for me beyond my dowry, yet I needed to hear the words from him myself.

The room appeared to quiet as Mr. Wickham finally lifted his eyes from Lydia and glanced my way. Recognition was instantly followed by a look of fear just before his normal carefree expression returned.

"Miss Darcy." He bowed. "It is a pleasure to see you again." He glanced about the room as I curtseyed and asked, "Is your brother not here?"

"No, Fitzwilliam remained at Netherfield today," I replied softly.

He nodded, then turned and continued speaking to the younger Bennet sisters. He dismissed me.

Unknowingly, I gripped Miss Elizabeth's hand and found myself immediately being led away into another room. As the door of the drawing room closed behind us, I realized Miss Bennet and Mrs. Annesley had followed.

"Oh, Miss Darcy, I regret you had to encounter that man here at Longbourn." Miss Elizabeth drew me into an embrace, and I laid my head upon her shoulder.

"Miss Darcy, are you unwell?" Mrs. Annesley asked as she brushed a curl from my brow.

Taking a deep breath, I forced myself to stand taller and release Miss Elizabeth. "It was a shock to see him again."

Miss Bennet tugged upon the bell pull as Miss Elizabeth motioned for the others to sit. When Mrs. Hill entered the room, Miss Bennet requested a fresh pot of tea. "Perhaps Mama's passion flower or lemon balm?"

I smiled weakly at the housekeeper as a slight frown crossed the woman's lips. Mrs. Hill nodded and left to attend her duties. As the door closed behind her, the room lit from outside and a roll of thunder followed immediately.

"Oh, it does not appear you shall be able to return to Netherfield any time soon." Miss Elizabeth looked anxiously toward the window.

"All will be well," I said as I laid a hand upon hers. As the others expressed their concern, it filled me with a comforting warmth. "I do not wish to be a bother to you. As I said, it was a shock to see Mr. Wickham again." I swallowed the emotions that had begun to well up within me. "But it appears my brother was correct; he felt little for me, else how could he greet me so coldly?"

"Forgive me, Miss Darcy, I am unaware of the details, but Lizzy did say you told her Mr. Wickham was not to be trusted. Perhaps he was uncertain of how you might react," Miss Bennet offered just before her brow furrowed. "Though he did appear concerned regarding Mr. Darcy's presence."

Suddenly I found myself laughing. "He was, was he not?" I brought a hand to my lips. "I suppose he thought Fitzwilliam might call him out."

"Papa certainly was not pleased with the prospect of housing the soldiers until the storm breaks," Miss Elizabeth giggled beside me.

Mrs. Annesley patted my hand and our eyes met. "It appears you are not as affected by Mr. Wickham as we feared."

The realization descended upon me and I felt my smile grow. "You are correct. I wonder now if I ever truly loved him."

"Love?" Miss Elizabeth scoffed. "You were but fifteen, no older than Lydia is now. Certainly she fancies herself in love …"

"Daily," Miss Bennet interjected as she rolled her eyes and we laughed.

"But she knows not what it truly means," Miss Elizabeth finished. "I am four years older than you, Miss Darcy, and I am certain I would not know love if it tapped me on the shoulder and introduced itself."

A could feel a blush slowly cover my cheeks. "You have been so kind to me. Please, Miss Elizabeth, Miss Bennet, will you not call me Georgiana? You are party to my deepest secrets; should we not be on more familiar terms?"

The sisters exchanged a glance before Miss Elizabeth responded. "Only if you will call us Jane and Elizabeth."

"Agreed," I replied, nodding.

"Well, this is quite a different sight," Mrs. Hill said as she entered the room with the tea things and set the tray on the nearest table. "Mrs. Bennet has requested the officers, Miss Darcy, and Mrs. Annesley remain for dinner as the rain shows no sign of ceasing."

"That is very kind of our hostess, but I fear Mr. Darcy will be quite concerned for us." Mrs. Annesley glanced at her timepiece and shook her head.

I was filled with guilt as I realized that had we been mindful of the time, we might have reached Netherfield before the rains had begun. "Is there any way to notify him of our change in plans?"

"Once the lightning ceases, I'll send a messenger to Netherfield," Mrs. Hill assured me before leaving the room.

"I suppose it is the best we can do." Unconsciously, I bit the inside of my cheek as my thoughts turned to Fitzwilliam.

Elizabeth patted my hand and leaned closer. "I can well imagine your brother may be one to worry; but he must know you would not venture out in such weather. Perhaps he will wisely deduce you remained here."

"Perhaps." I glanced toward the window as another flash of lightning lit the room. This time the thunder followed a moment later. "It appears the storm may be moving away."

"Then it will be that much sooner we can send word to him." Mrs. Annesley said reassuringly.

"And that much sooner that Papa will push the officers from his home." Elizabeth winked as she laughed again. "In the meanwhile, we have tea and lovely company. I can think of no better way to pass the time."

I found myself watching Elizabeth closely as the tea was poured and passed around. Finally, when we were all comfortably situated, I gave vent to my thoughts. "Do you honestly believe you will not know love when it comes to you?"

The corner of her lips turned up in a mischievous smile as Elizabeth set her cup in its saucer. "I doubt any will notice me while Jane is near; and with ladies such as Miss Bingley and her substantial dowry in the vicinity, I expect it shall be some time before a gentleman would deign to look my way. Hopefully by then I shall be wise enough to recognize it."

"Lizzy, you always say such things, but you cannot believe them." Jane shook her head before glancing toward me. "Please excuse my sister, Miss … forgive me, Georgiana. Lizzy speaks as though she will never fall in love, but she is a great romantic at heart."

Seeing an opportunity to further my brother's cause, I smiled at the eldest Bennet sister. "I am quite accustomed to it. Fitzwilliam tells me constantly it shall fall to me to produce an heir for Pemberley as he doubts he shall ever find a lady to whom he could entrust his heart."

Jane appeared confused for a moment, and glanced toward her sister. "Mr. Darcy? A romantic?"

"Oh yes! Though it amazes me how he can remain so with all the ladies throwing themselves before him. My aunt is the worse, telling everyone he is engaged to my cousin, but it is not true. Fitzwilliam says he will only marry for love."

Leaving the word hanging in the air, I sipped my tea and waited.

"I must say he hides it well," Elizabeth responded a bit coldly. "I am certain no one in Meryton would believe it could be so."

"Oh, but it is," I replied decisively. "He has told me many times that he would never marry for convenience. He says the Bible tells us woman was made as a helpmate to man so he would not be alone. The ladies of the *ton* look only at the position my brother can offer them. They do not think about how they could assist him." A thought crossed my mind, causing me to frown and I considered my words once more. "Could it be they do not understand what it means to be married?"

Mrs. Annesley looked favourably upon me. "As Miss Elizabeth has said, they know not what it *truly* means."

Nodding her head, Elizabeth looked to her sister. "They must all think as our friend Charlotte. She believes happiness in marriage is a matter of chance, and has decided it would be best to know as little as possible of the defects of the person with whom you are to pass your life. She seeks only a comfortable situation and would be content even with someone like my cousin."

"Speaking of Mr. Collins, I did not see him today." I suddenly felt uncivil as I realized he had not even crossed my mind until that moment.

"He has determined to spend the day with Papa. I heard him mention learning more about Longbourn." Elizabeth glanced toward the door. "Perhaps that is why Papa was so abrupt with the officers."

"And has your cousin persisted in his attentions?" I asked innocently.

"Miss Darcy," Mrs. Annesley spoke quietly in reprimand.

"No, it is quite alright, Mrs. Annesley. I have spoken to Georgiana before regarding my cousin's misplaced attentions." Elizabeth turned back to me. "He has attempted to do so, but with strategy worthy of the battlefield, my sisters and I have diverted him. My only regret is providing him with the opportunity to secure my first two dances at Mr. Bingley's ball."

I could not hide my disappointment upon hearing this. "How disappointing to begin the ball with one you dislike."

"Yes, well it is done. At least it will be over with early and I shall be able to enjoy the rest of the evening, whereas my sisters must wait in suspense to see which dance he chooses for each of them." Elizabeth's smile took on a wicked twist as she eyed Jane.

Her sister simply shook her head once more and refused to rise to the bait. "Will you attend the ball, Georgiana?"

"Brother has said I might watch the dancing and remain until dinner is served. I am not yet out, therefore, I cannot dance. But I look forward to seeing everyone in their finery. What colour are your gowns?"

A glimmer of excitement entered Jane's eyes as she responded. "Lydia has helped me remake my white silk by adding blue adornments. She is exceedingly talented, and I am pleased thus far. She does have a tendency to over embellish and I must watch her closely so that she does not lower the bodice more than is proper." Jane looked toward her sister. "Elizabeth has a gown our aunt gave her for her birthday last summer that is exquisite."

"Oh, tell me of it!" I begged as I set aside my teacup.

"I shall do more than that. I fear I have sat too long today and desire to move about. Come, we shall go to my room and I shall show it to you."

Anxiously I jumped to my feet just behind Elizabeth as she led the way. Jane and Mrs. Annesley followed at a more sedate pace. By the time the others joined us, Elizabeth was drawing the gown from her wardrobe.

"Oh, it is lovely!" I exclaimed. "The colour suits you wonderfully!" The dress was a green, the shade of young ferns, and put one in mind of the woods where Elizabeth loved to walk.

"Yes, my Aunt Gardiner insisted when she saw the fabric that I must have a ball gown. I attempted to convince her a simple sash would do, but I was pleased when she did not heed my request." Holding the gown before her, Elizabeth swayed as though she were dancing and a far off look entered her eye.

"As I said," Jane whispered behind me, "she is a romantic."

I felt my smile grow as I realized Fitzwilliam had a waistcoat that would complement Elizabeth's gown beautifully. "It is perfect!"

Chapter Eight

Elizabeth and I followed Jane and Mrs. Annesley into the dining room. The thunder was now a distant rumble, when it was heard at all, and a runner had been dispatched to Netherfield to make the inhabitants aware that everyone was safe and secure at Longbourn. No mention of the officers had been made.

Mr. Bennet took his seat at the head of the table, frowning as he placed his serviette in his lap. Mrs. Bennet had hardly stopped gushing over the officers since their arrival. Mrs. Annesley glanced my way before looking toward the Mistress of Longbourn. A quick smile reassured my companion, and Mrs. Annesley took the seat closest to the lady of the house, making every effort to mollify her effusions.

With the addition of the officers, the normal family seats had altered so the youngest sisters might sit closest to the gentleman each preferred. Jane and Elizabeth clearly made every attempt to sit by me, but it was not to be.

"Lizzy," Miss Mary called as we approached. She motioned for her sister to join her and their cousin on the far side of the table.

Elizabeth exchanged an annoyed glance with her eldest sister as she joined the others. It appeared Miss Mary was attempting to keep their cousin as far from their father as possible, but was having little success. With Elizabeth's assistance, he was finally seated toward the middle of the table with Miss Mary closer to Mr. Bennet.

In one voice, Mr. and Mrs. Bennet each called for their eldest two daughters and Jane attended her mother while Elizabeth stepped to her father's side. I smiled as each parent indicated the seat they selected for their favourite child, and the eldest were seated. A moment later, the smile slipped from my lips as I realized the only remaining chair was between Mr. Wickham and Mr. Bennet, across from Elizabeth. My friend's eyes widened as the realization struck her also and she began to rise, clearly about to offer me her own seat.

"Lizzy, whatever are you doing bouncing up like that? Take your seat," her mother reprimanded.

"Forgive me, Mama. I thought Miss Darcy might be more comfortable beside Mary." Elizabeth was about to step around the table when her mother's voice stopped her.

"Nonsense! Mr. Wickham and Miss Darcy are both from Derbyshire. They shall have much to discuss, I am certain. Now please be seated."

Reluctantly, both Elizabeth and I did as we were told. Once everyone was seated, Mr. Collins began to rise, obviously in preparation of blessing the food; but Mr. Bennet bowed his head and spoke a hasty thanksgiving. Before anyone could protest or respond, Mrs. Hill motioned for the dishes to be served.

Remembering that Elizabeth had told me earlier the family had yet to enjoy a hot meal since her cousin had joined them, I bit my cheek in an attempt to stifle a giggle. It was obvious Mr. Bennet and Mrs. Hill had found a way around him. I looked to my host and found him watching me. I was uncertain, but I thought he might have winked at me, causing my amusement to arise once more.

"I am pleased to see you looking so well, Miss Darcy."

The deep male voice to my left startled me and I turned toward Mr. Wickham, my mouth opened though I knew not what to say.

"Miss Darcy is a great favourite of ours," Elizabeth answered for me. "We think of her as one of our own, and do all we can to insure her happiness and well-being."

Mr. Wickham searched my countenance, a sad smile crossing his features. "As it should be. Miss Darcy is a treasure."

Dropping my eyes to my lap to hide my discomfort, I whispered my gratitude for his compliment. We sat in silence a moment longer before Lydia drew his attention away. Slowly, I raised my gaze to meet Elizabeth's as that lady smiled encouragingly.

"Well, Miss Darcy, I am certain this little thunder storm was nothing compared to those in Derbyshire," Mr. Bennet said as he cut his roast. "My sister-in-law is from that county and has told me of fierce storms rising the waters so quickly as to trap individuals in their homes."

"Oh, yes, the water coming off the peaks can be very dangerous," I replied, relieved for a change of topic.

"But you must not forget the hail," Mr. Wickham added, turning back to their conversation. "I am certain it is the largest I have seen in my life, no matter where I journey."

"And have you been many places, Mr. Wickham?" Mr. Bennet asked.

Lydia suddenly took interest in the conversation that was drawing Mr. Wickham's attention. "Oh do tell, Mr. Wickham. Where have you travelled?"

A roguish smile crossed his lips as he set back in a manner that included the entire table. "Well now, let us see. I was born in Derbyshire, but I went to school at Eton and then on to Cambridge."

"How fortunate, sir, that you have a gentleman's education," Mrs. Bennet gushed.

"My godfather saw to it," Mr. Wickham responded. It appeared he hesitated as though he intended to say more, but reconsidered. Instead, he returned to the original subject. "Following Cambridge, I spent some time in London."

"You did not return to Derbyshire? Did you dislike the country?" Kitty asked as she leaned forward to see him.

A pained expression crossed his eyes. "I found it was no longer my home. Both my father and my godfather had passed. There was nothing there for me."

"Is that when Mr. Darcy refused to give you the inheritance from his father?" Lydia asked, glancing maliciously toward me.

"Lydia!" Elizabeth, Jane and Mary all cried at once.

"What? Why are you looking at me like that? She turned her attention back to Mr. Wickham. "Tell them, Mr. Wickham," she urged.

"I believe you misunderstood me, Miss Lydia." Mr. Wickham's colour was high, but he showed no other sign of distress. "It was for Mr. Darcy to determine if I was suited for the position in the church. He decided against me in favour of someone else."

I sat quietly. This was not entirely true, but I did not want to insult my friends by calling their guest deceitful. Fortunately, there was no need for me to respond.

"I suppose it is for the best." Lydia smiled as she batted her eyes at him. "If you had been a simple clergyman, you would not be here with us now."

"You are correct, Miss Lydia." Wickham's laugh appeared to be one of relief.

"How should you have liked making sermons?" Elizabeth suddenly asked, catching the gentleman's eye and determinedly holding it.

Wickham swallowed as he composed himself. "Exceedingly well. I should have considered it as part of my duty, as you must, Mr. Collins. I am certain the exertion would soon have been nothing."

Before her cousin could respond, Elizabeth quickly continued. "I *did* hear that there was a time when sermon-making was not so palatable to you as it seems to be at present; that you actually declared your resolution of never taking orders, and that the business had been compromised accordingly."

Murmurs rushed about the table as Mr. Wickham's colour deepened. "Did you? Well, it was not wholly without foundation ..."

"Lizzy, what are you about? Leave Mr. Wickham be; it is unseemly to question him in this manner." Mrs. Bennet used her serviette to fan herself, worry marring her features as though she believed Mr. Wickham might take offense and storm out of the house.

Smiling, Elizabeth looked across the table at the gentleman in question. "Come, Mr. Wickham, do not let us quarrel about the past. In future, I hope we shall be always of one mind." Her brow rose in challenge, tainting the sweet innocence of her expression.

"Of course, Miss Elizabeth." Mr. Wickham bowed his head in her direction, before turning his attention back to her youngest sister.

I bit down on my lower lip in an attempt to suppress my laughter as I met my friend's gaze. Elizabeth winked before turning her attention back to her dinner.

"Well, that was an interesting exchange," Mr. Bennet said only loud enough for the Elizabeth and I to hear.

"Exceedingly so," I whispered as a soft giggle escaped me. The rest of the table remained distracted enough not to notice our private conversation.

"I suspect all will be explained, in detail, later?" Mr. Bennet looked to his daughter who nodded solemnly. "Very well." He motioned the servant forward to refill his glass and sank into silence.

I could not help but watch Elizabeth closely, wondering if her father would take her to task regarding the challenges she had presented to Mr. Wickham. She appeared unconcerned, so I decided all would be well and returned to enjoying my meal.

As the last course was served, Mrs. Hill entered the room carrying a missive, which she presented to me. "This just arrived, Miss."

"Thank you," I responded as I accepted the letter. Flipping it over, I noted my brother's seal and smiled before breaking it open. As I read the short note, my eyes widened. "Oh, dear."

"What is it?" Elizabeth asked as she leaned forward in concern.

"My brother says the bridge leading to Netherfield was damaged by the storm and he fears it will not hold the weight of the carriage. He insists we not return this evening."

Mr. Bennet held out his hand. "May I?"

I passed the letter to him as Mrs. Bennet began to gush. "Well, of course, you shall stay here and Mrs. Annesley too. I do hope the damage will be repaired before the ball. It would be dreadful if it should be cancelled due to an unsound bridge."

Mr. Bennet turned toward the housekeeper. "Who delivered the message, Hill? Was it Samuel? Did he report any other damage?"

"Yes sir, it was Samuel. He said the rest of the roads are good, but the brook is a bit higher than normal. A few trees were blown down, but nothing that would interfere with travel." She glanced toward the officers, her lips set in a firm frown.

"Thank you, Hill." Mr. Bennet's eyes appeared to convey a message as the housekeeper nodded her head and quickly left the room. The corner of Mr. Bennet's mouth twitched as though he fought a grin. "Well gentlemen, it appears conditions have improved to the point you are no longer forced to remain trapped amongst my silly daughters. Let us finish our meal so that you might be back on your way to your regimen. I am certain your Colonel will have work for you."

A pall fell over the group as the officers quietly finished their meal while Kitty and Lydia bemoaned the loss of their company. Afterward, as the gentlemen gathered their outerwear, Lydia stood at the drawing room window looking out.

"Papa, I believe it is beastly of you to send them out in this weather. It looks as though it might storm again at any moment."

"Well Lydia, you will be reassured to know the carriage has been readied to deliver them safely into Meryton. I would not have it on my conscience should some ill come to them." Mr. Bennet placed a hand upon his youngest daughter's arm and led her away from the window.

I sat by Elizabeth watching the scene. It was clear the soldiers did not wish to go out in the poor weather, but hearing the carriage would convey them appeared to brighten their countenances. They thanked Mr. Bennet for his generosity and Mrs. Bennet for the excellent meal. Captain Carter addressed Elizabeth regarding a book they had discussed earlier which she had offered to lend him, and she left the room to gather it.

Sensing a presence by my side, I looked up to find Mr. Wickham had approached. I swallowed my unease, and met his gaze directly. "Mr. Wickham?"

"Miss Darcy," he said softly. His eyes took on a soft, nearly watery appearance. "I fear I owe you an apology from the last time we were in company."

"Please, sir." I glanced about the room to see if any of the others were aware of our conversation. It appeared they were all partaking in their own leave takings and did not notice. Mrs. Annesley had left the room shortly before Elizabeth and I hoped she might return soon. With my companion not in sight, I held my head high and turned my attentions back to the man before me. "I have learned much since then. You must not be distressed for me."

He hesitated before finally responding. "No, I suppose not. I simply wished you to know that I meant you no harm, and I am sorry for the manner in which matters ended."

"I can well believe you would be," I replied coolly.

Mr. Wickham took a step closer to me. "Truly, Georgie, I never ..."

"Only my friends and family call me Georgie, sir. You are neither." My voice sounded cold, even to me.

Standing straighter, Mr. Wickham looked at me sadly. "You would be so cool to me? We were nearly ..."

I could feel my colour rise as the disbelief began to fill me. "We were nearly what, sir?" I whispered angrily. "You very *nearly* stole everything I hold most dear."

A look of contrition crossed his countenance and he bowed his head. "Forgive me; I suppose this was a mistake. I will not disturb you again." Mr. Wickham bowed before turning his attention to the other ladies and saying his farewells.

Uncertain how to interpret his reaction, I remained in my seat while the others saw the officers off. I was still in a pensive attitude when Mrs. Annesley returned to the room a few minutes later.

"Miss Darcy, are you unwell?"

Blinking, I turned toward her as I suddenly realized I was no longer alone. "Do not be concerned. I am simply perplexed."

The older lady glanced about as the Bennet ladies entered the room. "May I be of assistance?"

"Perhaps, but I wish to ruminate upon it first." I smiled, allowing the unease to slip from me as I turned my attention toward the Bennet ladies. "The officers are safely on their way?"

Miss Lydia flounced into the closest seat as she released a dramatic sigh. "Yes. We were such a happy party, but Papa ruined it."

"We shall see them at the Netherfield ball," Miss Kitty offered as she took a seat near her sister and took up a half-finished bonnet. "Captain Carter said Mr. Bingley extended an invitation to all the officers."

"Yes, but Mr. Wickham will not go." Miss Lydia pouted as she picked at a loose thread on the arm of the chair.

"Not go? Why ever not?" Mrs. Bennet demanded as she took her seat and picked up her needlepoint.

Throwing a displeased look in my direction, Miss Lydia explained. "I am certain he would not wish to be in the presence of those who think him beneath them."

Elizabeth frowned at her sister. "Lydia, I believe you are speculating upon something of which you know little. I am certain Mr. Wickham will attend the ball if he is able and, if he does not, there will be a simple explanation. Our enjoyment shall not be deterred should one officer not attend."

She took her seat next to me and slipped her hand over my own. Leaning closer, she whispered, "Pay no attention to Lydia. She is simply displeased as Mr. Wickham did not bestow all his attention upon her this evening."

Before I could respond, Lydia began speaking animatedly regarding the upcoming ball. "Oh, I can hardly wait to dance at Netherfield. I am certain I shall not sit out a single dance." Her lips turned up in what was meant to be a smile, but closer resembled a sneer. "Miss Darcy, how shall you like the dancing?" Again she spoke before I could respond, a look of false concern crossing her countenance. "Oh, but you shall not dance, shall you. Your brother has not allowed you to be out yet. Such a pity." She shook her head as she made a tsking sound.

Quite familiar with ill-behaved young ladies from my time in the finest finishing schools of England, and not prepared to allow someone of lower rank belittle me, I raised my head high. "No, I intend to observe the dancing. I am certain I shall be able to learn much regarding the proper," at this I looked down my nose at the youngest Bennet, "and *im*proper behaviour one sees at such an event."

Miss Lydia's jaw fell open, and she was about to respond, when Miss Kitty drew her attention to the bonnet, asking her sister's opinion regarding the most attractive placement of the ribbon. Shooting a wilting look in my direction, Miss Lydia stamped her foot and joined her sister.

Returning my attention to Elizabeth, I was surprised by the look of disbelief in her eyes. Immediately, I felt the sting of rejection and feared I had misbehaved. "Forgive me; have I said something I ought not?" I whispered.

"No." Elizabeth shook her head as she patted my hand once more, though in a distracted manner this time. "Lydia deserved a proper set down. I simply had yet to see you behave in such a manner."

My cheeks burned as I lowered my gaze to our hands. "I normally do not, but I have been the target of spiteful young ladies in the past. I learned it is best to fight back so they do not believe you weak, else they will grow more bold and hateful."

"Yes, I believe you are correct." Elizabeth looked at her youngest sisters and shook her head. "I believe that is why Kitty follows Lydia's lead and does not stand up for herself. Lydia can be quite cruel at times."

We sat in silence watching the youngest Bennet sisters until Lydia turned our way. Seeing us staring at her, a cruel smile crossed her lips and she raised her head higher.

Elizabeth sighed, shaking her head, and turned toward me. "I believe Hill has made up your room. Shall I show you the way?"

"Oh yes, please." I leaned forward a bit and lowered my voice. "I should not say so, but I am pleased I shall be staying here with you. The evenings at Netherfield are tedious. Miss Bingley is constantly fawning over my brother, and her siblings behave as though they are unaware. It can be quite embarrassing."

Giggling, Elizabeth pulled me to my feet. "I remember. Though I found it amusing, I can imagine it is not so to Mr. Darcy."

"No." My smile grew as I shook my head. "I suppose her behaviour could be seen as humourous, so long as you are not the individual she is addressing."

We left the drawing room and started for the stairs. "I have been exceedingly entertained by her conversations." Elizabeth's cheeks reddened as she lowered her eyes. "I fear during my stay at Netherfield I took pleasure in causing Miss Bingley to change her position on matters."

Laying a hand upon my friend's arm, I turned her so we faced one another. "Fitzwilliam mentioned something of that. However did you do so?"

Lightly setting her teeth against her lower lip, Elizabeth appeared to be considering her reply. Finally, she nodded her head and we began our ascent as she spoke. "One evening Mr. Bingley declared that *all* young ladies are accomplished. As I consider myself far from such, I would not have agreed with his assertion; but his sister and your brother took him to task." Taking on an overly innocent appearance, Elizabeth continued, "I felt as though I must come to my host's aide."

"Whatever did you say?" I asked as we reached the bedroom beside Elizabeth's.

After opening the door and following her inside, Elizabeth took a seat on the edge of the bed and patted the mattress for me to join her. "When Mr. Darcy declared he knew only half a dozen ladies who were really accomplished and Miss Bingley agreed, I mentioned that they must comprehend a great deal in their idea of an accomplished woman. Well, that was all Miss Bingley needed to hear. She began a list as long as my arm of all that a lady must possess; many I am certain she met, and the rest she believed to be true." Though she appeared ready to say more, Elizabeth hesitated and a crease appeared between her brows.

"What is it? Do you not remember what happened next?" I asked.

"No, the opposite actually. Mr. Darcy agreed with all Miss Bingley said, but added that a truly accomplished lady must also improve her mind by extensive reading."

I smiled broadly. "Oh yes, Fitzwilliam quite dislikes the society ladies who are unable to hold an intelligent conversation. He much prefers being able to debate a topic; unfortunately they normally bow to his opinions."

Rallying herself, Elizabeth returned my smile. "Well I certainly supplied his need during my visit. In response to his comment, I stated that I was no longer surprised by his knowing only six, and doubted he knew one. At which time Miss Bingley did not disappoint my expectations; she and her sister quickly declared they now knew *many* women that fit the description. I fear I had to leave the room soon afterward in order not to laugh outright."

"And how did my brother respond?"

Elizabeth frowned. "I am uncertain. I fear I was quite distracted by my hostess's response." She shrugged her shoulders. "In any case, Mr. Hurst declared they were not paying attention to their cards and I left the room."

Her eyes took on a distant look once more, and I decided to sit quietly for a moment. Eventually, when she appeared thoroughly lost in her thoughts, I cleared my throat quietly and asked, "What are you thinking?" I was surprised when Elizabeth's countenance reddened as though she had been caught at something quite terrible.

"I do not wish to say."

Suddenly ill at ease, I looked about the room and gasped. "Oh, but this is not a guest room. Has my presence forced someone from their bed?"

Smiling once more, Elizabeth took my hand. "This is Jane's room; she shall share with me while you are here. We are accustomed to sharing a room, and I thought you may prefer to be near us."

"Oh yes!" I embraced my friend, before I quickly stepped back. "Forgive me, but I feel so close to you." I hesitated and looked nervously about the room once more. "What is it like to have so many sisters?"

"Noisy!" Elizabeth laughed.

"I only have Fitzwilliam," I said as I examined the miscellaneous items laid out on the table beside the bed. "He is a wonderful older brother, but there are so many years between us. I have spent time with my cousin, but she has always been very determined to marry well. She spoke of little else. I cannot imagine growing up with so many women about me."

I heard a soft sigh and turned to see a far off look in Elizabeth's eyes just before she spoke. "I have often dreamed of being part of a smaller, quieter family. Of course, I would not sacrifice Jane for all the world, but I always enjoyed visiting my aunt and uncle in London. They have children now, but when they first wed, it was so quiet and refined there. I would imagine I was their only child and think of how my life would be different." Her eyes twinkled with mischief as she met my gaze. "But then I would return home and realize I had truly missed my sisters and their constant banter."

Turning back to the table, I picked up a small seashell and turned it over in my hand. "Will you prefer to live in London or the countryside when you wed?"

"I had not thought of it," Elizabeth said in a contemplative tone. "I suppose, *if* I wed, I shall live wherever my husband chooses."

"But, if you were given a choice, where would you prefer?" I asked insistently.

"Oh, the country by far. I fear when I am in town, I quite despise the restrictions. I cannot walk alone as I do here at home, though I suppose my husband would not allow me to do so wherever I may be." Placing a stern look upon her face, she turned to meet my eye. "It is quite improper; scandalous even."

"I believe your husband would love you so much, he would allow you to do as you please." I smiled brightly.

"Oh, dear, if only such a man existed." A dreamy expression passed over Elizabeth's countenance before she shook herself. "But I am certain he does not; and should he, I doubt he would even notice me."

Placing the seashell back on the table, I stood and walked about the room. "After we left Ramsgate, Fitzwilliam and I spoke of men and marriage. I asked him what he desired in a wife." Pausing, I glanced over my shoulder to gage Elizabeth's reaction. She sat still, not meeting my gaze, so I continued. "I suppose I anticipated a list of accomplishments; but he simply said he hoped to find someone he could esteem, who treasured him, and could love Pemberley as he does."

"Of course they must be of the upper ranks in society," Elizabeth said softly.

"No. Brother said nothing of society. In truth, I do not believe he enjoys being in town. He would be ever so much happier at Pemberley, if he were not alone." Turning so I could see Elizabeth's response, I waited patiently.

A moment passed before Elizabeth's shoulders drew back and she sat taller. "Georgiana, I fear you believe there to be some connection between me and your brother. Mr. Darcy has made it abundantly clear that he dislikes my family. I must admit that, since you have arrived, I have seen a different side of him; but I would not have you think more may come of it. We are too different."

"And I believe you are very much the same." I faced her directly. "You are both educated and speak your opinions decidedly; you each have a tendency toward prejudices which cause you to err in judgement;" Elizabeth began to interrupt me, but I continued. "And you are both determined to have a marriage of affection. I believe if you lowered your guard and actually spoke to one another, you would recognize how perfect you would be together."

Elizabeth stood, her eyes flashing passionately. "Firstly, I am not prejudiced."

"What of your reaction to my brother?"

"He insulted me!"

"He apologized."

Taking a deep breath and turning her back on me, Elizabeth stood quietly while I waited for a response. I began to feel none was coming, when Elizabeth finally turned back.

"I suppose you are correct," she said softly. "If I must be honest with myself, I was quite hurt when Mr. Darcy called me only tolerable. He was the most handsome man I had seen in our small town. I quite fancied him at first. Besides his insult, it was his manner that made me dislike him so. He appeared above everyone, as though we were not good enough."

"I have often been called shy because I am uncomfortable around people I do not know." I stepped forward and took Elizabeth's hand. "I believe Fitzwilliam feels the same way. When he is uncomfortable, he becomes very distant and stiff. You have been so kind, putting me at ease. Could you not do the same for him?"

"Georgiana, I ..." Elizabeth appeared to be searching for a response.

"Please, do not say anything now, but would you think on it?" My head tipped to the side much like a puppy I once had as a child. It had been nearly irresistible, and I hoped I had the same effect on Elizabeth.

Finally, Elizabeth sighed and nodded. I released a quiet squeal as I threw my arms around her.

"Shall we rejoin the others?" Elizabeth asked though she looked a bit weary.

"Oh, yes." I am fairly certain my countenance beamed from the victory I perceived I had won.

"Very well, since you are so pleased with yourself, you shall accompany me to my father's book room so we can explain the reasons behind my comments to Mr. Wickham."

Though my smile slightly dimmed, I nodded and slipped my hand about Elizabeth's arm before we left the room.

Chapter Nine

The rain beat against the windowpane in a staccato rhythm, gradually drawing me from my slumbers. Stretching my arms above my head, I arched my back and twisted first left, than right, before relaxing back into the pillows. Opening my eyes, I glanced about the unfamiliar room as I slowly remembered where I was.

Memories of the previous evening rushed back, and I rolled onto my side, trying to see out between the curtains. Mr. Bennet had listened intently as Elizabeth told what she had learned about Mr. Wickham. I was most impressed with the way she had alluded to my improprieties without revealing details or names. Mr. Bennet most likely suspected the naïve heiress was me, but could not say for certain.

The sound of distant thunder made me shiver and I snuggled deeper into the blankets and sighed. After leaving Mr. Bennet's book room, we rejoined the others. Miss Lydia had continued in her rude behaviour, leaving me no option but to eventually ignore her completely. The worse had come when we retired for the evening.

"I fear the rain has begun again and shows no sign of slowing." Elizabeth shook her head as she drew the curtains in the parlour. "I doubt you shall be able to return to Netherfield in the morning, Georgiana." Elizabeth chewed her lip as her gaze passed over each of the ladies in the room before returning to her youngest sister. "Lydia, you shall have to loan Georgiana a morning dress."

"Me? Why me?" the young girl sputtered.

"Because you are the tallest of us. Any of my dresses would be positively improper. Our maid, Maggie, might be able to let out the hem on one of yours so that Georgiana's ankles will not show." Elizabeth smiled at me.

Looking about, I realized I stood a full head taller than most of the Bennet ladies. She was correct, Lydia was the closest to me in height, but even she was several inches shorter.

"No!" Miss Lydia crossed her arms and looked down her nose at her sister. "I have nothing to lend her."

"Lydia!" Mrs. Bennet scolded. "You most certainly do. Your pink dress will look lovely on Miss Darcy."

As a crimson hue covered Miss Lydia's countenance, she turned large eyes toward her mother. "No! It is my absolute favourite. I will not allow it to be let out, or for anyone to wear it but me."

"Lydia," Mrs. Bennet's voice lowered as she glanced about the room and smiled apologetically toward Mrs. Annesley and me. "You shall choose a dress for Miss Darcy to wear tomorrow, or you shall remain in your room for the remainder of the week."

In the time we had been at Longbourn, I had come to learn that Mrs. Bennet would give in to most all of Miss Lydia's whims, unless it risked making her appear to be a poor hostess. Apparently, her reputation as Mistress of Longbourn was the one thing Mrs. Bennet cherished over her youngest daughter's happiness.

A cruel smile slipped across Miss Lydia's lips as she cut her eyes in my direction. "Very well then. I suppose I could find *something*."

"See that it is presentable, Lydia." Elizabeth frowned at her sister. "In fact, I believe it best if I choose something for Georgiana from your wardrobe."

The scowl which overtook Miss Lydia's features was fearsome indeed, but the other Bennet sisters appeared not to notice; they were obviously accustomed to the youngest's fits of temper. I sighed, hoping the rains would lessen and I would be able to return to Netherfield by the following evening.

Now I glanced toward the pale blue dress that lay across a chair at the foot of the bed. Elizabeth had brought it to me the previous evening. I could tell she was exceedingly displeased, but she was reluctant to mention it. The walls at Longbourn were not so thick as to block out Miss Lydia's cries of misuse as her sister 'stole' her belongings.

Another roll of thunder, this one close enough to rattle the windowpanes, caused me to jump. I wondered what time it was and lay still to listen for movement in the house. It appeared no one was up and about. Propping myself on my elbows, I lifted my head to feel the heat radiating from the fireplace and was grateful that one of the maids had slipped in at some time to build up the fire in an effort to chase away the morning chill.

Reluctantly, I turned back the counterpane and sat up on the side of the bed. Stretching my legs out in front of me, I wiggled my toes as I had done since I was a small child. I could vaguely remember my nurse, or perhaps it was my mother, tickling my feet during this morning routine. A sigh escaped me as I thought of my family.

My mother had died when I was but a toddler. My father, who cherished boys over girls, rarely visited the nursery. Only Fitzwilliam made a point of seeing me each day. We had been very close when he was home, and he wrote me often when he was away at school. While at Pemberley, I would sometimes come upon him in the portrait gallery, sitting in a chair he had set before our mother's painting. Not liking to see him sad, I would climb up in his lap and tell stories until he laughed.

Another sigh slipped from my lips as I wondered how life would have been had Mother lived longer. Shaking my head decidedly to dispel my melancholy, I slid my feet into the slippers Elizabeth had loaned me and pulled Jane's dressing gown about my shoulders. The chilly air brushed against my bare shins as I crossed to the window and looked out. The rain was coming down even harder now and I leaned my forehead against the cool glass.

"Well, I am awake, so I should get dressed," I said aloud before turning back to the little room. Taking up the morning dress, I looked it over. The hem had been let out completely, but I doubted it would touch the tops of my slippers. "There is nothing to be done about it. Luckily, the rain will keep visitors away."

Examining the garment closely, I determined I should be able to dress myself. Being in a strange home, and knowing the Bennet sisters shared a lady's maid, I was reluctant to request any special attention. I laid the dress back upon the chair and took a seat at the dressing table.

Smiling, I looked over the little odds and ends scattered before me. Jane was all that was lovely and feminine. In front of the mirror sat a few bottles of flowery scents, most likely created in the still room Elizabeth had shown me yesterday. I lifted the stoppers, sniffing each one by one, before replacing them unused. The oils were a bit too sweet for my tastes.

I removed the tie from my hair and loosened my braid before I began brushing it. A bit of Jane's favourite scent lingered in the hairbrush and I wrinkled my nose. "Well, there is little can be done now," I said as I finished my task; putting my hair in a simple twist low on the back of my head.

Removing the borrowed dressing gown and nightgown, I pulled my petticoat on over my chemise; hoping it would cover what the dress did not. As I was about to slip into the garment, I heard a soft knocking. Returning the dress to the chair, I donned Jane's dressing gown once more before crossing to the door.

"Yes?" I called softly.

"Miss Darcy, it is Kitty. May I come in?"

I opened the door a crack and saw Miss Kitty looking about anxiously. "May I help you?"

"Please," the young girl said anxiously. "May I come in before she knows I am here?"

Puzzled, I opened the door and allowed her entrance.

Slipping inside, Miss Kitty quickly closed the door and looked about. "Oh, good, you didn't put it on." She crossed to the chair and picked up the blue dress. "I gave Maggie my yellow dress to let the hem out. It was Lydia's, but she didn't like the colour so she gave it to me. It should fit you as well as this one would have. She will bring it up as soon as it is ready."

Miss Kitty started toward the door, but I stopped her, puzzled by her actions. "Why?"

Refusing to meet my gaze, Miss Kitty fingered the trimming on the blue gown. "I am uncertain regarding the reason, but Lydia dislikes you."

"Yes, I had noticed. I fear Mr. Wickham has told her things regarding my family that may not be entirely true." I waited to see what else the Bennet sister would say.

Miss Kitty raised her eyes as she shook her head. "Mr. Wickham didn't say anything bad about you, just your brother." She swallowed and looked down again. "I think Lydia believes he likes you, and that is why she is being so cruel."

"Well I do not particularly like Mr. Wickham." I laid a hand upon her arm. "He is not a man to be trusted, Miss Kitty. He has been given many advantages in life, but has squandered them all. He wishes everything to be given to him, but does not feel as though he should pay for anything."

"He sounds like Lydia," Kitty muttered.

"What did Lydia do to the dress?" I asked, no longer able to wait for an explanation.

Miss Kitty swallowed hard. "I am uncertain, but I believe she put pins or something in it. She was giggling about how uncomfortable you would be in it before she fell asleep last night. I arose early this morning so I could stop you from wearing it."

I was shocked by the extent of Miss Lydia's cruelty. "Thank you, Miss Kitty." I watched as she began to move toward the door again, but suddenly felt the urge to know her better. "Would you like to stay for a few minutes?" I asked quickly.

Miss Kitty looked at me, clearly confused. "But my sister ..."

"Miss Lydia did this, not you. You warned me, and gave me one of your own dresses. I would like to learn more about you." I smiled, hopeful she would trust me.

Glancing uncertainly toward the door, Miss Kitty chewed her lip in contemplation. Finally, she nodded and went to sit in the chair where the dress had been earlier. "I cannot stay long. Lydia might wake up."

"Are you always with Miss Lydia?" I asked as I took the seat before the dressing table.

Miss Kitty nodded. "Jane and Lizzy are normally together, when Lizzy is not off walking somewhere. Mary is always reading or playing the pianoforte. Lydia makes me go everywhere with her because Mama does not like her to be alone."

"Do you prefer to be with Miss Lydia?" The puzzled expression had returned to Miss Kitty's countenance, and I suddenly realized no one had ever asked the girl about her preferences before. "If you were able to choose, how would you spend your day?"

Slowly, with a thoughtful look in her eyes, Miss Kitty began to disclose her interests. "I believe I would spend my mornings sketching. The light is best then."

"What do you sketch?" I asked with interest as I leaned forward.

Miss Kitty shrugged. "Once I drew a bird who came to sit on our window sill every morning. Each day I drew a bit more." The smile that had begun as she spoke suddenly fell away. "Lydia tore it up. She said it was terrible and didn't even look like a bird. She made me sketch a new dress for her instead."

So, Miss Kitty has talent and Miss Lydia is jealous. Running a finger over the trim of my dressing gown, I spoke softly. "From what I have seen, Miss Lydia would not have asked you to sketch a dress if she did not believe you had talent."

Tipping her head to the side with a contemplative gaze, slow understanding overtook Miss Kitty. "She had the pink dress made from the sketch."

"The one she declared was her favourite last night?"

Miss Kitty nodded. "She never said she preferred the design, or even thanked me for drawing it."

"Forgive me, but it sounds as though Miss Lydia is extremely selfish. If she were my sister, I believe I would find ways to spend my time in other pursuits." I watched Miss Kitty closely. "You are sixteen, are you not?"

"Yes, my birthday was last month."

"As was mine!" I exclaimed, pleased that we had something in common. "What day?"

"The twenty-third." Miss Kitty leaned forward expectantly.

"It cannot be," I leapt from my chair and took hold of her hands. "That is my birthday as well! We must be connected in some manner."

"Miss Darcy, it is hard to believe …"

"Please, we share the same birthday, you must call me Georgiana, or Georgie."

"Well, since I am called Kitty, you shall be Georgie!" Kitty giggled as she squeezed my hands.

A knock on the door startled us both and Kitty's joyous expression disappeared instantly. I crossed to the door and asked who was there. Smiling reassuringly at my newest friend, I opened the door to reveal Maggie holding the promised dress. Within moments, I was ready for the day and the blue garment whisked away.

"What shall we do now?" I asked Kitty who looked at me questioningly. "You said you prefer to sketch in the morning as the light is best, but it is raining today. I know Elizabeth prefers to walk in the morning as she has promised to show me her favourite views, but that also is not possible. What do the Bennets do when it rains?"

"Sit in the parlour and listen to Lydia complain while Mary plays a ponderous piece on the pianoforte." Kitty frowned. "Jane stitches while Lizzy reads. If Lydia becomes too loud, Lizzy goes to our father's book room."

"At Pemberley I play bright, happy pieces to lift everyone's spirits. Even Fitzwilliam comes from his study to listen." I pressed a hand to my lips as a memory came to me and I was suddenly filled with mirth. "Once it had been raining for several days and a few of the tenants' homes were damaged. Fitzwilliam had them come to Pemberley until the rain stopped and repairs could be made.

"Being inside for so long, everyone was becoming irritable and displeased with everything. Fitzwilliam called us together in the ballroom and asked me to play a reel. He escorted Mrs. Reynolds, our housekeeper, to the head of the line and everyone followed. It was such fun!" I looked up to see an incredulous look upon Kitty's countenance, and paused.

"Mr. Darcy danced a reel? With servants?" Kitty asked, clearly doubting every word.

"Well, Mrs. Reynolds is nearly a second mother to us, and there were more tenants than servants in the room; but yes, my brother danced a reel. You have seen him dance while he was in Hertfordshire, have you not?" I began to feel a bit defensive.

"Yes, but only with Mrs. Hurst and Miss Bingley, and then he did not appear to enjoy the experience." Kitty hesitated before she continued. "Mr. Bingley insisted he dance with Lizzy, but Mr. Darcy refused."

I shook my head, wondering just how many more things I would learn about my brother's behaviour. "I have heard what he said about Elizabeth, and he has apologized to her. Has there been any other dancing since then?"

Kitty stuck out the tip of her tongue as she thought very hard. "Since meeting Mr. Darcy? Oh, Lydia made Mary play a jig for us to dance at Lucas Lodge. I believe Mr. Darcy was talking to Sir William. He did not appear pleased with those of us who were dancing, even though Mr. Bingley was partnering Jane."

"Oh dear, it is worse than I thought." I began nibbling on the nail of my first finger.

"What is worse?" Kitty asked, laying a reassuring hand on my arm.

I studied her closely for a moment, trying to determine if I should include her in my plans, before asking, "Can you be trusted with a secret?"

Slightly taken aback, Kitty nodded slowly. "I believe so. I have kept many of Lydia's secrets from our family."

Curious regarding Lydia's secrets but knowing it was impolite to ask, I grasped Kitty's hands instead while looking directly into her eyes. "You must swear to tell no one; especially not your sisters or parents."

Kitty nodded solemnly, her eyes opened wide in curiosity.

"I believe Fitzwilliam likes Elizabeth," I said in a rush before holding my breath in anticipation of Kitty's response.

Slowly a smile spread across her lips and a moment later she was laughing. "Lizzy? But he thinks she is only tolerable. He said it himself."

"I told you, he apologized." I released Kitty's hands, throwing them away from myself, and began to pace. "You have not seen them when they are together. He never stops looking at her; as though he is memorizing everything about her."

"But I have seen him," Kitty insisted. "The night at Lucas Lodge he followed her everywhere. Most of the time he looked quite displeased. Everyone in Meryton believes he looks at her to find fault."

Nibbling on my nail once more, I shook my head. "I was correct; it is worse."

Kitty leaned closer. "Georgie, you truly believe he likes her?"

"He is positively smitten. I have never been more certain."

"Oh dear, but Lizzy has declared she shall never dance with him. I believe she quite dislikes him."

I stopped pacing and sat on the edge of the bed. "When I first met Elizabeth, I would have agreed with you; but I have seen them together since then and she also could not stop looking at Fitzwilliam. I believe they feel something for each other, but neither is taking action."

Kitty joined me on the bed, her brow creased in thought. "I wonder …"

"What?"

"Well, there is a ball in a few days, maybe we can arrange for them to dance. Mr. Darcy appeared to be a good dancer, even if he was not enjoying himself." Kitty sat quietly, muttering under her breath. "Lizzy normally will not allow people to appear exceedingly serious. She would definitely make him speak while they danced. If she knew what topics would interest him …"

"I could tell her things he likes," I offered quickly. "I have seen her gown, and Fitzwilliam has a waistcoat which would complement it perfectly. I shall tell his man to prepare it. I do hope it is not in town. If so, he will have to send for it."

"Georgie, you have to be at Netherfield to do so," Kitty reminded me.

"Oh, this wretched rain!" Another thought crossed my mind and I fell back upon the bed. "The bridge! What if it does not stop raining in time and they are unable to fix the bridge? Is there any other way to Netherfield?"

Kitty shook her head sadly.

"Oh, Kitty, however are we going to bring them together?"

The sound of doors opening and closing as individuals greeted each other and went below to break their fasts interrupted my thoughts.

Kitty stood and held out her hand. "I suppose we shall have to watch for any opportunity."

Nodding, I accepted her hand and we crossed to the door. I was about to open it when a thought occurred to me and I stopped and turned back. "What about Miss Lydia?"

Though her complexion blanched, Kitty held her head high. "I believe Maggie will have told Hill what Lydia did. If Mama hears of it, Lydia may be sent to her room as was threatened."

"Do you believe that will happen?" I asked doubtfully.

"No, but I will not spend the day listening to her when I can be speaking with you." She smiled timidly. "I am glad I told you about the dress."

"So am I." I could feel the grin spreading across my countenance and I reached out to embrace Kitty. "I have never had a friend who shared my birthday before. We are as good as sisters!"

Kitty giggled. "Yes, as good as sisters!"

Chapter Ten

Miss Lydia's eyes widened as Kitty and I entered the dining room arm in arm. She glanced down at the yellow morning dress and frowned before turning to glare at her sister. Kitty was so busy whispering to me, she did not even notice.

We took seats next to one another near Mr. Bennet's end of the table, with one chair separating me from the youngest Bennet, and waited for the remainder of the family to join us. We did not wait long before Jane and Elizabeth entered together, looking about anxiously, probably for me. Relief flooded Jane's smile when she saw me already in attendance, but Elizabeth peered at me curiously.

"I forgot Kitty had Lydia's yellow dress. It suits you very well, Georgiana; but was there some problem with the blue?" She looked suspiciously toward her youngest sister who fiddled with the serviette and refused to meet her gaze.

"Kitty brought it to me this morning and we agreed it might be a more *comfortable* fit." I smiled at Kitty as I squeezed her hand under the table.

"I see." Elizabeth glanced between the three of us. It was clear she suspected more, but she soon took her seat as though she would not pursue it further at this time.

Mrs. Bennet and Mrs. Annesley entered next, with Miss Mary close behind them on Mr. Collins' arm. After seating her between Mrs. Annesley and Jane, his countenance revealed his realization that the only remaining seat was between Miss Lydia and myself. Drawing himself to his full height, which was surprisingly closer to Fitzwilliam's than I had originally believed, he rounded the table and stepped in front of the available seat; but he remained standing.

A moment later, Mr. Bennet entered the room and moved to his place, just as Mr. Collins cleared his throat. "Shall we bow our heads in thanksgiving to the bounties supplied by our wondrous Lord?" He folded his hands before his thick middle as Miss Lydia's sigh reverberated about the room.

I could not resist the urge to peek at my friends who sat across from me and felt the need to bite down on the inside of my cheek to suppress my grin. It appeared Mr. Collins was determined not to be overlooked, and we all knew we would not be enjoying a hot breakfast this morning.

I felt my eyes begin to glaze over as the man recited the numerous blessings bestowed upon himself, repeatedly thanking his creator for the wisdom and guidance of Lady Catherine de Bourgh. It took most of my inner strength to maintain my silence as the man beside me made every argument for my insensitive, demanding aunt's sainthood. *No wonder Fitzwilliam was so ill at ease in his presence.*

Finally, as Kitty began to lean heavily against my arm, Mr. Collins closed his prayer and took his seat. Glancing about, I noticed everyone blinking rapidly as though waking from a dream or realizing the droning sound of the man's voice had ended, effectively breaking a spell under which they had fallen. As I nudged Kitty back into her own seat, I saw the corner of Mr. Bennet's mouth turn up and thought I heard him whisper, "Well played, Cousin."

As expected, the food had cooled, but Mrs. Hill made certain the tea and coffee were hot. We ate little and soon adjourned to the front parlour, while Mr. Bennet disappeared into his book room before Mr. Collins could address him. Kitty and I took the window seat and stared out at the gloomy day.

"The rain appears to be slowing; perhaps it will stop so repairs can be made to the bridge." Kitty smiled hopefully in my direction before taking up her sketchpad.

The light was not the best, but I sat in the brightest spot, looking out at the rain dripping from the bare branches of the massive elm. Kitty moved to a chair close by and tapped her pencil against her lips as she studied me, before finally beginning to draw.

Approximately half an hour later, I stared at the reflection in the glass and saw Elizabeth stepping silently up behind Kitty and viewing the drawing over her sister's shoulder. "Why, Kitty, that is very good."

Startled, the younger sister clutched the sketchbook to her chest and looked up at Elizabeth. Reluctantly, she lowered it again. "Do you really think so?"

"Oh, yes. You have perfectly captured the curve of Georgiana's nose and chin. I am anxious to see it completed."

I smiled, happy to see my friend receiving Elizabeth's praise. Returning to my position so Kitty could continue, I stared absent-mindedly out the window. Kitty had been correct; the rain had slowed, and even appeared to be stopping. My eyes focused on a distant movement as I wondered whether I would be able to return to Netherfield today.

"Oh!" I cried a moment later and leaned closer to the window, trying to get a better view of what appeared to be approaching. "I believe someone is coming."

"Where?" Kitty asked, dropping her sketchbook and joining me in the window seat. "It appears to be someone on horseback."

"Who?" Miss Lydia rushed forward, pushing her way between us, and looked out. "Is it one of the officers?"

"I did not see red," Kitty replied, trying to see around her sister.

"Bah," Miss Lydia cried as she turned away. "It is only Mr. Bingley and Mr. Darcy." Flouncing down into the seat Kitty had just vacated, she picked up the sketchbook. "What is this scribble?"

Kitty snatched the book from her sister's hands as I stood to get a better look out the window. I had only seen one rider and had not suspected it to be my brother. Now, as they drew closer, I realized it was indeed as Miss Lydia had said. I looked excitedly toward Kitty who grinned in response.

"Mama," Kitty called as she carried her book away from Miss Lydia. "There are gentlemen approaching."

"Gentlemen? Good gracious!" She looked about the room and quickly determined all was satisfactory. "Mary, see to tea."

I watched Fitzwilliam and his friend dismount and stride toward the front door. It appeared he carried a portmanteau and I hoped it contained some of my belongings. I did not wish to borrow any more from the Bennet sisters, particularly not Miss Lydia.

The gentlemen were announced and I stood patiently by as my brother addressed the Mistress of Longbourn.

"Forgive our intrusion, Mrs. Bennet. I fear with the continued rains my sister must trespass upon you another day and I believed she would prefer to have a few of her things." Fitzwilliam turned toward me with a searching gaze. "Mrs. Hill has taken your bag to your room, Georgiana."

"Thank you, Fitzwilliam." I stepped forward and smiled reassuringly before embracing him. For the first time since Ramsgate, his concern for my well-being did not upset me.

"You are all consideration, Mr. Darcy," Mrs. Bennet crooned before turning her attention toward his friend. "Mr. Bingley, I hope the continued rains will not cause the ball to be delayed."

"Certainly not!" the man cried. "Darcy and I saw the men at work on the bridge before leaving Netherfield. I pray the rains hold off for a few hours so the work might be completed. Miss Darcy and her companion may be able to return this evening."

"Oh, but we quite enjoy having her here. Miss Darcy is such a joy, Mr. Darcy. You must be exceedingly proud of her." Mrs. Bennet waited for his answer, a frown slowly overtaking her features as none was forthcoming.

Puzzled, I turned my attention to my brother and found him quite distracted. Following his gaze, I realized he was watching Mr. Collins.

The man had taken up position by Elizabeth, who appeared quite discomforted. In the arrival of the gentlemen, Miss Mary had gone to the kitchens per her mother's orders. Mr. Collins had seized the distraction to claim the place on the small sofa beside Elizabeth and was speaking quite intently.

As a silence fell over the room, Elizabeth's soft response was clearly heard. "But I have agreed to dance the first with you, sir." She looked up, realization that they were now the centre of attention crossed her countenance and her eyes begged for assistance.

"Miss Elizabeth," Mr. Bingley stepped toward her. "I had hoped during our visit to secure a dance with each of the Bennet ladies."

A grateful smile crossed her lips. "Of course, Mr. Bingley. I am engaged for the first set, but the second is available."

"Excellent!" He turned toward Jane and intently held her gaze. "Miss Bennet, might I hope to dance the first with you?"

Jane's colour rose as she demurely granted his request. I held back my amusement as Mrs. Bennet nearly bounced in her seat with joy. I looked toward my brother to judge his reaction, but his eyes still lingered upon Elizabeth.

"Miss Elizabeth, I too wish to secure a dance. I fear I am engaged to dance with Miss Bingley and Mrs. Hurst during the third and fourth dances, but am hoping you are available for the dinner set. You would then be guaranteed to sit by Georgiana during the meal."

His voice was even, but I noticed his fingers twitching by his side. He had not done this in years. It was a trick he used when speaking to dispel his unease. He had only disclosed it to me after he had done it while holding my hand during his address to the Pemberley servants following our father's death. The distraction of his twitching fingers allowed him to conceal his anxiety, but went mostly unnoticed by those about him.

"I would quite enjoy Georgiana's company at dinner, sir." Elizabeth's relief in his offer was palpable, so much so that I began to wonder if Mr. Collins had been pressing for that very dance, and more, whether my brother was aware of it.

Glancing once more at Fitzwilliam before returning my attention to Elizabeth, I suspected a silent conversation to be playing out between them. I quietly excused myself and returned to Kitty in the window seat, where I waited expectantly for what might transpire next.

"Do you think they will speak aloud?" Kitty whispered.

I glanced at my friend, whose eyes remained glued to her sister and the silent suitor. "I am uncertain. Has anyone else noticed?"

Kitty shifted as she glanced about. "Mama is too busy with Jane and Mr. Bingley; and Lydia is pouting in the corner. Mrs. Annesley is watching us, so she may know what we are discussing. Mr. Collins appears confused. Do you think he might move so your brother can sit there?"

"I believe he is torn between fighting for Elizabeth and praising my brother for his connection to Lady Catherine." I felt the giggle over the man's ridiculousness rise in my throat and was unable to stifle it.

"That is quite a predicament," Kitty agreed, joining me in my merriment.

Mrs. Annesley's eyes narrowed and we quieted, hoping no one else had noticed us. Nonchalantly, I turned to take in the others in the room and found Miss Lydia watching me closely, a frown set upon her countenance. I smiled in response, but felt a chill run through me as Miss Lydia turned her attention toward Fitzwilliam.

He had taken a seat in the chair closest to the sofa and was carrying on a quiet conversation with Elizabeth, completely excluding Mr. Collins. Their heads were bent toward one another in an intimate manner.

I looked back to Miss Lydia and found the young girl now had a rather disturbing smile playing about her lips. *Surely Miss Lydia would not do anything to separate Fitzwilliam and Elizabeth. What interest could she have in them?*

All conversations and contemplations ceased as Miss Mary returned with a maid carrying the tea service. Mrs. Bennet called for Kitty to help her sister, and they began to pour out the tea and hand it about.

I debated moving closer, but decided my current seat allowed full view of the room and its occupants. I was grateful for my choice a moment later as Miss Lydia began slowly drawing closer to my brother. Unfortunately, I realized her intentions too late to be of any assistance.

Reaching Fitzwilliam's seat, Miss Lydia met and held my gaze as she leaned forward and spilled her drink upon his hand. The heat of the fresh tea caused him to startle, upsetting his own cup upon Elizabeth. In an instant, the entire room was in an uproar.

"Oh, how clumsy of me." Miss Lydia exclaimed as she reached for something to soak up the spill.

It took me only a second to suspect the paper Miss Lydia handed my brother was from Kitty's sketchpad, which she had laid on the table by Elizabeth.

"Lydia, what are you doing? Fetch a towel." Elizabeth ordered as she reached out toward Fitzwilliam. "Your hand is quite red, sir. You must allow me to bandage it."

Clearly, Fitzwilliam was in no small amount of pain, but he turned his full attention to his companion. "I am well, Miss Elizabeth, but please reassure me you are uninjured."

Looking down at her dress, Elizabeth chuckled softly. "This was never a favourite, sir. Lydia has given me reason to remake it. Perhaps I should have it dyed to match the colour of the tea?"

I watched my brother's shoulders relax as he met Elizabeth's gaze. Only Miss Lydia dropping a towel upon his injured hand caused him to wince.

"I insist, sir." Elizabeth took the towel and wiped the remaining tea from her dress before she stood and held out her hand to Fitzwilliam. "If you will accompany me to the still room, I have a cream which will relieve your discomfort."

Fitzwilliam took up the towel she had discarded and wiped away any moisture from his trousers. Reluctantly he stood and offered his arm to her while holding his injured hand protectively at his side. "Lead the way, Miss Elizabeth."

Fluttering her hands, Mrs. Bennet nodded toward her daughter. "Yes, yes, Lizzy. Tend to Mr. Darcy. Hill!" Mrs. Bennet called as the housekeeper stepped into the room. "Oh, thank goodness. Hill, please see to this mess. Lydia bumped Mr. Darcy and now tea is everywhere."

As I watched, the housekeeper picked up the paper, now soaked with tea, and tossed it into the fire. Finally free from my surprise, I jumped from my seat and rushed over in time to see the drawing, on which Kitty had worked so hard, begin to smoke.

"Oh, Kitty," I muttered.

"It wasn't very good, anyway."

I turned to see Miss Lydia standing a few steps away; a smug smile lingered upon her lips.

"I saw what you did; all of it." I glared at her. "Keep your distance from my brother."

"Perhaps it would be better should you and your brother return to London where you belong." Lydia's tone was sweet, but her expression hard.

I was about to reply, but Mrs. Hill moved toward us shaking her head ever so slightly. Taking a moment to look about, I realized we were drawing attention. I straightened my shoulders and raised my chin. "I much prefer the country," I replied in a haughty voice and walked away.

My anger grew as I neared Kitty, but I forced a smile. "I fear I do not remember where the still room is. Kitty, would you show me the way so I can see to my brother?"

Though she looked at me oddly, Kitty nodded and we left the room. "Are you well, Georgie?" she asked when we were alone in the hall.

"Lydia spilled her tea on Fitzwilliam on purpose," I said through clenched teeth.

Kitty gasped. "But why?"

Reaching out to take my friend's hand, I felt tears fill my eyes. "She used your sketch to mop it up."

Slowly, Kitty's look of surprise gave way to disbelief and finally anger. "For being displaced as the centre of attention, she would injure your brother and destroy something of mine."

I glanced over my shoulder as the parlour door opened, but saw only Mrs. Hill. "Come; let us find Lizzy and Fitzwilliam. Perhaps they might be able to suggest what actions should be taken against Lydia."

Kitty nodded and led me down a hallway toward the stillroom. We were about to enter when we heard laughter from inside. Exchanging a startled glance, we leaned forward as one and pressed our ears against the door.

"Mr. Darcy, you must hold still." Elizabeth laughed once more. "Have you always been a terrible patient?"

"I am not so bad as you insinuate, Miss Elizabeth." I could hear the amusement in my brother's voice. "I am simply attempting to assist you."

"As you have only one good hand and I have two, I believe it would be best if you allowed me to finish, sir."

Silence reigned for a moment before Elizabeth declared she was finished. "I do not understand how Lydia could have been so clumsy."

"Young people often are. I remember frequently tripping over my own feet when I was her age. Have you never taken a spill with no one to blame but yourself?"

We strained to hear Elizabeth's response, but Fitzwilliam's laughter told us she had admitted to it.

"Are you certain you are uninjured, Miss Elizabeth?" Fitzwilliam's voice was soft and caring. "I must know if my reaction caused you harm."

We could hear Elizabeth's laughter again, but this time she sounded nervous. "Merely my dress, sir."

"Then I shall see you have a new one," Fitzwilliam responded, nearly in a whisper which I had to hold my breath to hear.

"That will not be necessary, sir." Elizabeth's voice was also much softer and almost distracted.

We pushed against the door as close as possible, attempting to hear more, but only succeeded in releasing the latch and making our presence known. As we stepped inside the stillroom, Elizabeth quickly stepped back from Fitzwilliam and turned so her back was toward us.

"Georgie, what are you doing here?" Fitzwilliam snapped before forcing a smile. "I am well. It was only a mild burn, and Miss Elizabeth has seen to it."

I did not miss the look of longing in my brother's eyes as he gazed at my friend. I wished I could back out of the room and leave them alone once more, but the damage was already done.

"I am pleased you were not badly injured, Brother." I hesitated and glanced toward Kitty. Neither of us were certain of the best way to disclose Miss Lydia's actions.

Fitzwilliam straightened and took a step toward us. "Georgie? What has you concerned?"

Elizabeth drew closer also and addressed her sister. "Kitty? It is obvious the two of you had other reasons for seeking us out. Has something occurred?"

We both nodded, but it was Kitty who spoke. "Georgie saw Lydia purposely pour the tea on Mr. Darcy."

Elizabeth inhaled sharply as Fitzwilliam turned toward me. "Is this true?"

Nodding, I could feel the tears begin to sting my eyes once more. I brushed them away and told Elizabeth and Fitzwilliam all I had seen. "I do not know her reasons, but I suspect it may have been her way of defending Mr. Wickham. If not, it was simply to destroy Kitty's sketch." I shook my head. "Could she truly be that spiteful?"

"I have no idea how that girl's mind works," Elizabeth mumbled before turning toward Fitzwilliam. "I must apologize for my sister, sir; though there is no excusing her behaviour."

"Hush," Fitzwilliam whispered as he leaned toward her. "There is no reason for you to apologize, Miss Elizabeth." He took her hand in his good one and laid it upon the arm of his injured hand before meeting my gaze. "I believe we must visit Mr. Bennet to enlighten him on what has occurred."

"Yes," Elizabeth agreed. "I fear he shall be forced to discipline her now." She sighed longingly. "When the bridge is repaired, perhaps Kitty and I might accompany you to Netherfield in order to avoid the uproar."

"And face Miss Bingley?" I asked, attempting to adopt Elizabeth's teasing tone and lighten our moods.

"She, at least, has never caused me bodily harm." Fitzwilliam grimaced before glancing at the lady by his side. "Though I could not speak for *your* safety."

A pleasant blush passed over Elizabeth's features and she laughed softly. As she turned away, she motioned for Kitty and I to follow them and they led the way to Mr. Bennet's book room. After pausing at his door to assure everyone was prepared, she knocked and waited to be admitted.

"Enter."

Elizabeth took a deep breath and pushed open the door revealing Lydia sitting in a chair before their father's desk, her face streaked with tears.

"Ah, it appears all parties are now present. Shall we discuss today's events?" Mr. Bennet asked, obviously displeased.

Chapter Eleven

I reached out for my brother's hand as we entered the small room. He squeezed my fingers reassuringly, but released them again to assist Elizabeth to the sofa. Once Kitty and I were seated on either side of Miss Lydia, he took the remaining seat at Elizabeth's side. We all looked expectantly at Mr. Bennet.

That gentleman had watched as we entered and found our seats; his brow arching as Fitzwilliam had finally claimed his own. My stomach felt as though it were turning flips when his eyes roamed over each of us before he finally spoke. "Lydia came to me regarding certain tensions which have been felt within this house in the last day. Normally I would dismiss her and call her silly; but a guest has been injured, and I believe this must be dealt with so that it might not occur again."

He turned toward Fitzwilliam, the corner of his lip pulling upward. "I assume sir that your injury is not severe and you have been ministered to adequately?"

"Miss Elizabeth has cared for my hand proficiently, sir. One could not ask for a more accomplished nurse." His eyes lingered upon her, so he did not see the smirk which grew on our host's countenance.

"Yes, yes. With three younger sisters and herself always into something, Lizzy has become quite efficient in her doctoring skills." He turned back to us, the three younger girls directly before him, and his smile slipped away. "I have been witness to several upheavals in my home over the past day, and I find I am unable to avoid them. Lydia has disclosed her insight, now I wish to hear from the others involved."

My posture stiffened and I saw Kitty sit taller. I was sure we both wondered who would be called upon first. As quickly as he turned toward us, he looked back to my brother.

"Mr. Darcy, I might ask for your counsel. There is merit in having each girl tell their tale separately, unknowing of what has already been said; but some may say they deserve to know what has been accused."

Fitzwilliam drew his gaze from Elizabeth as he stroked his chin with his good hand. "I see your dilemma, sir." He turned back to the lady at his side. "Miss Elizabeth, how would you counsel your father?"

Looking at each of us girls closely, she pursed her lips in contemplation. "I believe each may reveal their perspective on what they have seen. Perhaps it would be best should they tell their tale in the order it occurred."

Mr. Bennet nodded as he looked at each of us. "Very well then, Lizzy, we shall begin with you and last night's dinner."

Elizabeth appeared startled, quickly glancing at Fitzwilliam and away again. "But, Papa, we discussed that last evening."

"You are correct, Child, but Kitty and Lydia were not present and do not know what was said."

Hesitantly, Elizabeth drew a breath and looked to her younger sisters. "I was rude to a guest in our home last evening, but I have explained my reasoning to Papa. Mr. Wickham …"

"Wickham? What was he doing here?" Fitzwilliam clasped her hand.

Mr. Bennet responded for his daughter. "Unfortunately, a few officers were also trapped at Longbourn due to the storm and were forced to dine with us. They were seen back to Meryton once your missive was received and we determined they would arrive safely." He motioned for Elizabeth to continue.

I watched as she carefully slid her hand from under Fitzwilliam's, as though she were trying not to draw attention, and placed it in her lap. "Mr. Wickham had made certain claims which Lydia believed to be true …"

"You believed him too, Lizzy, when he told you at Aunt Philips. Why should you say it was only me?"

"Quiet, Lydia! Lizzy, continue." Mr. Bennet eyed his youngest, his patience clearly nearing its end.

A look of exasperation crossed Elizabeth's countenance as she looked at her sister and her words were harsh when she spoke. "As Lydia decided dinner was the appropriate time to mention Mr. Wickham's lies, I felt it necessary to shed more light on the subject. It was clear Lydia was attempting to make Georgiana feel ill at ease, and I wished to protect her."

Lydia leaned forward as though to protest, but her father's glare silenced her.

"I questioned Mr. Wickham regarding his interest in the church as I was aware he had refused the position and received remuneration for it." Her gaze fell, and a moment later I saw Elizabeth lay her hand upon Fitzwilliam's twitching fingers just before she looked back at her sisters. "I was aware Mr. Wickham was not what he appeared to be, and I should have warned you both away from him prior to then."

"Very well, Lizzy." Mr. Bennet glanced at her hand, which she quickly moved back to her lap, before he turned his attention to his other daughters. "As I am now aware of the man's habits, I have decided he shall not be welcome at Longbourn. What's more, you shall not be seen in the presence of officers unless one of your older sisters is with you. As I doubt I can trust you to follow this dictate, you shall not venture to Meryton without one of your older sisters."

"Papa! No! Are we simply to believe Mr. Darcy?" Lydia cast a disdainful glance toward my brother.

"As he has a longer acquaintance with Mr. Wickham and documentation to support his claims, yes." Mr. Bennet's expression held no amusement as he stared down his youngest daughter.

Begrudgingly, Miss Lydia looked away first as she crossed her arms and sulked in her seat. "But what of today?"

"No," Mr. Bennet said softly, still watching her. "There is one more incident which occurred last night." Leaning forward, he waited for Miss Lydia to raise her eyes to his. "A guest was in need in our home, and you refused to provide assistance."

I could feel the heat rise in my cheeks as I knew Mr. Bennet was speaking of the dress. My gaze fell to the yellow skirt I wore and I picked lightly at an embroidered flower.

"Have you nothing to say for yourself? You were quite vocal last evening." Mr. Bennet ignored the others in the room, focusing completely on Miss Lydia.

"I suppose I might have simply given Miss Darcy one of my dresses." Her tone suddenly changed from repentant to petulant. "But Lizzy pushed her way into my room and began rummaging through my things."

"Is this true, Lizzy?"

"Having seen Lydia's suspicious expression when she finally agreed to lend Georgiana a dress, I thought it best to choose one myself for fear our guest would come down in rags this morning or something else that was inappropriate." Elizabeth shot a disapproving glance at her sister. "As it was, Lydia still made attempts to injure Miss Darcy."

"Yes, yes, I shall get to that." Mr. Bennet waved her away. "Well Lydia, what have you to say for yourself?"

"I did nothing to that dress!"

"To what dress?" he asked sardonically.

Suddenly uncertain, Lydia glanced around until her eyes fell on Kitty. "Lizzy took the blue dress from my room. I did not see it again. I do not know why Miss Darcy was wearing Kitty's yellow dress this morning. Perhaps Kitty did something to the blue one."

"Well, Kitty?" Mr. Bennet asked in a bored manner.

A moment passed while Kitty twisted a stray thread about her finger. Slowly, she raised her eyes and glanced across Miss Lydia to meet my gaze. I nodded encouragingly. "Last night, before we fell asleep, Lydia said Miss Darcy would find the blue dress uncomfortable. I woke before her this morning, as I had barely slept, and took my yellow dress to Maggie to let the hem out so Georgiana could wear it instead."

"Yes, Mrs. Hill brought the blue dress to my attention this morning. It appears gravel had been rubbed into the seams. I can imagine it would cause the wearer to be quite uncomfortable."

Everyone looked to Miss Lydia, but she was sitting quietly staring at her lap. From my vantage point, I could see my brother was becoming exceedingly displeased, but it appeared Elizabeth was reassuring him.

"So, we now come to the events which led to Mr. Darcy's injury." Mr. Bennet leaned back in his seat and took a deep breath. "Lydia informs me that she was quite disturbed by Miss Darcy's glares and stumbled over the leg of the chair causing her to spill her tea on Mr. Darcy's hand. She came to me as she was afraid she would be accused of doing it intentionally."

I sat taller in my chair, mouth agape in astonishment. I was about to respond when Elizabeth came to my defence.

"I find that quite difficult to believe, Papa, as I witnessed Georgiana giving Lydia the best imitation of Mr. Darcy's glare just last evening and Lydia was completely unmoved."

"'Tis true, Papa." Kitty nodded rapidly. "In fact, Lydia appeared about to confront Georgiana, so I asked her to assist me with my bonnet. Lydia was not in the least daunted by Georgiana."

"Very well, then what did happen, Miss Darcy?" Mr. Bennet turned toward me; his expression was neutral, but humour glinted ever so slightly in his grey eyes, allowing me to lose a bit of my unease.

My voice was soft when I spoke, but I was pleased it did not shake and reveal my nervousness. "Miss Lydia witnessed Kitty sketching my likeness and appeared most displeased. When she attempted to look at the drawing, Kitty took it away and sat it beside Elizabeth. Tea was being served and I saw Miss Lydia step up behind my brother. I could not understand why she stood where she did. I turned her way and that is when she looked me directly in the eye and leaned forward, pouring her tea on Fitzwilliam's hand." I lowered my gaze and took a shaky breath. "She then used Kitty's sketch to soak up the spilled tea."

"Is this true, Lydia?" Mr. Bennet turned once more to his youngest daughter and waited for her response.

Lydia looked around the room at each of us. Slowly, her lower lip began to tremble and tears filled her eyes. "Papa, they have all contrived against me to make up these lies. I never would injure anyone by design. How can they think so ill of me?" She sobbed into her hands.

"You have hurt me repeatedly!" Kitty suddenly cried out, jumping from her seat. "Papa, do not believe her! I have bruises covering my legs from where she kicks and pinches me when she does not get her way. Shall I show you?"

"Oh, Kitty," Elizabeth stepped quickly to her side and drew her into an embrace. "Why did you not speak of this before?"

"No one would listen. Mama told me that I must go with Lydia wherever she goes as no one else would; she never asked if I wished to do so. All that matters is what Lydia desires." She broke down in tears upon her sister's shoulder.

"Hush now," Elizabeth comforted her. A glance passed between her and her father who nodded and she led Kitty from the room.

As the door closed behind them, Mr. Bennet sighed. "I am grieved this played out before you and your sister, Mr. Darcy."

"I assure you, sir, neither of us will speak of it." Mr. Darcy approached my chair and took my hand. "I do, however, believe it best that I be going."

"I would agree; but how shall you manage your horse with your injured hand?" Mr. Bennet shook his head. "No, I fear it may be best that you remain our guest until we determine the safety of the bridge to Netherfield. You would do better to return in the carriage with your sister and her companion."

"I would not wish to be a burden, sir."

"Nonsense. I believe a few of the ladies will be pleased with your presence." He smiled in my direction, his eye nearly closing in a wink. "Miss Darcy, would you show your brother back to the parlour while I speak with my daughter?"

"Yes, sir." I stood and took my brother's arm as we left the room. Once outside, I felt as though my legs would not hold me and Fitzwilliam slipped his arm about my waist as I clung to him.

"Georgie?" The concern in his voice nearly undid me. "Has it been terribly unpleasant staying at Longbourn?"

Suddenly a giddiness filled me and I trembled with the effort to restrain it.

"Georgie?"

A giggle escaped as I shook my head. "No, Brother. Only Miss Lydia has been a trial. Mrs. Annesley and I have both been welcomed warmly here. Jane allowed me to spend the night in her room so I would be closer to them and not have to hear Mr. Collins snoring through the night, Miss Mary has invited me to practice with her on the pianoforte this afternoon so we might play a duet this evening, and of course Elizabeth and Kitty have been quite wonderful."

Fitzwilliam smiled. "So Jane, Elizabeth, and Kitty, eh? I suppose by the end of this day it shall be Mary also?"

"Oh, I hope so." I squeezed his arm as we approached the parlour. "I do like being around so many women close to my age. I would very much like to call them my sisters." I felt a slight bounce enter my step. "Kitty and I share the same birthday. We have decided we are as good as sisters already."

"Already?" he asked nervously.

"I hope Kitty will be well. I cannot believe Miss Lydia was being so cruel to her." I continued, turning the subject as we made to enter the room. Fitzwilliam appeared to hesitate, but followed me without another word.

"Oh, Mr. Darcy!" Mrs. Bennet exclaimed as we entered and she eyed his bandaged hand. "I must apologize again. I cannot imagine how this could have happened. Please, take a seat here. Hill has brought fresh tea with willow bark to ease your discomfort." She poured a cup and handed it to me. I carried it to Fitzwilliam and joined him on the settee.

Mr. Bingley looked up, as though just noticing his friend's return. "I say, Darcy, I suppose we should return to Netherfield." Reluctance was clear in his voice and countenance.

"Unfortunately, Mr. Bennet has insisted I remain. He fears I will be unable to ride with my injured hand." He held the offending limb up for his friend to see.

"Oh," Mr. Bingley appeared puzzled. I wondered if he would mention having seen Fitzwilliam ride with one hand in the past, but then his eyes grew brighter. "Yes, of course, how foolish of me. Mr. Bennet is a wise man; it would be best that you not ride."

"No, no," Mrs. Bennet quickly agreed. "I believe you both must stay for dinner. Perhaps the bridge will be mended by then and you may take the carriage back to Netherfield."

"May we send one of your stable boys to learn of the progress?" Mr. Bingley asked.

"Of course!" Mrs. Bennet rang for Hill who appeared almost instantly. "Hill, send Samuel to see how things are progressing on the bridge. Mr. Bingley and Mr. Darcy shall be joining us for dinner."

"Yes, mum." Hill curtseyed and left the room. It appeared I was the only one who noticed the smile crossing the woman's countenance as she closed the door.

Chapter Twelve

I entered the dining room at Longbourn, dressed in my own gown, with my arm linked through Kitty's. The host and hostess were already by their seats. I was amused and smiled inwardly to myself. Mrs. Bennet was speaking animatedly to Mrs. Annesley on her left. I watched as Mr. Bingley escorted Jane to the table and held her chair for her to sit beside my companion. When Mr. Bingley slipped into the seat beside her, Kitty nudged me and we giggled softly.

"Mr. Darcy, I believe I must apologize. I fear your sister's time amongst my silly daughters may be having a less than desirable affect upon her." Mr. Bennet motioned toward the chair to his left as Elizabeth took her normal seat on his right.

Fitzwilliam claimed the offered chair and smiled in my direction. "I am pleased to hear Georgiana laugh again. She has been in poor spirits for some time now. I doubt a few days with your lively family will completely undo her years of training."

"Oh no, I can only attribute your lack of concern to a diminished understanding of the gentler sex. Take the word of a man surrounded by the fair creatures; sense and rationality are more novelty than habit." He winked at Elizabeth, who shook her head but said not a word.

Kitty pulled earnestly upon my arm and quickly led me to the chairs closest to Mrs. Bennet's end of the table. A moment later, Mr. Collins took the place beside me with Mary on his other side next to Fitzwilliam. I was disappointed not to be sitting between the younger Bennet sisters, but pleased my brother would not be overwhelmed with Mr. Collins' presence.

Something was odd about the dining room this evening, but I was unable to determine what it may be. The inhabitants were genial and quiet conversations abounded, but something was amiss. I took a deep breath and the distant smell of roasted pheasant tantalized my hunger. *Distant?* I looked to the sideboard, but saw only a few covered dishes there.

With my brow creased in confusion, I glanced toward Mrs. Hill who stood near the doorway as though awaiting a cue, her eyes trained on the master of the house. I followed her gaze and found that man smiling mysteriously.

"Mr. Collins," he said as his lips twitched suspiciously. "Shall we have the blessing?"

The gentleman to my right startled, obviously unaccustomed to Mr. Bennet's ready acquiescence. He mumbled his assent, stood, and began another recitation of the many reasons for thanksgiving. I knew I should lower my head, and I did, as far as possible while still maintaining a view of my host and his housekeeper.

Kitty again began leaning heavily against me and others seemed to sway as the Rector continued in a droning manner. A motion from Mr. Bennet caught my attention, bringing me back to full awareness, and I saw Mrs. Hill slip from the room. When Mr. Collins finally said his amen, for what seemed to be hours later, though it was only minutes, Mrs. Hill reappeared with several servants carrying steaming platters to the sideboard.

I found it difficult not to laugh aloud. They had finally found a way to serve a hot meal. She glanced about the table, but Elizabeth appeared to be the only Bennet to notice. Her head was bent and she was whispering to her father who nodded as his grin widened.

Though amused by their interchange, I slowly felt a growing unease and looked about the room once more. After counting places a second time, I realized Miss Lydia was not amongst us. With wide eyes, I turned toward Mr. Bennet. He met my gaze with a kind smile before responding to a question from Fitzwilliam.

My brow drew together in concern and I leaned toward Kitty. "Lydia is not here," I whispered.

Kitty looked at me oddly before lowering her eyes to her lap. "She is in her room." My friend's voice was so low I could barely hear it. "Papa was forced to take action against her."

"But do you not share a room with her? Are you not afraid she shall seek revenge on you for speaking against her?"

"Lydia is being moved back to the nursery which is Mary's room. Mary and I shared Lydia's and my room before, until Lydia demanded they switch."

"So she shall have a room to herself? I would think that should please her very much." I was undecided if Lydia was truly being punished.

A slight flicker of mischief entered my friend's eye as she shook her head. "Lydia hates being alone and the room is very small. She shall be quite miserable, I assure you. Papa says that if she is going to behave like a child, she shall return to the nursery and there she shall remain until she can do better."

I glanced about to see how everyone was reacting to Miss Lydia's banishment, and saw Mrs. Hill step quietly up between Mr. Bennet and Fitzwilliam. She leaned over and spoke softly so I was unable to hear what was said. I watched as my brother nodded and then glanced in my direction.

"My dear, I have glad tidings," Mr. Bennet called to his wife. "The bridge leading to Netherfield has been repaired. There shall be no delay to Mr. Bingley's ball."

"Oh, how wonderful!" Mrs. Bennet gushed, but when her eyes fell upon me, her enthusiasm waned. "Oh, but that means you and your companion shall return to Netherfield, Miss Darcy. We have so enjoyed your company. I am loath to see you go!""

Before I could respond, my brother cleared his throat. "I am certain my sister has enjoyed her time here at Longbourn, and you shall all be together in a few days at Netherfield. Georgiana will be attending the first half of the ball, though she will not be dancing."

"That is good to hear," Mr. Bennet smiled in my direction. "She will be able to keep Kitty company as Lydia will not be attending the ball."

"Not attend?" Mrs. Bennet asked. "Why ever not? The officers will be so disappointed. My Lydia adores a ball! She will be greatly missed. I cannot have that! No, Mr. Bennet I think –"

"We will discuss it later, *Mrs. Bennet*."

I was as surprised as my hostess by the finality in Mr. Bennet's voice. I saw her open her mouth to respond, but a severe glance from him caused her to close it again. The Bennet sisters sat in stunned silence staring at their mother as she returned to her conversation with Mrs. Annesley. Even I, in the short time I had known her, could not explain Mrs. Bennet's easy submission to her husband, though I had never seen that man look so displeased either.

The dinner ended with little excitement. Mary was able to consistently deflect Mr. Collins' attempts to flatter Fitzwilliam; though I was not so blessed. After hearing his thoughts on Anne De Bourgh's grace and beauty repeated twice, I adopted a partial smile and nodded whenever it appeared appropriate. Kitty did assist when possible, but the man rarely paused to draw breath and therefore, aside from rudely interrupting him, there was little else I could do.

Once the final course was finished, Mrs. Bennet rose and led the ladies into the drawing room. As the door closed behind us, she took Jane's hands and squealed happily. "Oh, Jane! Mr. Bingley barely noticed anyone else at the table this evening. I am certain he shall propose!"

"Mama," Elizabeth spoke cautiously. "You cannot know his mind. Please do not assume that it shall be."

"Oh, little you know, Lizzy. You and your father and Mr. Darcy had your heads together discussing who knows what. You were not paying attention as I was." She squeezed her daughter's hands once more. "Five thousand a year and Netherfield so nearby! Oh, I shall go quite distracted!"

"Mama, please," Jane begged. "I would not want Mr. Bingley to believe I would marry him solely for his fortune."

"Well of course not," Mrs. Bennet scoffed. "Your dispositions are exceedingly well suited. But is it not grand that he is a gentleman of such standing? Oh, I was sure you could not be so beautiful for nothing!"

The Bennet sisters, nearly as one, released sighs as their mother continued with her effusions. Mary motioned for me to join her at the pianoforte and I willingly followed.

"Poor Jane," Mary whispered as she straightened the sheets of music before us.

I frowned. "Does she not like Mr. Bingley?"

"Oh, no, I am certain she is on her way to being deeply in love with him; but Mama's behaviour can be … Well, would you wish to live so near such a woman? I fear, should Jane and Mr. Bingley wed, Mama will be always at Netherfield. Were Mr. Bingley wise, he would end the lease and look elsewhere to establish himself."

Mrs. Bennet clapped her hands together in delight. "Oh, and this will throw you girls in the way of other rich men! I shall have all my daughters married and well settled. Oh what a fine thing!"

"Thank Heaven I shall be away from here," Mary muttered under her breath.

"Wherever shall you go?" I asked before realizing she had not meant for me to hear the comment.

Mary's countenance reddened as she stared at her hands.

"Forgive me, Mary, it was impolite to ask."

"No," she shook her head and looked up. "I simply do not wish Mother to know. She has encouraged Mr. Collins to pay his addresses to Lizzy, even though it is clear your brother much prefers her." Her hand flew to her lips and her brow rose. "Oh, I did not mean …"

I laughed as I reached out a hand to Mary. "No, it is well. I believe you are correct regarding Fitzwilliam's feelings. He has even taken actions to improve her opinion of him. Do you think Elizabeth might welcome his attentions?"

We turned and studied the lady who sat beside her eldest sister, lending her support and making every attempt to quiet their mother. "*Should* Mr. Bingley propose to Jane, I imagine Lizzy will often be in their company. As your brother is a close friend to Mr. Bingley, they would frequently be together. Perhaps, if Lizzy is able to swallow her pride, she will realize that Mr. Darcy is most likely the only man who will accept her impertinent manner."

"Do you truly see your sister so poorly?"

Eyes wide in innocence, Mary looked at me. "Oh no! I love my sister, but her faults are plain to see. She would admit them herself, if asked, and often has. I doubt many men would want a wife so outspoken, but your brother seems to appreciate it. Had he not insulted her, I am certain they would already be courting."

Uncertain how to respond as I knew my brother possessed his own pride which could interfere in such a courtship, I decided to redirect the conversation. "But you said you were pleased you would not be here."

The door opened and the gentlemen entered the room as the ladies stood. "No," Mary whispered determinedly, "I am doing what I must to secure my future. Now, shall we play the duet we practiced?" A pleasing smile crossed her lips as she looked across the room. "Mr. Collins, will you not turn the pages for us?"

****

As the Darcy carriage pulled away from Longbourn, I stared across at my companions. Mr. Bingley's lovesick expression was highly amusing, but my brother's brow, creased in deep thought, concerned me.

"Though I am pleased to be returning to Netherfield, I shall miss the Bennets exceedingly," I said to Mrs. Annesley.

"Oh, indeed. They are such a loving family; willing to share their home and table with any in need. I doubt there are a dozen families of the *ton* who would welcome unexpected guests in the open and caring manner in which they do. Mrs. Bennet may be a bit officious, but I choose to see it for what it is; a woman who only wishes the best for those she loves."

Fitzwilliam and I stared at her, both of us shocked that the normally quiet woman would speak her opinion so plainly. Before either of us could respond, Mr. Bingley released a sigh followed closely by a deep chuckle.

"Most assuredly. I cannot imagine a more loving mother."

"Bingley, have you lost your senses? You would consider Mrs. Bennet an excellent mother-in-law?" Darcy suddenly sat forward and turned an amazed expression upon his friend.

"A sight better than your aunt, I am certain." Mr. Bingley chuckled again, but his humour dispelled when he caught Fitzwilliam's eye. "Forgive me, old man. I meant no disrespect. I would simply prefer a wife with a loving, doting mother in contrast to the demanding, calculating society mothers I see in town. Tell me you do not feel the same."

A derisive snort escaped Fitzwilliam as he settled back against the squabs. "I begin to fear for you, Bingley. Mrs. Bennet is just what the mothers of society are, only with far less sophistication."

"Perhaps she would treat you better had you not insulted her daughter," Bingley challenged.

Even in the now dimly lit carriage, I could sense my brother's embarrassment. "I believe Mrs. Bennet would be more favourable toward you should she know you apologized, Brother. Perhaps Mr. Bennet will enlighten her when they speak regarding Miss Lydia."

"You apologized?" The incredulity in Bingley's voice startled me.

"But of course he did. Why would he not? Once he knew Elizabeth had heard him, my brother could not avoid apologizing." Unfortunately, my confidence dwindled as I spoke, and my voice reflected my uncertainty.

"I doubt he was unaware at the time of the occurrence. I believe the entire room knew of the insult before we left that evening. Darcy and Miss Elizabeth were in each other's company many times in the following weeks and this is the first I have been made aware of an apology." Bingley crossed his arms as though waiting for his friend to dispute him.

"Perhaps I do not reveal everything to you." The moonlight fell across Fitzwilliam's lap, revealing his hands tugging at his gloves as he stared out the window.

Bingley huffed, but turned his attention to the passing trees on his side of the equipage. We rode in silence the remainder of the way; dismounting quickly once the door was opened.

"I believe I shall retire early," Fitzwilliam said to all and none as we entered. "I fear my injured hand has made me unsuitable for company."

"Oh, Brother, does it hurt terribly?"

His expression softened as he saw my concern. "No, Georgie, but it does ache. I shall have my man, Preston, see to it."

"May I accompany you? I wish to see to your comfort, Fitzwilliam."

He leaned forward, conspiratorially. "You mean you wish to speak to me privately." I nodded and he released a soft sigh. "Very well. Allow me a few minutes to change and come to my room."

I nodded once more and allowed Mr. Bingley to escort me to the drawing room where Miss Bingley and Mr. and Mrs. Hurst sat. I endured the ladies' commiseration over being *trapped* at Longbourn until I felt enough time had passed, and excused myself saying I would retire early.

Climbing the stairs slowly, I debated what to say to Fitzwilliam. I had been so certain things were improving between him and Elizabeth. Reviewing the evening, I was able to determine it was when the men rejoined the ladies that his demeanour had changed. *What might have been said while we were not in the room?*

Chapter Thirteen

I stood before my brother's door, hand raised to knock, yet I hesitated. My mind continued to race over the events of the day, before quickly returning to Fitzwilliam. *What shall I say to him?* In my distraction, I barely noticed the door opening until the object of my reflection stood before me.

"Fitzwilliam!" I startled from my thoughts.

He took my raised hand in his own and led me into the room. "I wish to retire, Georgie, else I would have waited to see how long you would have remained in that position." His eyes flashed with amusement and I relaxed.

My gaze fell to his freshly wrapped hand. "Are you much improved now that Preston has tended your injury?"

"Somewhat." He crossed to the set of chairs before the fireplace and waited for me to sit before he took his place in the companion. "What did you wish to discuss, Georgiana?"

"I could not help but notice your change of spirits following dinner. I was concerned something occurred after we ladies left the room." Though avoiding his direct gaze, I watched my brother surreptitiously.

He stared into the flames as he turned his signet ring ever so slightly. After doing so for some time, he took a deep breath and turned toward me decidedly. "I am aware you believe I should offer for Miss Elizabeth. I see your reasoning; she does seem to draw me out of my normally quiet ways. She is intelligent and quick witted." A small smile played about the corners of his lips. "I can well imagine she would be a challenge to any society matron."

"I believe our aunts would be delighted by her." I saw his brow rise and pursed my lips to hide my smile. "Well, until they realized your affections for her."

"Georgie ..."

"Do not tell me you have no feelings for her, Fitzwilliam. I saw your eyes just now when you spoke of her, and the manner in which you conversed with her at Longbourn." I stared into his eyes, my own pleading for him to admit this one thing.

I saw the moment he relented, though he did not speak. His shoulders slumped and he dropped my gaze. The look of complete defeat was not lost on me. "I do not understand why you are so saddened by finding such a woman."

"Because I cannot have her; she can never be my wife."

"Why not?" I cried out in utter amazement.

"Georgie, I am the Master of Pemberley. I must think of all that entails. Our estate is grand and would survive a marriage that brought no fortune, but no connections also? What would that do for your prospects? For my children's prospects? Yes, one marriage would be well and good, but what if my son is unable to bring a lady of wealth and connection to wife due to his mother's lack of connections? What if we have five daughters, as Mr. Bennet? Could I dower them all and have Pemberley remain what it is?"

He pushed from the chair and began pacing before the hearth. "Do you not believe I have carefully considered this? That I have not imagined her at my side at Pemberley? She would be the best of Mistresses to the tenants, but can I risk their future?"

"Forgive me, Brother, I had not thought of those things." I lowered my gaze to my lap as I twisted my fingers. I was certain he had used every one of these arguments with himself over the time we had been in Hertfordshire, but it still did not explain why his mood had changed so drastically this evening. "Was something said following dinner which brought this to mind once more?"

He stopped his pacing and folded his arms against the mantel as he lowered his head to rest upon them. "Bingley spoke to Mr. Bennet. It is clear he is ready to ask for a courtship. Mr. Bennet told us precisely what the sisters could expect as dowries before describing his wife's connections in detail. I believe he did so to weed out any squeamish suitors."

"And he succeeded in one," I murmured softly.

Fitzwilliam's posture changed once more as he reached for the poker and began agitating the wood. "Mr. Collins was quick to announce he took no issue with the ladies' lack of dowry and hoped to claim a Bennet sister as his wife. I saw the look of recognition which passed over our host's countenance. He would sacrifice *her* to that drivelling fool!" Sparks shot from the abused log as he struck it.

Realization settled upon me and I fought the urge to laugh outright at his jealousy. "Are you certain?"

He turned toward me, incredulous. "You have been witness to his fawning over her. I secured the

159

dinner dance as I heard him attempt to cajole it from her when all could see her discomfort. She is the one of his choosing."

"But he is not the one of her choosing."

"He is the heir to her father's estate. Clearly she is Mr. Bennet's favourite and he would prefer to have her as Mistress of Longbourn when he is gone."

"Not if she must sacrifice her happiness." As I finished speaking, Fitzwilliam looked at me suspiciously. "Elizabeth and I have discussed Mr. Collins' attentions. She has made every attempt to dissuade him as she does not wish to embarrass the man, but she is convinced her father will not force her to accept him."

My brother stared at me, as though he had not fully comprehended my words. Slowly, enlightenment struck him and he straightened. "But, should she refuse him and her father passes, what would become of her? I doubt Mr. Collins would be generous enough to allow her to remain at Longbourn without making her very existence miserable."

I lowered my gaze, suddenly uncomfortable to speak of what I had learned from my new friends. "I believe Mary has taken it upon herself to encourage Mr. Collins' attentions."

"Miss Mary? Does she hold a tender for Mr. Collins?" His lips curled in disgust at the very idea.

I quickly shook my head. "I do not believe it to be so. I fear she only looks to her security and well-being." I frowned. "Truly, I doubt she has even considered her sisters in her choice. I know not how the unwed sisters would be treated once Mr. Collins is the Master of Longbourn."

Fitzwilliam shuddered. "Elizabeth shall leave, I am certain. I know, were I in her position, I would be unable to watch that man assume my father's place."

"It would be best were she wed before that occurred," I murmured and saw him nod, though he was deep in thought.

From just behind me, a man cleared his throat. "Pardon my interruption, sir. Will there be anything else tonight?"

Fitzwilliam ran a hand over his brow. "Perhaps a tonic for my head, Preston, and then you may retire."

"Very well, sir." The valet returned to the dressing room.

I sat quietly a moment, but it was clear my brother no longer noticed my presence. Silently, I stood and entered the dressing room. "Mr. Preston," I said softly to make him aware of my presence.

"Miss Darcy." He hid his surprise well, but not his curiosity. "May I be of assistance?"

"I am most hopeful, sir." I turned toward Fitzwilliam's wardrobe, scanning for a specific item. Upon spotting it, I smiled broadly and drew it from the cabinet. "I believe this waistcoat to be one of the finest my brother owns; do you not agree? It suits him well and would set him apart at Mr. Bingley's upcoming ball." I met his eye, hoping I need not say more to enlist his assistance.

His head tipped slightly to one side as he eyed first me and then the item in my hand. Finally, a twinkle entered his eye as his lips turned up on one side. It was the closest thing to a smile I had ever seen on the man. "I must agree, Miss Darcy. I should have chosen it myself. I believe it would reflect the light in another's eyes beautifully."

Realizing he understood more than I anticipated, I could barely contain a squeal of delight. I leaned forward, pointing to some of the embroidered threads, and whispered, "Her dress is just this shade."

Preston suddenly stood taller, the light in his eyes still visible behind his now stern demeanour. "I know not of whom you speak, Miss, but I shall see that your brother is properly attired that evening." He took the waistcoat from me and set it aside for pressing.

Turning, I saw Fitzwilliam move toward the dressing room and quickly stepped out to meet him.

"Whatever are you doing, Georgie?" he asked in a wearied voice.

"I was asking Preston about your hand as you appear to be in discomfort. Perhaps a bit of laudanum would do better than a tonic. Are you in great pain, Brother?"

He eyed me suspiciously for a time. Finally, he took a deep breath and replied, "I do not believe that is what was being discussed, but I have no desire to press the issue this evening. I beg of you, Georgie, allow me to retire and end this conversation."

Stepping closer, I laid my hand against his chest, just over his heart. "I do not wish to see you ill or discomforted, Brother. I shall end this for tonight, but only on the condition you do not close your heart to her. I have heard your arguments against Elizabeth, but I believe the good she could bring to our family far outweighs any concern you might have. Our times are changing, Brother. Even titled men have married penniless brides from the landed gentry, and I dare say a few from trade." I paused and reflected. "She makes you happy when you are with her and that is enough for me. You deserve happiness, Fitzwilliam." Going up on tiptoe, I kissed his cheek and left the room.

As the door closed behind me, I whispered a prayer that my brother, for once, would not be so obstinate.

Chapter Fourteen

The day of the Netherfield Ball, I was nearly as anxious as Mr. Bingley. All day, the two of us could be seen 'grinning in a most ridiculous manner', according to my brother. Sitting on a chair by the ballroom doorway, I ran my fingers over the fringe of my silk shawl and attempted to calm my excitement. Though I had been sent to my room that afternoon to rest, I had been unable to close my eyes. Now I sat with Mrs. Annesley and waited.

It appeared as though all of Meryton had arrived, and still no Bennets. My brother stood in a corner, frowning at the number of red-coated officers in the room, but there was no sight of Mr. Wickham and I hoped he had decided not to attend. I was suspicious, however, of the looks that passed between the officers who were there as they, in turn, watched Fitzwilliam.

Before I could give it a second thought, there was movement and a familiar cry at the door and all eyes turned to see the Bennets make their entrance. As I drew closer, I saw Jane speaking quietly to Mr. Bingley, oblivious to her family's behaviour, but Elizabeth's cheeks appeared flushed as she eyed her mother.

Mrs. Bennet gripped her hostess' hand. "Oh, Miss Bingley, I am so enchanted by your use of fall flowers to decorate the entryway. However did you know they are Jane's favourites? I am certain she must feel exceedingly welcome."

"I am so pleased," Miss Bingley responded through clenched teeth.

Elizabeth bowed to our hostess, but moved quickly past her until she was before me; we linked arms as we greeted one another. "Oh, I feared we might never arrive," she whispered as we began to make our way around the room. "Lydia came below, dressed and ready to accompany us. Papa had to send us ahead while he dealt with her. He shall arrive later, if he decides to come at all. He really does dislike balls for the most part."

By the time Elizabeth finally drew breath, I realized her recitation was due to nervousness. I glanced about the room, but did not see anyone who might cause Elizabeth's discomfort. These were friends, accept perhaps the officers, but she had never appeared affected by them in the past. As we drew near Fitzwilliam, Elizabeth's voice drifted away. It was clear to see the strong attraction they bore towards one another.

He stepped forward and took her hand in his, bending over it as she curtseyed. "Miss Elizabeth," his voice was hesitant. "You are a vision."

"Thank you, Mr. Darcy." Elizabeth responded, a quiver in her voice. Her eyes fell to his waistcoat. "It appears we are well suited this evening."

His eyes followed her gaze as though it were the first time he saw what he was wearing and a smile passed over his countenance. "So it would seem. I wonder how my valet knew."

They both glanced toward me, but by that time I had moved back toward my companion to allow them time alone; though I was careful to stay near in order to hear what was said.

"I believe your sister wishes to see us together, sir."

"Yes, so it would appear." Silence stretched between them and he reluctantly released her hand.

"I suppose she is much like Kitty, believing in fairy tales where the handsome prince falls madly in love with the poor peasant girl and defies society to marry her."

"You think me handsome?" he teased.

"I had not realized you were royalty, sir." Mirth flashed in her eyes.

"I suppose not, for you are most decidedly *not* a peasant girl, Miss Elizabeth."

"No, but I am certain Miss Bingley would want her brother to marry someone of a higher standing than my family. How much more so would you?" Her eyes fell. "Mr. Darcy, I must apologize for what occurred at my home ..."

Fitzwilliam reached out toward her. "Please, you need not apologize for your sister's actions."

"No, you misunderstand me. I was speaking of what occurred in the stillroom."

He inhaled sharply and looked about before returning his gaze to her. "It is I who should apologize, if I felt the desire to do so. I took advantage of our proximity while you cared for my burn. I hope you have nothing to regret. I do not."

Slowly she raised her eyes to his and I could see they glistened with unshed tears. *Whatever could have happened in the stillroom?*

A sudden tug on my arm drew my attention. "Have I missed anything?" Kitty asked as she took in the ballroom. "Ooh, it is spectacular! Has the dancing begun? I do hope we have not missed the first dance. Well, perhaps, for Lizzy must dance with Mr. Collins and I would hope she could avoid it."

I glanced back in time to see the very man leading Elizabeth toward the dance floor. "No, the first dance appears to be starting now." I looked back to my brother who scowled at the retreating forms. "Come, Kitty, you may sit by me if you do not have a partner."

"You do not appear overly excited. Is this not your first ball? I thought you would be as happy as I."

"I was, but ..." I glanced toward Mrs. Annesley who was speaking with Mrs. Bennet and Lady Lucas. Leaning closer to my friend, I whispered, "I overheard Elizabeth and Fitzwilliam. Something *did* happen in the stillroom."

Kitty's eyes grew large. "What do you think it was? Could they have kissed? Did he compromise her? Oh, if only we had opened the door sooner, we might have seen them and then they would have to marry."

"Kitty! You would want them forced into marriage when they do not wish to be?"

Rolling her eyes, Kitty motioned toward Fitzwilliam. "Does he look as though he does not want to marry my sister? If Mama sees him looking at her in that manner, she shall set her sights upon him." Distracted by movement close by, she looked away. "Oh, here comes Miss Bingley."

"Miss Bingley? I thought she would be dancing." I strained to see a large feather bouncing its way through the crowd until it stopped before my brother.

"Mr. Darcy, you are not dancing." Miss Bingley gazed over the edge of her fan.

"Neither are you, Miss Bingley," he responded while continuing to watch the dancers.

"I had left this dance open for fear I may be needed, but now I am without enterprise."

Fitzwilliam nodded, but made no comment.

Kitty and I exchanged a glance and covered our mouths to smother our giggles. Miss Bingley clearly wanted Fitzwilliam to ask her to dance, and he refused to satisfy her. Mrs. Annesley flashed us a gentle warning glance, and we both turned our attention back to the dance floor.

Unfortunately, we were just in time to see Mr. Collins turn wrong and step on Elizabeth's hem. That it was torn was obvious. The lady's response was all that was commendable, but her ire was clearly raised. She left the floor directly in search of the retiring room in hopes that it could be mended, Mr. Collins following after her apologizing profusely.

Kitty took hold of my arm and pulled me from the room so we could follow. As we entered the hallway, Elizabeth turned upon Mr. Collins.

"You, sir, have done enough. I beg of you to return to the ballroom and leave me be."

No one had seen Mary behind them until she took hold of the Rector's arm. "Please, Mr. Collins, my sister is correct. It would not be seemly for you to be seen with her in such a state. Come join me in the ballroom. I dislike dancing and would prefer to spend the evening in discussion. Do you not agree that is the better way?"

Reluctantly Mr. Collins allowed Mary to lead him away and Elizabeth continued down the hall. Kitty and I called out to her and she turned in time for us to see the tears falling down her cheeks.

"Lizzy, what is it?" Kitty asked as she took her sister's arm.

I stepped to her other side and we swept her into the retiring room. Leading her to a chaise lounge, we forced her to sit while we knelt before her and inspected the damage. Kitty handed Elizabeth a handkerchief to wipe away her tears.

"Is it very bad?" Elizabeth asked timidly.

It appeared as though the dress could be repaired, but all would know it had been damaged. We looked at one another questioningly before answering her. Kitty raised her shoulders, uncertain how to respond.

"I shall get Hannah. She will know what to do." I leapt from my place and rushed from the room. I rounded the corner and was confronted with the solid form of my brother.

"Is Miss Elizabeth unwell?" he asked, taking hold of my arm to balance me.

"Her gown is torn. I was going for Hannah to see if she can repair it."

Fitzwilliam nodded, but did not release me. "You should not be in the hallways alone when a ball is in progress, Georgie." He looked about and motioned a footman toward us. "Find Mrs. Nicholls and have her send Hannah to the retiring room."

"Yes, sir." The servant scurried off toward the kitchens.

My brother frowned as he turned back to me. "Have you forgotten what we discussed? That you should never be alone?"

Suddenly uneasy, I glanced about. "No, I remember, but I was not thinking of myself. I wished to assist Elizabeth. She is so upset. The gown was a special gift from her aunt and uncle, and now it may be ruined after only one dance."

"Georgie, do not exaggerate. I am certain something may be done to make the dress presentable."

My eyes drifted down from his countenance, falling upon his cravat. "Brother, I thought Preston had prepared a green neck cloth for you to wear this evening."

Fitzwilliam frowned. "I am not accustomed to this new style. I prefer the white."

I clapped my hands excitedly. "Perhaps the gown can be repaired after all. Will you fetch the neck cloth?"

His brow drew together in a frown, but I opened my eyes wide and allowed my lip to pout. With a sigh, he motioned me toward the retiring room and turned away.

I skipped into the room, but stopped when I saw the tears flowing down Elizabeth's cheeks. "Oh, do not cry. Hannah is on her way and I believe I know how to make the gown even better than it was before."

The Bennet sisters looked at me quizzically, but I refused to say more. Hannah entered a moment later and inspected the tear while we anxiously watched.

"Well, I can mend it, but it will be noticeable," she announced as she sat back on her heels.

Just then there was a knock upon the door and a voice followed. "Georgie?"

Jumping up from my place beside Elizabeth, I rushed to the door and opened it for Fitzwilliam. "You have it?"

He handed me the green neck cloth, though his gaze fell just behind me. A tender smile crossed his countenance as he bowed his head.

Glancing over my shoulder, I saw a blush cover Elizabeth's chest and countenance. I pushed my brother from the room and closed the door.

"Hannah, what can you do with this?" I waved the neck cloth.

"Ooh, it's the perfect colour!" Kitty exclaimed. "Lizzy, it will look as though it was meant to be there."

"If we can attach it correctly." Hannah frowned as she laid the cloth across the damaged gown. "It is not long enough to wrap the whole way around." She bit her lip as she laid the cloth one way and then another. Suddenly inspiration struck her. "Miss Elizabeth, will you stand please? I must see how tall you are."

"Oh, I feel so ridiculous," Elizabeth muttered as she stood. She glanced at Kitty and me. "You need not stay with me. I am certain Hannah will be able to make me presentable, but it will most likely take some time. I do not want you to miss the ball."

"Are you certain?" Kitty asked, clearly eager to return to the dancing.

"Go!" Elizabeth smiled and waved us away.

I hesitated, but Kitty grabbed my hand and pulled me toward the door. "Come now; Lizzy will be displeased if we miss the fun by sitting here with her."

"She is correct, Georgiana. You may leave me knowing I am in capable hands." She smiled at Hannah who nodded absent-mindedly as she began pinning the cloth to the gown.

"If you insist," I responded hesitantly. I was at the door when I stopped and turned back to Hannah. "She must be ready for the supper dance." I looked at Elizabeth. "I wish to dine with you."

"I shall join you for dinner, even if I am too late to enjoy your brother's dance." Elizabeth's smile was not as bright as it normally was, but I nodded and left the room.

Once in the hallway, I could hear scattered footsteps, but did not see anyone. I remembered my brother's words of warning and glanced about, searching out the small, somewhat private areas he had mentioned. I was shocked when I saw a flash of red in an alcove down the way and heard a faint, feminine giggle. Shaking my head, I gripped Kitty's arm tighter and moved quickly toward the ballroom.

We entered at the far end and I could see Fitzwilliam coming down the line of dancers with Jane. As they reached their places, the music ended. It appeared as though he might escort her toward them, but Mr. Bingley was soon by his side offering Jane refreshment. Fitzwilliam bowed and made his way toward me.

"Did the neck cloth suffice?" he asked as he glanced about for Elizabeth.

"Hannah believes it will do well, but Elizabeth sent us away to enjoy the ball." I finished speaking just as the feather appeared behind my brother.

"Mr. Darcy, I believe this is our dance." Miss Bingley wrapped her hands about Fitzwilliam's arm possessively, not looking at anyone else in our party.

"Of course, Miss Bingley." He bowed to her before turning back to Kitty and me. "If you will excuse me." He bowed once more, a look of pain crossing his face, before he turned and led his partner to the head of the line.

Kitty giggled. "Your brother is nothing like we believed."

I frowned. "And what was that?"

"Well, he was always so stiff and proper. He would stand to the side and look down on everyone. Of course I suppose part of that is because he is so tall, he must look down; but we believed he was too proud to speak." She glanced about, hopeful for a partner. "Do all the women act like Miss Bingley when they are near him?"

I shook my head as I watched our hostess attempting to flirt with Fitzwilliam while they danced. "Unfortunately, yes."

"I suppose that could be fun for a time, but it would soon become tiring I should think." Kitty gripped my arm and stood taller as an officer approached.

"Miss Catherine, may I have this dance?"

"Of course, Mr. Pratt." She smiled to her companion as she took the officer's arm and was led away.

I looked about for Mrs. Annesley and finally found her by Mrs. Bennet and Lady Lucas. I began to make my way toward them when I came upon Mr. Bennet, who had just recently arrived. His complexion was pale and he scanned the room as though in search of someone.

"Mr. Bennet, you appear distraught. May I be of assistance?"

"I beg your pardon?" He glanced down and smiled as he recognized me. "Ah, Miss Darcy, I believe you *can* be of assistance. I see your brother is dancing, but I do not see Lizzy."

"There was an accident, sir. She is in the retiring room having her gown mended."

"An accident?" A look of unease crossed his countenance and I quickly reassured him.

"Nothing so bad. Mr. Collins stepped upon her gown and tore it at the bottom. I suspect Hannah shall soon be finished stitching it, and Lizzy will return to the dancing."

Mr. Bennet looked toward Fitzwilliam once more as though he was deciding something. "Miss Darcy, I must speak with your brother, but I do not wish to cause an uproar."

"After this dance, he is to partner Mrs. Hurst. I am certain he will have a moment between dances," I sighed, "if we are able to separate him from Miss Bingley."

The corner of Mr. Bennet's lips twitched and his eyes sparkled momentarily. "And should I require your assistance in that endeavour, may I count on you?"

I smiled brightly. "Most certainly, sir."

He returned my smile, but it faded quickly. I took a guess as to what had the gentleman so unusually concerned. "I understand Miss Lydia wished to accompany you this evening."

The creases on his brow deepened. "Yes. I fear she is the reason I must speak to your brother."

"Fitzwilliam? I do not understand."

Mr. Bennet took a deep breath and glanced about once more. I was sensitive to his anxiety; it appeared Miss Bingley had arranged for this to be the longest dance of the evening. When Mr. Bennet took my hand and placed it on his arm, I was surprised, but allowed him to lead me about the room.

"I suppose it would be best to warn you, as it may be some time before I speak to your brother." His voice was soft and he had donned a false air of amusement as he glanced at the dancers we passed. "In her ranting, Lydia revealed she had arranged to meet Mr. Wickham here. It was to be a surprise as he had told the other officers he was unable to attend."

I felt as though the air had been forced from me. Mr. Bennet patted my hand, meeting my eye for a moment in an encouraging manner. I forced a smile and glanced toward my brother who was looking in my direction and appeared about to step out of the dance line, so I laughed as though Mr. Bennet had just told a witticism, not delivered unwanted news. When he relaxed and returned his attentions to his partner, I gripped my escort's arm tighter and spoke through clenched teeth.

"Did she mention where or when?"

"No. Once she realized what she had revealed, she refused to say more." He muttered something I was unable to hear, but was certain it was an oath of some sort. "She is in her room with Mrs. Hill watching over her."

I nodded, deep in thought, as we made our way closer to the matrons of Meryton society. When we reached Mrs. Annesley's side, Mr. Bennet assisted me to a chair and bowed to the ladies.

"Oh, Mr. Bennet," Mrs. Bennet cried upon seeing him. "I am so pleased you were able to arrive before the supper dance. You know, Lizzy is to dance with

Mr. Darcy, and they appear to be getting on exceedingly well together."

"Mrs. Bennet, I would ask that you not begin matching our daughter with Mr. Darcy. Though I believe he may be the best of men, I do not desire her living so far away." Before anymore could be said, he turned and left the circle of hens.

"He apologized, you know," Mrs. Bennet continued to Lady Lucas, oblivious to her husband's words. "I am certain he has found Lizzy to be so much more than tolerable." She giggled behind her fan.

I watched as Mr. Bennet made his way toward the far end of the room in order to be near Fitzwilliam when the dance ended; all the while listening to his wife continue her speculation regarding a match between Fitzwilliam and Elizabeth while observing the activity in the room.

Kitty was dancing enthusiastically with the officer, while Miss Bingley and Fitzwilliam appeared ill at ease. Mr. Bingley smiled broadly at Charlotte Lucas, though his glances often followed Jane who danced with Mr. Denny. As I watched, I noticed that Jane's gaze was frequently drawn toward her host as well. A movement to my left drew my attention and I turned to find Mary and Mr. Collins sitting together speaking animatedly, perhaps of the dancers as they motioned that direction frequently.

A smile crept across my lips as the importance of a ball resurfaced in my mind. Yes, they were entertaining, but there was so much more just below the surface. This was a marketplace, and the merchants presented their wares to the best of their abilities in hopes of capturing a customer. Miss

Bingley was using the opportunity to show her skills as hostess in an attempt to impress Fitzwilliam. He had no desire for her, but she was incapable of recognizing it. Most everyone in the room had seen the attraction between him and Elizabeth, thus beginning Mrs. Bennet's conjectures.

"Oh, to see two daughters wed!" that lady suddenly decreed to her friend before turning and seeing her third daughter. "Perchance three." She pointed and all eyes turned to Mary who was unaware of the sudden attention.

Yes, the ball was the lead into courtship with expectations of matrimony. No wonder Fitzwilliam had attempted to avoid them for so many years. I giggled softly until I felt Mrs. Annesley's eyes upon me. *She must believe I have been in the punch.* This brought on another round of giggles.

Finally, the dance ended and I watched as Mr. Bennet stepped quickly up to Fitzwilliam, bowed to Miss Bingley, and led her escort away. The lady's eyes blazed, but she drew herself to her full height and moved decidedly toward her sister where her countenance displayed every indignation as she spoke.

I turned my attention back to my brother, but he and Mr. Bennet were no longer in the room. Keeping my eyes on the doors, I was pleased when they returned a few minutes later escorting Elizabeth. Fitzwilliam scanned the room, obviously searching for me, so I stood and waved to draw his attention.

"Miss Darcy," Mrs. Annesley stepped up to my side. "Was there something you required?"

"Oh no, Fitzwilliam is looking for me." I pointed toward the approaching group.

"Mrs. Annesley," Fitzwilliam bowed as he neared us. "I must ask that you be even more attentive this evening. I fear the presence of an unsavoury character." He hesitantly turned toward me. "Forgive me, Dearest, I believe it would be best that you retire for the evening now."

"Fitzwilliam ..." I began to protest, but he stopped me.

"No, Georgie. I insist you go upstairs now."

My eyes dropped to the floor, where I noticed for the first time how expertly Hannah had attached the cloth to Elizabeth's gown. It looked as though it was part of the original design, and matched perfectly with my brother's clothing so everyone would suspect it had been planned.

"Could I not at least see you dance with Elizabeth?" I pleaded.

"Mr. Darcy," Elizabeth leaned closer to him. "I understand your concern, but would it not appear odd for Georgiana to leave prior to the appointed time? And, more importantly, is she not more protected in a room full of people than alone upstairs?"

"Miss Elizabeth, your argument has merit, but we are dealing with an unpredictable foe. I know not what he may say or do, but I firmly believe, whatever his actions, the object will be to injure me."

Her brow arched as she observed him. "You are so certain? I understand there has been a long history between you, but is there no chance that he may simply wish to make more of his life? And may I point out that the only word we have of his possible arrival here tonight is from my sister; a highly unreliable source."

"Please, Fitzwilliam. I promise I will remain by Mrs. Annesley; stay away from doors and windows; whatever you require." I looked at him with wide pleading eyes. Elizabeth stepped forward to stand by my side.

With a great sigh, Fitzwilliam relented. "Very well; I fear I am unable to resist the two of you together."

"Oh, thank you!" I stepped forward and placed a kiss upon his cheek.

"Yes, well," he looked reluctantly about. "I fear I am delayed in collecting my next partner. Do I ask too much that you both remain here until I return?"

Elizabeth slipped an arm through mine. "We shall not move from this very spot." She looked about. "Well, we may take those seats over there, but there we shall remain."

Though he attempted to appear stern, it was beyond his power. He bowed and went in search of Mrs. Hurst instead as Mr. Bennet sighed loudly.

"What is it, Papa?" Elizabeth asked in concern.

"Oh, I was simply considering the cost of traveling to Derbyshire." He turned his attention toward me. "I understand your home boasts a most extensive library."

"It does indeed, sir. I believe you would be quite at home within it." I smiled as I squeezed Elizabeth's arm.

Chapter Fifteen

"Oh, Elizabeth, I am so pleased Hannah was able to repair your dress." I squeezed her hand as we sat together watching the dancers.

"It would have been atrocious if not for your brother's neck cloth. I hope he did not expect it returned to him." She fingered the silk cloth, which Hannah had cut into strips and sown into a pattern on the front panel of her gown. "Do you think anyone will notice?"

I shook my head decidedly. "Fitzwilliam prefers white neck cloths. I purchased the green for him for his birthday, but he has never worn it. And I doubt anyone will think twice regarding the change to your gown, unless they studied it closely when you first arrived." I shrugged my shoulders as I looked out at the dancers. "Besides, many people saw the damage done by Mr. Collins, or heard word of it, and would be pleased you were able to return to the ball."

"I suppose." Elizabeth ran a hand nervously over the material once more. "Georgiana, did you suggest your brother wear a green waistcoat?"

"I did not mention it to Fitzwilliam," I replied innocently, while not looking directly at her.

"I see." There was a slight silence and I was about to turn around when Elizabeth spoke again. "Do you frequently speak to his valet regarding Mr. Darcy's clothing choices?"

Feeling heat rush to my cheeks, I lowered my gaze. "Will you forgive me, Elizabeth? When I saw your gown, I was immediately reminded of

Fitzwilliam's green waistcoat. I knew you would appear stunning together."

"Georgiana, I must ask you to stop pushing your brother and I together. I quite like you and hope that we may be great friends; but I do not wish to be constantly concerned that our visits may make your brother uncomfortable."

"Why would you believe he is uncomfortable?" I tilted my head to the side, studying Elizabeth who gazed at the dancers most intently.

"Whenever we have been in company, he has stared at me in such a manner that I am certain he is attempting to find fault. My family has certainly proven itself quite ridiculous before him on several occasions. My own sister has attempted to maim him and conspired with his enemy. However could we overcome such obstacles?"

The dance ended and Fitzwilliam quickly dispatched his partner to her husband and hurried across the room in our direction.

"Does he appear desirous to avoid you?" I whispered just before he arrived in front of us.

Elizabeth's blush was exceedingly becoming as Fitzwilliam bowed over her hand and led her to the floor. She glanced over her shoulder in my direction, flashing a reluctant smile of acceptance as he laid his injured hand over hers, which rested upon his arm.

"Oh, how I wish I could hear what they say," I said under my breath.

"That would be highly improper," Mrs. Annesley responded causing me to jump.

"Forgive me," I said as I took my seat and the lady followed. "I had forgotten you were there."

"You and Miss Elizabeth were speaking quite intently. I did not wish to interrupt."

"Do they not look beautiful together?" I watched as Fitzwilliam led Elizabeth through the pattern and returned to their places. It was clear he was favouring his hand and she was making adjustments to protect his weakness. "Did you see how he looked at her just now?"

"Now Miss Darcy, her mother is doing enough speculating without your assistance."

I glanced about until I found Mrs. Bennet, surrounded by her friends, speaking animatedly as she motioned toward the dancers. My eyes then moved over the onlookers and found that many were watching both of the eldest Bennet sisters and their partners. Slowly I began to understand Elizabeth's words. Expectations were being raised, if my brother decided not to court Elizabeth, future visits to Hertfordshire could be exceedingly awkward, to say the least.

A sigh escaped me and Mrs. Annesley laid a hand upon mine. "Your brother is a sensible man and Miss Elizabeth is wise for her years. I am certain all will be well."

Nodding slowly, I promised myself I would do no more to force the couple together. "So long as no one presses the issue. I fear I have done more than was proper."

Mrs. Annesley sat straighter and looked me up and down. "I know I may not have been as attentive as normal, but I have not seen any misstep on your part. Why do you believe you have injured them? From what you have told me, I find you have simply smoothed the way toward friendship."

"What of Fitzwilliam's waistcoat?"

"A most lovely coincidence."

"Will others not believe it was planned?"

Mrs. Annesley shrugged her shoulders. "Is it important? They look very well together, but it is their behaviour that may cause talk, not the colour of his clothing or hers. Should your brother pay sole attention to her, fawn over her, or stare moon eyed ..."

"As Mr. Bingley?" I giggled as I glanced at our host who was grinning like a schoolboy at the eldest Bennet daughter.

"Precisely. Expectations have formed regarding *their* future. I would not be surprised if they announced a courtship before the week ended. Prying eyes will then turn to Miss Elizabeth, but they still remember her initial reaction toward Mr. Darcy, as well as his insult. They will not quickly accept such a reversal in feelings."

I fell silent, deep in thought, and missed the remainder of the dance. There was so much I had not considered when attempting to secure what *I* believed would be my brother's happiness. Absentmindedly I rubbed my temple.

"Georgie? Are you unwell?"

I looked up to find my brother and his partner standing before me. "Oh, has the dance ended?"

Fitzwilliam frowned. "Did you not rest this afternoon? Perhaps you should take a plate to your room and retire early."

Elizabeth laid a hand upon my cheek, concern showing in her eyes. "You are not warm; does your head ache?"

Smiling at the loving attention, I shook my head. "I am well, thank you. I was simply lost in thought and am now disappointed that I did not see the whole of the dance."

My brother's eyes narrowed as he studied me. Though it was clear he did not fully believe me, he held out his hand. "Then let us go into supper before you miss more of the festivities."

I smiled gratefully as I rose and took his arm. I noted Elizabeth held his left arm as he cradled that injured limb against his chest.

"Does your hand pain you, Fitzwilliam?"

He glanced down at the wrapped appendage before allowing his gaze to drift toward his companion. "During previous dances, it did; but Miss Elizabeth was most attentive to my comfort."

"As the injury occurred in my presence, I was most mindful of it, sir. I would not like you to believe the Bennets were determined to always cause you harm." Her brow rose as she smiled at him in a teasing manner.

"Are you my protector, Miss Elizabeth?"

Her lips drew together in an attempt to hide her amusement. "That will not do, Mr. Darcy. You have promised to guard your sister and me. You cannot abdicate your responsibility so easily."

"No, I suppose you are correct," he sighed. Turning slightly, he winked at me. "Though Georgiana shall be retiring after supper."

Elizabeth's light laughter carried us into the dining room. "And when it is just the two of us remaining behind, you would place protection upon my shoulders?"

"Never," he said softly as he led her to her place. Once she was seated, he assisted me, and then claimed the chair between us.

I watched as he questioned Elizabeth regarding her preferences. He flinched as he served her, and I was pleased to accept the young officer to my right when he offered to fill my plate. It was obvious to me that Fitzwilliam was in more pain than he acknowledged. I wondered how to send word to Mr. Preston. Perhaps I could ask Fitzwilliam to escort me to my room and he could have his hand tended to at that time.

"Georgie?"

I looked up to see my brother frowning at me. "Forgive me, Fitzwilliam. I ..."

"Mr. Darcy, I apologize for stepping over my bounds and attending your sister. You may not remember me, but I served with your cousin, Colonel Fitzwilliam. My name is Jacobs, Captain John Jacobs." The man bowed his head.

"Jacobs? I do remember you. Were you not ... an *intricate* member of my cousin's squadron?"

I looked between the men. I could tell my brother meant to say more, but was uncertain that he should. While the young officer was attempting to provide information without speaking.

"Yes, yes. I was wounded in battle and returned to England to recuperate. The Colonel suggested I spend some time with the militia, see over certain *interests*, and regain my strength before returning to his side." His brow rose upon the word 'interests' and I wondered what my cousin was about.

"I see." Fitzwilliam glanced at me and then back to the young man at my side. "Perhaps we should speak after supper."

"I believe it would be wise, sir."

My brother looked at him a bit longer before turning to me. "Georgiana, may I introduce Captain Jacobs. Captain, my sister, Miss Darcy."

Feeling as though I had been passed along, as one would pass a precious trinket to a trusted companion to guard, I lowered my head in acknowledgement to the introduction.

"Miss Darcy, I feel as though we are already acquainted; your cousin speaks of you frequently."

I glanced toward my brother, but he was speaking quietly with Elizabeth and I was unable to hear what was said. "Well, you have me at a disadvantage, sir. Unfortunately, my cousin rarely speaks to me of his work or his troops."

Captain Jacobs blushed. "No, I suppose he would not. Shall I tell you of myself and how I came to be friends with your cousin?"

Looking back at my brother once more, I nodded and turned my full focus to the man at my side. As he spoke, I realized he was not as young as I originally thought. Though his features were youthful, the creases about his eyes spoke of years in the elements.

"Like the Colonel, I am a younger son; however, I did not grow up longing to serve my King as he did. That decision came later. My father is the Earl of Suthridge."

"Suthridge? I know that name. Your father and my uncle are friends, are they not?"

"Indeed, tis how I became a soldier." The Captain motioned a servant forward to fill their cups as he continued telling his story. "I was captivated by philosophy when I was a lad, but my father feared my outspokenness would not fit well within the Church. When he learned your cousin had entered the Army, he determined I should follow in his footsteps. Our fathers were able to force hands a bit, and I was placed under the Colonel's command. He is a good man."

"Yes, Richard and my brother are the best men I know." I took a spoonful of soup and waited for him to continue.

"I have been pleased to serve with him, and to now be of some assistance here."

"You mentioned that earlier. Does Richard know Mr. Wickham is in Hertfordshire?"

I was forced to look away when Captain Jacobs began coughing on the piece of meat he had bit into just before my statement. Obviously, he believed me to be ignorant of that man's presence. Before he could fully recover and respond, I continued. "I believe Fitzwilliam wishes to tell you we suspect Mr. Wickham will make an appearance this evening."

The man eyed me suspiciously. "He has told the officers he will not attend."

Nodding, I picked up my glass and brought it to my lips. After taking a sip, I replaced it and turned my attention to him once more. "It appears he had made plans to meet with … a young woman this evening." Though I tried, I was unable to call Miss Lydia Bennet a lady.

Captain Jacobs' eyes narrowed as he studied me. "And will that rendezvous continue?"

My jaw fell open. "It is not me!" I glanced about to be certain no one had noticed my reaction. "Her father is aware of her intentions and has taken measures to thwart their plans," I said in a calmer tone.

"I am pleased to hear it." He smiled before returning his attention to his plate. "I understand you are not yet out, so you will be retiring following dinner?"

"Yes. My brother had thought to have me retire earlier, but Elizabeth and I convinced him it would be better for me to remain below."

"Miss Elizabeth is a wise lady. I believe it would be best to determine Mr. Wickham's whereabouts before you leave the safety of the ball."

I turned to catch his eye. "But would it not be odd if I remained beyond the time expected? Would people not talk?"

The Captain shrugged. "They may simply believe your brother is unable to refuse your wishes." He smirked. "I am certain you are not the only young lady of the first circles who has been spoiled by her family."

I straightened, suddenly taking offense. "I beg your pardon? I am not spoiled."

"Are you not?" His lower lip curled out as though he considered my words doubtful. "Yet most young ladies are. Those I have encountered are exceedingly accustomed to having their way."

Doubt tickled my conscience, but I held my head high. "I do not see that as being spoiled. I am not like other girls who faint or cry to gain their heart's desires."

His countenance became exceedingly serious as he studied me. "I believe you."

I was just about to smile when he continued.

"You are far too intelligent to use such simple means. No, I suspect you prefer to eavesdrop and manipulate what you hear to your advantage." His eyes narrowed a bit more, just before a slow smile spread across his features. "Though I see pouting is not beneath you."

Realizing my lip had indeed begun to do as he said, I pulled it back in and turned away. A low chuckle drew my attention back to him.

"Forgive me, Miss Darcy, I meant no offense. I have several sisters, you see, and am quite familiar with the means they execute when they are most desperate to have their way." He laughed again as he took up his glass and tipped it toward me. "A truce?"

Reluctantly, I took up my glass and nodded. "I believe I understand why Richard likes you."

The man laughed once more and the lines, which aged him moments earlier, now appeared what they should have been all along; signs of a joyful life. "I suppose the Colonel and I do share a similar outlook; we have been known to find amusement in situations when those around us are bereft of humour."

"I suppose a soldier's life is not often a pleasurable one." I moved the food about my plate as I considered the man at my side. "How was my cousin when you last saw him?"

His countenance became serious once more. "He was well. I fear I am unable to say more." He laid his hand on the table between us. "The Colonel is an honourable man who is unwavering in his support of his King and country. It is men like him who will win this war."

Lifting my glass once more in his direction, I forced a smile. "May it end soon."

"Here, here." He drank with me.

The glasses were returned to the table and we said little while we finished our meal. I was about to ask the Captain what he thought of Hertfordshire when Fitzwilliam once more turned in our direction.

"Captain Jacobs, if you have a moment, I would like a word with you."

"Certainly, sir." The officer bowed to Elizabeth and myself as he and Fitzwilliam stood and left the room.

Elizabeth looked at me, a strange smile gracing her lips. "I suppose they must go and fortify the castle walls."

Having been lost in contemplation of my earlier conversation with the Captain, I responded with a weak smile. Suddenly feeling exceedingly guilty for my behaviour, I reached out to my friend. "Elizabeth, I must ask your forgiveness. I realize I have been quite horrid in my actions of late. I have not behaved as a proper lady would at all."

Concern flooded Elizabeth's countenance as she moved to the seat Fitzwilliam had vacated and took my hands in hers. "How so? I have seen nothing inappropriate."

I shook my head. "I have listened while you and Fitzwilliam spoke privately, and tried to force the two of you together though you both asked me to stop. I have been so disrespectful."

The corner of Elizabeth's mouth twitched as she patted my hands. "Oh, you behaved like any sixteen-year-old girl. I believe that is forgivable."

I shook my head again. "But I knew I should not do so." I lowered my eyes, afraid to meet Elizabeth's gaze.

"True, and of course every young girl knows what is right and does it faithfully. It is obvious you are the only one to act so truly horrible." There was a pause, but I refused to look up. "And what is more important are your motives. I am certain, for you to feel so terrible, that you did these things solely for your own benefit."

This brought my head up, my eyes opened wide in innocence. "No. I wanted only what I thought was best for you and Fitzwilliam."

Elizabeth smiled brightly. "Of course, you did." She laughed quietly. "Dear Georgie, I am beginning to believe you are a puzzling combination of all that is sweet in Jane and all that is puckish in me." She slipped an arm about my shoulders. "Come; let us go see what is keeping your brother."

"But will he not be displeased? I am certain he would not want us wandering the halls." I blushed as I remembered his words earlier. "He told me couples sometimes steal away during balls, and I must remain with a large group so I am not found in a compromising situation."

"Oh? Well I suppose that may be true in town, but I doubt the watchful eyes of the Meryton matrons would allow such here. I am certain they know where every young maiden is at all times, or so I was led to believe when I attended my first ball." She winked and took my arm as we stood. "If your brother is displeased, we shall simply tell him we were on our way to the retiring room before the dancing began again."

"I suppose." I bit the inside of my cheek as we left the dining room. My mind returned to the couple I had glimpsed in the hallway earlier. *Obviously the matrons' skills are slipping.*

Chapter Sixteen

The thought of the mysterious couple still lingered in my mind as Elizabeth and I walked down the hall leading away from the ballroom. My brother was nowhere to be seen. As we approached the alcove, I allowed my gaze to linger there.

It was a simple recess, unremarkable really; in fact, it appeared exceedingly barren. I wondered why Miss Bingley had not filled it with some notion or other; perhaps a table, bench, or pedestal holding a flower arrangement. Of course it was November and few flowers were to be found, those that were graced the front hall.

As I was turning to continue on my way, I noticed something on the floor. Disengaging my arm from my companion, I bent to pick it up.

"What is that you have found?" Elizabeth asked as she looked over my shoulder.

Frowning, I passed the bit of fabric to my friend as I stood. "I am uncertain. Could it have been torn from someone's gown?"

"Hmm," Elizabeth studied it closely. "It appears to be a token."

"A token?"

"Yes, to a passer-by it might look like a bit of fabric and lace, perhaps torn from a gown or a handkerchief; but see here? It feels as though there is a lock of hair sown inside. The gentleman could wear it close to his heart and people would think nothing of it." She sniffed it. "And it has been scented, most likely with the lady's favourite fragrance." Her brow creased and she sniffed it again.

"What? Is there something odd about the scent?" I leaned closer in an attempt to smell it.

Elizabeth shrugged her shoulders and handed it to me. "Not odd, I simply thought I recognized it. It isn't rose or lavender as many ladies wear, but it seems familiar to me for some reason."

I smelled the bit of linen and lace, but shook my head. "What should we do with it?"

"Do with what?" my brother's voice came from behind me.

"Oh, Fitzwilliam. We found this on the floor in the alcove." I held it out to him, but he frowned as though he had no desire to touch it.

Captain Jacobs stepped forward and accepted it instead. After studying it closely, he leaned forward. "Mr. Darcy, see here. There appear to be initials stitched into the fabric."

Taking the token, Fitzwilliam stepped closer to a wall lamp and examined the spot the Captain had indicated. "I cannot make it out."

Elizabeth crossed to his side, smiling. "Perhaps I might be of assistance. My stitching was quite ill when I was younger. I may be able to read another's lettering." She leaned forward and stared at the material in his hand. "Could that be an M? See how the second stitch is quite close to the first? At first I thought it was a backwards N."

Lifting it closer to the light, Fitzwilliam nodded. "I believe you are correct. Do you think the next might be a K?"

"Yes. M K?" She thought a moment before her eyes widened. "Mary King! And that is the scent she wears. It was a gift from her grandfather when he travelled to Paris. Since he passed, she has worn it frequently."

I looked to my brother who had continued to study the remaining stitches.

His lips pursed as he handed the token to Captain Jacobs. "If I am not mistaken, the remaining letters are G W, though the W does resemble an N." He turned toward Elizabeth. "You said her grandfather has passed? Is she an heiress?"

Elizabeth's eyes widened as she looked to me and then back to Fitzwilliam. "I have heard it said she inherited ten thousand pounds."

"Oh my," I murmured as I began chewing my nail.

"What is it, dearest?" Fitzwilliam took my hand, lowering it to my side.

"I found it in that alcove." I pointed to the spot just behind me. "Earlier this evening, when Kitty and I were walking from the retiring room to the ball room, I heard noises coming from there and saw a flash of red."

"Why did you not speak of this earlier?" Fitzwilliam questioned me brusquely.

"I doubt she thought it important." Elizabeth slipped an arm about my shoulders as her eyes flashed at Fitzwilliam.

"Not important that Wickham was here?"

"How could she know it was him?"

"Forgive my interruption," Captain Jacobs said just loud enough to draw their attention. "Miss Darcy, this was before you were aware Mr. Wickham may be at the ball?"

"Yes," I responded timidly.

"And were you able to see anything other than the colour red?" He smiled reassuringly at me.

"Nothing. I was glancing over my shoulder as I walked in the other direction. I heard a woman's giggle and soft voices and looked back to see who was there."

My brother's frown deepened. "We have discussed these matters, Georgie. I am surprised you said nothing."

Elizabeth shook her head. "I am surprised the couple was able to elude the matrons."

"Did anyone see Miss King arrive?" Captain Jacobs asked, but we all indicated we had not. "Perhaps he was able to draw her away before anyone was aware of her presence."

"What of her companions?" Fitzwilliam asked, clearly doubtful anyone could be that unobservant of a young charge.

I could not help but raise my brow, shocked at his sudden naiveté. "She could easily have given some excuse, such as wishing to visit the retiring room, and sent them ahead."

Elizabeth nodded and appeared about to voice her agreement when the musicians began tuning their instruments. "It appears the ball is recommencing." She looked to the gentlemen as though determining what would be done now.

Sighing, Fitzwilliam glanced at the Captain. "We conducted a thorough search of the public rooms, but have not found him."

"It is uncertain if he has remained." The officer appeared thoughtful before turning suddenly to Elizabeth. "Have you seen Miss King at all this evening?"

Her jaw fell open slightly and her eyes took on a faraway look, as I had seen her do before when searching her memory. "I do not believe I have. Her mother was speaking to Lady Lucas and my mother before dinner; I assumed Miss King was dancing."

The gentlemen exchanged a worried glance before Fitzwilliam took Elizabeth's hand and placed it on his arm. "Let us return to the ballroom and ascertain her whereabouts. Will you be able to find her in a crowd?"

"Most definitely, sir. She is exceedingly fair with vivid red hair. I am certain none would miss her."

Fitzwilliam stopped in mid stride. "I believe I know of whom you speak." His gaze fell upon me. "She cannot yet be my sister's age."

"I believe she has just celebrated her sixteenth summer. She and my youngest sisters are the same age." Elizabeth followed his gaze and frowned. "Miss King, Lydia; it appears Mr. Wickham prefers to prey upon the young and inexperienced."

For a moment, it felt as though a hand wrapped about my chest and it was difficult to take a deep breath. I felt the tears well up, but the thought of Miss King being drawn in by Mr. Wickham was enough for me to shake away the panic which threatened to overwhelm me. Mustering my strength, I straightened my back and lifted my chin.

"Fortunately he is unaware that we know of his duplicity." I turned toward the gentlemen. "If Miss King is no longer at the ball, what can be done to find her?"

A look of admiration crossed my brother's countenance before he replied. "I doubt Wickham is foolish enough to remove the girl from a public gathering. I suspect they have arranged to meet afterward or on a later date."

Captain Jacobs frowned. "I would agree, but for the information I shared with you earlier, sir. It is probable he is looking for an immediate exit from Hertfordshire."

"What information?" Elizabeth and I asked in unison.

The gentlemen looked at each other, a hint of amusement in their gaze, before Fitzwilliam shrugged and nodded.

"Colonel Fitzwilliam has had several individuals watching Mr. Wickham for some time. When they learned he joined the militia, your cousin arranged for me to be part of the training command. Earlier this week, it became apparent that Wickham had not changed his ways." He frowned and glanced at Fitzwilliam once more.

"What has he done?" I asked coldly.

"Accumulated debts, as before; but ... there is at least one merchant who is reporting a more serious transgression."

My brow drew together in puzzlement until I saw Elizabeth's blush. My eyes opened wide in shock. "He has ..."

Fitzwilliam quickly interrupted. "I suggest we return to the ballroom before it is too crowded to locate Miss King easily."

"I fear it may be too late." Elizabeth tilted her head as the first notes of a dance began.

We turned as one toward the music and entered the ballroom. Fitzwilliam suggested we split up in search of the young girl. As only he and Elizabeth knew what she looked like, he took my arm while Elizabeth accompanied Captain Jacobs.

We circled the room in opposite directions until we met on the other side. None had seen the young lady. To be certain, we continued on our way, coming together once more at the doors where we began. Still no red haired lass had been sighted.

Rising up to her full height, Elizabeth scanned the crowd once more. "It appears Mrs. King is not in the room either."

Suddenly hers eyes widened and I followed her gaze to see Mrs. Bennet speaking animatedly to Lady Lucas who simply shook her head, lips pursed in disapproval. As one, we began moving toward the matrons to learn what scandal had occurred in our absence.

"...such a sweet girl, but to act so irresponsibly ..." Mrs. Bennet was saying as we approached.

"Mother, are you unwell?" Elizabeth asked, slightly out of breath from our dash across the room.

"Oh, Lizzy, it is such a scandal! Mary King has gone missing! She arrived with her mother, but cannot now be found. None remember seeing her at dinner."

I asked breathlessly, "What is being done to locate her?"

Frowning, Lady Lucas responded, "Mrs. King has looked in all the public rooms and the retiring room. She has just gone to speak to Mr. Bingley."

We turned in time to see Fitzwilliam and the Captain approaching, but moved past them in the direction we had last seen our host. The gentlemen followed behind.

Mr. Bingley was not easily located, and I quickly explained to my brother what we had learned. With a nod, he took my arm and turned me toward the hall. Once outside, in the relative quiet, he glanced about.

"Were I Bingley, with a house full of guests and one missing, I would take Mrs. King away from the others so as not to create a panic or unnecessary concern should it simply be a misunderstanding." He led the way toward the study.

As we approached, we could hear weeping and a soft reassuring voice. Fitzwilliam knocked before opening the door and stepping inside. He held up a hand for the rest of us to remain in the hall as he closed the door behind him.

Though we did as he requested, Lizzy and I leaned closer to the door in hopes of hearing what was said. I noticed the Captain's lip twitch as he watched me, and I straightened and turned away. *Irritating man!*

The door opened a moment later, and Fitzwilliam motioned Elizabeth and me into the room. "Please attend to Mrs. King. We will ask that you be brought tea while we do a thorough search for Miss King."

With a puzzled expression, I nodded and took a seat beside the distraught woman. *Have we not just searched?* I watched as Elizabeth held Fitzwilliam's gaze longer, her own eyes betraying the same question. He leaned forward and spoke softly with her before leaving the room with their host.

Elizabeth sat at Mrs. King's other side and took her hand. "Mr. Bingley and Mr. Darcy will leave no stone unturned to find Miss King. They shall search from the attic to the cellar and anywhere else she may be."

"What could have become of her?" The woman wailed. "I cannot bear to lose her, not so soon after her father and then her grandfather. Oh, where can she be?"

"Hush now," Elizabeth pressed a fresh handkerchief into Mrs. King's hand. "Did Miss King say she was to meet anyone? Was she anticipating the dance for any particular reason?"

Taking a shuttering breath, the widow shook her head. "So many gentlemen have called recently. Mary is quite popular amongst them, you know. I am certain she shall marry ere long."

"Were there any gentlemen who were more attentive than others?" I asked in a small voice.

"A few of the officers had spoken of dancing with her tonight." Her tears began to flow freely once more. "Though she has disappeared before they could. Oh, if only we had not been late arriving!"

"Forgive me, I had not realized." Elizabeth tilted her head to the side and glanced at me. "Did something occur?"

"The carriage arrived later than planned. Mr. Wickham apologized for the inconvenience."

"Mr. Wickham?" I leaned forward anxiously.

"Yes, he had offered to accompany us to the dance as it is only Mary and me now. My brother has business in Liverpool and has been unable to come to us."

A knock at the door drew our attention and Elizabeth nodded for me to see to it. I opened the door to find the maid with a tea service. Motioning the servant into the room, I attempted to stay between her and the whimpering woman. *The least amount of talk, the better.* I thanked the girl and hurried her from the room before returning to pour tea for everyone.

With a cup in hand and clutching the least damp handkerchief, Mrs. King seemed to settle a bit. "Mr. Bingley will not let anything happen to my Mary, will he?"

"Of course not." Elizabeth patted the widow's shoulder reassuringly, though I saw the doubt in her eyes.

I glanced at the mantle clock and tried to determine how long Miss King had been missing. If the couple had been in the alcove, they had not left immediately upon arriving at the ball. Perhaps they had not gone far.

"Oh, I hope Mr. Bingley has found Mr. Wickham. He may know where my Mary is." Mrs. King clutched her teacup.

"I am certain the gentlemen are searching for him." Elizabeth sipped her own tea, refusing to meet anyone's eyes.

I stared at the older woman, a sense of disbelief settling about me. Was it not obvious that Mr. Wickham was at the centre of the girl's disappearance? I was about to speak when the door opened and Mr. Bingley stepped into the room.

"Mary? Have you found my Mary?" Mrs. King jumped from her seat.

Bowing, Mr. Bingley begged her forgiveness. "I fear we have not, but Mr. Darcy and Captain Jacobs have not given up hope. Miss Elizabeth, may I have a word with you?"

Mrs. King collapsed back onto the settee, weeping uncontrollably. Elizabeth hesitated, but I waved her away as I consoled the older woman.

"Hush now, Mrs. King. My brother and the Captain will certainly find Miss King. They are the best of men."

The woman turned to lay her head on my shoulder, her tears unabated. By the time Elizabeth returned, without Mr. Bingley, my bodice felt as though it was wet through and through.

"Mrs. King," Elizabeth eased the woman from my embrace and handed her a serviette from the tea tray. "Mr. Bingley was simply looking for my father in hopes he may be of assistance. Please, try not to upset yourself so."

Taking up the widow's teacup, Elizabeth refilled it. I noticed she added something to the tea before handing the cup to the woman and urging her to drink it. Within a few minutes, the woman began to quiet, and shortly after that she drifted off to sleep.

"Laudanum," Elizabeth said before I had a chance to ask. "She was about to work herself into a full attack of hysterics."

"About? I fear she already had." I took up a serviette and wiped at my tear stained dress. "Why did Mr. Bingley want to speak to your father?"

"The gentlemen are hoping Lydia will know where Mr. Wickham and Miss King have gone." Elizabeth chewed lightly on her lip. "I only hope she cooperates and tells them what she knows. I suggested they point out that Mr. Wickham deserted her for Miss King. If she is angry enough, she may tell them everything."

I sat quietly, deep in thought. "Could Lydia have been acting like Mrs. Younge when she encouraged my attachment to Mr. Wickham?"

Elizabeth stared at me, her brow drawn together in deep thought. "I had not thought of it before. Why did Mrs. Younge assist Mr. Wickham? What would she hope to accomplish? I realize, of course, that Mr. Wickham would have access to your dowry; but how would that be of benefit to her?"

"Afterward, when I thought back on our meetings, I began to believe Mrs. Younge was in love with Mr. Wickham. The way she looked at him, as though she did not want to look away. She was always praising him and telling me what a wonderful man he was." I could feel the heat rise in my cheeks as I remembered a particularly uncomfortable conversation with my former companion. "She suggested he would be a caring lover."

"Do you believe she and he ... they ...?" Elizabeth cleared her throat, but did not finish her question.

Shrugging my shoulders, I shook my head. "I did not think of it at the time; but now, in hindsight and knowing what I do of him, I believe they had been intimate." The warmth in my countenance began to feel as though I stood before a blazing fire.

Elizabeth shivered and looked back to the older woman, whose mouth had fallen open releasing a most unladylike snore. "I suppose we should make her more comfortable."

The distraction of adjusting Mrs. King's posture, placing a pillow beneath her head, and raising her feet helped me dispel the images that had entered my mind. We moved the tea things back to the tray and sat quietly, waiting for one of the men to return with news. We remained comfortable in each other's company so that no conversation was necessary. After a few minutes in this posture, I began to feel the effects of not resting earlier in the day and my eyes grew heavy.

Chapter Seventeen

There were voices, whispers actually, but I could not make out what was being said. With great difficulty, I opened my eyes. Mrs. King still slept on the lounge beside me, but Elizabeth was no longer on the other side. Glancing about, I found her across the room in a tête-à-tête with her sister, Jane.

I opened my mouth, but only a soft croaking sound escaped. Clearing my throat, I tried once more. "What time is it?"

The sisters jumped at the sound and turned toward the lounge. Relief was clear in Elizabeth's eyes when she determined Mrs. King had not awakened.

"It is quite early in the morning, Georgie. Would you like to seek your bed?"

"No," I shook my head, coming more fully awake each minute. "Have the men returned?" I asked over a yawn.

The sisters exchanged a glance, but shook their heads.

"Have you heard whether Lydia was of any assistance?"

Once again a look passed quickly between Jane and Elizabeth before they glanced at Mrs. King. Finally, when I was becoming a bit upset at their reluctance to speak, Elizabeth stepped closer to me.

"We are hoping Lydia is with them."

"I beg your pardon? Why?" I sat forward, now filled with alarm.

"Papa did return and told us Lydia was no longer at Longbourn. Apparently, she pretended to be sleeping and, when Mrs. Hill left the room for a moment, she slipped away."

"And her being with Mr. Wickham and Miss King would be a good thing?" I rubbed my eyes in a weak attempt to clear my mind as well as my vision.

"Do you not see?" Elizabeth glanced once more in Mrs. King's direction and lowered her voice further. "If they are both with Mr. Wickham, they may not be considered ruined."

"But where are they?"

"The gentlemen are searching for them now. Mr. Bingley … he remained behind as he was the host of the ball and it would appear odd should he be gone. He told Jane that Mr. Darcy has ridden towards Clapham hoping to intercept them on the way to Scotland while Captain Jacobs returned to London in order to inform your cousin and gather assistance."

I sat back and shook my head. "I fear your hope is in vain. Has there not already been gossip? Mrs. Bennet and Lady Lucas were speaking of it in the ballroom last evening."

Surprisingly, Jane and Elizabeth smiled before the eldest responded. "When Mr. Bingley explained what had occurred to Papa, he spoke to Mama before leaving for Longbourn. Within a few moments, the word circulated the room that all was well and Mrs. King had taken her daughter home."

Turning first to look at the inert form beside me, I returned my gaze to the sisters.

"Everyone has left now," Elizabeth replied to the unspoken question. "No one knows she is here but us."

"But what will occur if someone takes it upon themselves to visit the Kings today? I am certain people are curious and will want to know why Miss King disappeared from the ball." I closed my eyes and rubbed the spot between my brows. I was surprised the Bennets would be so slow to see the danger of this deceit unravelling.

Elizabeth shook her head. "Georgie, the ball went very late. Though people will visit to discuss the event, it will be later in the day."

"And what of Mrs. King's servants? Will they not dispel the belief that Mrs. King arrived home last night with Miss King?"

"It would not be the first time my mother has gotten a story wrong. That is the problem with gossips, you know, they do not usually have all the facts." Taking my hand, Elizabeth knelt by my side. "We can only pray your brother and the Captain are able to find them quickly. If Miss King is returned unharmed, there will be nothing to conceal."

Jane perched on the edge of the nearest chair. "Papa has sent an express to Mrs. King's brother making him aware of the situation. I am certain he will arrive as soon as possible."

Once again, my eyes travelled to the woman beside me. "And what of Mrs. King? We cannot keep her sedated until her daughter is found."

The look which crossed Elizabeth's countenance clearly questioned why we could not do that very thing.

"Will no one come looking for her?" I asked in exasperation.

"I believe you should go to your room and rest," Elizabeth said softly as she stood. "There is no need for you to become upset by this. I promised your brother I would look after you."

"*That* is what he said." My eyes fell to my lap. "I wondered what he told you. Does he believe I am ill-equipped to handle such a situation?"

Dropping onto her knees, Elizabeth took my hands in her own and forced me to meet her gaze. "No! He was concerned you would see too much of your own situation in Miss King's. He asked me to stay with you and see to your needs."

"It could have been me." My voice sounded small, even to me.

"But it was not," Elizabeth replied with determination.

"No, thanks to Fitzwilliam it was not."

"And now he is doing what he can to assist Miss King." Elizabeth squeezed my hand again. "Your brother is a good man and he will not rest until they are found."

Jane stood and crossed toward the door. "I believe we could do with that tea Mr. Bingley promised." Opening the door a few inches, she spoke softly to someone outside before closing it and returning to her seat.

We sat quietly, each in solitary contemplation of what had occurred, until a thought caused me to moan softly.

"What of Miss Bingley and Mrs. Hurst? Are they not suspicious of why you remained behind and why Fitzwilliam left?"

A slow smile pulled at Elizabeth's lips. "As we all left the ballroom together, Mr. Bingley told her you invited me to spend the night and we retired early, weary of the dancing."

My jaw fell open in dismay. "And she believed him?"

An unusually devilish gleam entered Jane's eye as she responded. "I believe she was more concerned regarding the sleeping arrangements, than the reason for Lizzy spending the night. She left the ballroom immediately, but returned a short time later to announce that Mr. Darcy's valet said he was not to be disturbed and Mrs. Annesley confirmed that the ladies had all they needed."

Understanding my brother to be behind the ruse, I was able to relax some. He would do whatever was necessary to protect all our reputations; even the Kings' whom he did not know before this evening.

"But what of you, Jane?"

"Mother insisted I remain with Lizzy, of course. Mr. Bingley agreed immediately, and Miss Bingley was unable to deny the request. Papa has taken the others home, but he will return shortly with clothing for Lizzy and me. Your brother decided it was best to send news here to Netherfield and for Mr. Bingley to coordinate all efforts."

"Mr. Bingley?" I understood that it was Mr. Bingley's home, but I had not considered him up to such a challenge. After all, Fitzwilliam was here to assist him in managing an estate.

As if reading my mind, Elizabeth sat forward. "Your cousin is expected to either come to Netherfield or send someone to assist in the endeavour."

"My cousin is not available at present. Therefore, I suspect he will send someone, though Richard would never willingly relinquish the opportunity to face Mr. Wickham if it could be helped. They have never been friendly."

A male voice from the doorway broke into our quiet conversation. "I believe that is an understatement."

I flew from my seat at the sound of his voice. "Richard! However did you arrive so quickly? I did not realize you had returned to London."

Sweeping me up in his arms, he twirled me in a circle before setting my feet upon the floor and embracing me. "Well, Poppet, I am simply pleased it is not you I have come to rescue."

I broke from his embrace, but linked my arm through his as I drew him closer to the ladies. Mr. Bingley, who had entered with my cousin, followed behind us and took up position beside Jane.

"Richard, I must introduce you to my friends. Jane, Elizabeth, may I present my cousin, Colonel Richard Fitzwilliam, second son of the Earl of Matlock. Richard, this is Miss Jane Bennet and her sister, Miss Elizabeth, of Longbourn."

The appropriate curtseys and bows were interrupted by a most unladylike snort and moan. As a group we turned toward Mrs. King. Though she had not awakened, it was clear she would soon.

In a soft voice, Richard turned toward his host. "Perhaps we might go to your study, Bingley ... Oh," Richard glanced about, "this is your study, is it not? The library then?"

"Of course," Bingley replied. He glanced toward the ladies. "If there is anything you require ..."

Jane's smile was reassuring as she interrupted him. "We have requested tea, but if you would ask Mrs. Annesley to join us, I believe she could be of assistance."

"At once." He bowed over her hand and their eyes lingered a moment longer before he turned and led Richard from the room.

As they reached the door, my cousin turned back, flashed an impish smile in my direction, and left the room, closing the door behind him.

"Oh, poor Mr. Bingley," I whispered.

"Mr. Bingley?" Jane asked anxiously.

"Forgive me. I did not mean to speak aloud." I looked to my friends hoping to say no more, but their curious gazes drew me out. "Richard can be ... well, he is very observant. Sometimes he sees things others do not *want* him to see, and he takes great pleasure in making them *aware* that he saw them."

Elizabeth glanced at her sister. "I believe Georgiana is trying to say her cousin noticed Mr. Bingley's attentions toward you and will tease him mercilessly."

"Oh." Jane's eyes grew large, but humour overtook her features. "I suppose you should hope that Mr. Darcy does not return while his cousin remains."

Glancing in my direction and back to her sister, Elizabeth whispered, "I do not take your meaning, Jane."

"Do you not? Simply, if the Colonel is as observant as Georgiana says, I believe Mr. Bingley will not be the only one who suffers his wit."

A soft knock at the door stopped Elizabeth's retort. Jane opened the door and helped Mrs. Annesley bring in the tea tray.

I was disappointed the conversation had ended and surprised to find the tray from the previous evening had been cleared. I had obviously slept through quite a bit of activity.

Mrs. Annesley crossed to my side and laid a cool hand upon my cheek. "Are you unwell, Miss Darcy? This has not been too much for you?"

"I am fine." I smiled at my companion's motherly manners. "Though I fear Mrs. King will need our attentions shortly. She appears to be waking."

Indeed, the widow had begun to stir and was looking about. "Where …?"

"You are at Netherfield, Mrs. King. Do you remember me?" Mrs. Annesley motioned for me to move aside and she took the place beside the confused woman.

"Mrs. Antsly?"

"Annesley, yes. You have had a difficult night. Would you like to go upstairs and refresh yourself?"

Mrs. King was clearly confused and began to nod, but instead her eyes grew wide and filled with tears. "My Mary?"

Mrs. Annesley wrapped her arms about the woman. "We are waiting word of her. Mr. Darcy will send an express the moment he finds her."

The woman began to sob and Mrs. Annesley began rocking very slowly as she spoke softly. "Now, now, Mrs. King. You will make yourself ill and of no use to your daughter. An express has been sent for your brother. You do not want him to worry for you also."

"My brother? He is coming?"

Everyone was so focused on the widow we had not heard the door open until Mr. Bingley stepped forward.

"Indeed, Mrs. King. I have just received his response. He anticipates arriving late tomorrow morning or perhaps this evening if he is able to obtain good horses along the way."

"Oh, he will be so displeased." Mrs. King began to whimper.

"He speaks only of concern for you and your daughter, ma'am." Mr. Bingley bowed to her and turned back toward the rest of us. In a lower voice, he asked "Miss Bennet, would you be able to assist the Colonel? He has questions regarding the area which I am unable to answer."

"I would love to be of assistance, sir, but I believe Lizzy knows the countryside better than I."

"Of course," Mr. Bingley blushed. "How foolish of me. Miss Elizabeth, will you join us in the library?"

Elizabeth nodded, but slipped her arm through Jane's. "Of course, but Jane may be able to help also." She laid a hand on my arm. "Are you able to remain here and assist Mrs. King?"

We all looked toward the older ladies to find Mrs. Annesley assisting Mrs. King to her feet. Looking up at us, my companion gave a reassuring smile.

"I believe Mrs. King will feel better after refreshing herself and taking a bit of nourishment. We are going upstairs and will have food sent to my room. We are of a similar size; I have a dress she can wear. Miss Darcy, I would ask that you remain with the Bennets."

"Yes, ma'am." I dipped my head to the older ladies as they left the room.

"Well, Mr. Bingley," Elizabeth said brightly, "shall we invite the Colonel back to the study to take tea with us while we answer his questions?"

"An excellent idea."

Mr. Bingley left the room at once and returned quickly with Richard. While they were gone, we straightened the room and were pouring out the tea when the gentlemen entered. Once everyone had possession of a cup and a plate of goodies, my cousin began to speak.

"Captain Jacobs has been keeping me abreast of Wickham's actions for some time, so I was not surprised that he would choose the night of a ball to make his escape. I was on my way to Meryton when I met the good Captain on the road."

"Travelling so late at night?" I asked suspiciously.

"Well, it was your actions which drew me here, my dear. I had been reading the Captain's missives the moment they arrived, but saved your letter for a time when I could savour it. Last evening I sat down in your brother's study with a fine glass of port and broke the seal. Imagine my shock to learn you were in the very vicinity of that scoundrel? I spilled the port! A terrible waste."

I laughed and shook my head at my cousin's antics.

"I set out at once to be certain you were safe and Wickham was not up to his old tricks. Jacobs and I met up at a posting inn while changing horses. We sent word back to London requesting reinforcements, and he rode on to catch up with Darcy."

"But why did you come here?" I asked, surprised once more that he had not gone after Mr. Wickham himself.

Sitting his cup and saucer upon the table, Richard leaned forward. "I know not if it is simple experience or a visceral reaction, but I fear Wickham is not yet gone from the area. Since arriving here and learning of Miss Lydia's involvement, my skin is nearly crawling with certainty that they are not bound for Scotland."

"Then where could they be?" Elizabeth's cup rattled against her saucer and she quickly set it down.

"That is why I wanted to speak to you. I understand you are familiar with the surrounding countryside."

Elizabeth nodded, but Jane responded. "Lizzy probably knows every inch of the country surrounding Longbourn and Meryton, but for what are you looking?"

"A place they could hide. Perhaps an abandoned farm house?"

I shook my head. "I do not understand. Why would they not simply go to Scotland? Mr. Wickham has what he wants, an heiress to wed. Why not do so and be done with it?"

Richard looked at each of us before turning his full attention on me. "I doubt Miss King's dowry is sufficient to meet Wickham's needs. I fear his eye is set on a larger prize."

Dropping my gaze to my lap, I whispered, "Me?"

"Georgie, you know that winning your dowry would both meet his financial needs and quench his thirst for revenge upon your brother. I believe it best if you remain within Netherfield. I do not want you to be alone at any time."

I stared into his eyes, choosing to focus on the strength of his love for me and not the worry, which threatened to overwhelm me. "Very well," I agreed with a shaky nod.

Chapter Eighteen

Once again I stood at my window, watching the Bingley carriage roll down the drive. I was still uncertain as to how it had occurred so quickly, but the Bingleys and Hursts were on their way back to London.

After declaring I was not to be left unattended, Richard had begun a discussion with Elizabeth regarding the surrounding countryside. Before much could be discussed, there was a knock on the door. All eyes turned to Mr. Bingley who answered it, slipping outside and remaining gone for some time.

"I fear Caroline's suspicions are growing," he announced upon his return. "I was to leave for London this morning to address business concerns. She wonders that I have not yet gone and that Darcy has not risen."

"Who says he has not risen?" Richard replied. "Tell her he rode out this morning to meet up with several officers. This way it will not appear odd should he return with Jacobs."

"And my journey?"

Richard glanced about. "I suppose it would be best that you go." A thoughtful expression overtook his features. "Would your sisters not prefer to accompany you?"

"I am certain they would *prefer* to be in London, but what of our houseguests? It would be inconceivable to leave them here alone." Bingley held out his hands toward the ladies.

"Your sisters do not know of Mrs. King's presence, correct?"

Mr. Bingley shook his head. "Not that I am aware."

"Well then, should the Bennet sisters return to their home, only Georgiana and her brother would remain." He turned toward me. "I cannot convince you to return with the Bingleys, can I?"

I held my head a bit higher as I responded that I would remain in Hertfordshire.

"Very well, then you are waiting for your brother. He will decide if you will travel to London or wait for Bingley to return. Your companion is with you." Richard returned his attention to the maps strewn before him.

"But is it proper," Mr. Bingley asked, "to leave guests unaccompanied?"

With a sigh, Richard settled back in his seat. "Have you not visited Pemberley when Darcy was called away? I am certain he insisted you remain until his return. How is this different? Georgiana was not of an age to act as hostess. It was left to Mrs. Reynolds, the housekeeper, to see to your needs. Is your housekeeper insufficient?"

"Of course not! Mrs. Nicholls is exceedingly competent."

"Then how is this not conceivable?"

Mr. Bingley chewed upon his lower lip before he spoke. "But will Caroline leave Netherfield knowing Darcy remains behind?"

"How should I know, man? She is your sister. Imply that Darcy and Georgiana will be leaving once he returns." Richard was obviously becoming annoyed with Mr. Bingley, but all were saved any further discussion when the door to the study opened unannounced and Fitzwilliam entered, followed closely by Captain Jacobs.

"Darcy!" Richard stood and crossed the room to shake my brother's hand. "I didn't expect you back so soon."

Fitzwilliam's eyes narrowed as he eyed our cousin. "Yet you did anticipate my return. I presume you are aware that no one within one hundred miles recognized the descriptions I provided. It is clear they are not gone to Scotland."

Frowning, Richard returned to his maps. "I was afraid that would be the case."

With disgust, Fitzwilliam brushed the dust from his leg and moved in my direction. After settling a kiss upon my forehead, he looked me over. "Have you not slept, my dear? You are still in your ball gown."

A warmth spread across my cheeks as I shook my head. "I did sleep a bit here while we looked after Mrs. King."

"And how is the good lady?" His concern was clear in his voice as he took my arm and led me to a seat.

"Mrs. Annesley has taken her upstairs so she can bathe and change. It has been some time since they left; I believe she may have been convinced to rest again."

"And so you should do also." He looked up at the Bennet sisters. "All of you have had a long night."

"I have need of them, Darcy." Richard glanced up for a moment before motioning toward the papers before him. "Miss Elizabeth, can you tell me anything of this area?"

"Colonel," Mr. Bingley spoke up. "Darcy is correct; the ladies have not slept and we still have to discuss what is to be done regarding my sisters."

"But I thought that was concluded." Richard looked about as he drew a deep breath. "Darcy is now returned. Take them back to London and he will give his blessing. Surely he can assume his Master of Pemberley air in order to chase Miss Bingley away."

Mr. Bingley appeared doubtful, but left to speak to the others.

"Georgie." Fitzwilliam squeezed my hand. "I believe it best you retire to your room before the others come down. If they see you dressed so, they will question it."

Nodding, I turned toward the door, but stopped when Richard called after me.

"I thought we agreed you would not be alone."

Releasing an exasperated sigh, I eyed my cousin. "And who is to accompany me? My companion is in her rooms with Mrs. King, and you have need of the Bennets."

Jane stood and moved in my direction. "No, he has need of my sister. I shall go with you."

My expression softened. "Thank you, Jane. You should rest also."

We linked arms and moved noiselessly through the halls toward my room, hoping we would not be seen. When the bedroom door finally closed behind us, we both released a sigh of relief.

Now wearing a fresh morning dress, I sighed as I stood at the window. I glanced over my shoulder at Jane who slept comfortably on my bed with the counterpane gently placed over her. I had attempted to rest, but sleep would not come. The Bingley carriage was no longer in sight and I wondered what I should do now.

As if in answer, another carriage made its way up the drive and stopped before the front steps. I watched as Mr. Bennet stepped out carrying a portmanteau, most likely carrying clothing for Elizabeth and Jane. Glancing once more at my friend deep in slumber, I crossed to the door and out into the hall.

"Miss Darcy, may I be of assistance?"

I jumped at the sound of the man's voice so nearby and turned slowly, but released a sigh of relief when I saw Captain Jacobs a few feet behind me.

"Captain Jacobs, you gave me a start. I saw Mr. Bennet arriving and was going to collect Miss Bennet's things. She is resting."

I am certain a blush crept across my cheeks as I spoke. I was not sure why I explained my actions to this man. Oh, I knew it was because my cousin had forbidden me to be unattended, but I was uncertain whether the Captain was aware of that.

The corner of his lips turned upward in a slightly mocking fashion. "I see. Well I have just finished refreshing myself from the road, so I am in time to escort you below."

He held out his arm in a most demanding manner, and I knew immediately he was most definitely aware of his commander's orders. Laying my hand upon his arm, I allowed him to escort me below without saying another word; though I wished I were able to remove the impudent grin from his countenance. Once we reached the bottom of the stairs, he led me to the study where the men remained with Elizabeth.

"Georgie, I thought you were resting." Fitzwilliam's voice was as weary as he appeared.

"I am well, but you have not slept." Relinquishing the Captain's arm, I approached my brother and took his hand. "It will not do for you to exhaust yourself. There are others who can take up the search while you rest."

"Indeed, Poppet," Richard nodded from his place behind Mr. Bingley's desk. "I have told him as much myself. Perhaps you may have more success."

I eyed my cousin. He looked as though he was also fatigued, but I knew he was accustomed to fighting through a lack of sleep. The determined gleam in his eye told me he would not rest until Mr. Wickham was found.

Turning toward Mr. Bennet, I smiled. "Sir, I believe you have delivered clothing for Jane and Elizabeth?"

"Yes, Mrs. Nicholls is seeing to it."

"Then I shall show Elizabeth to my room where Jane is resting and she can do the same." I turned back to Richard and gave him an imperial smile. "I am certain you have gained all the information you need for a time?"

Elizabeth looked to Richard who nodded. Wearily she stood and moved toward me.

Once we were together, I turned toward my brother once more. "Come, Fitzwilliam. You must escort us and then continue on to your own room."

A harsh laugh resounded about the room. "You heard her, Darcy. You are being called to do your duty, and a delightful one at that." Richard's intelligent eyes scoured the trio, his lips twitching with merriment.

"Miss Darcy," Captain Jacobs stepped up beside me. "Will you be remaining above with the Bennet sisters?"

I could feel my cheeks burn once more, knowing I had every intention of returning below once Elizabeth was settled.

As if knowing my response, the soldier continued. "Perhaps Mr. Darcy should escort Miss Bennet alone if you are inclined to return."

Seeing Richard's brow furrow, I quickly turned toward my brother. "Perhaps the Captain is correct. As I am not to be unattended, it would be best if you escorted Elizabeth and I remained here." I glanced back to the officer, bowing my head as I said in a sarcastic tone, "Thank you, sir, for being so thoughtful."

"At your service, miss." He bowed deeply, his actions as mocking as my words.

My brother frowned as he glanced between us. "I believe it would be better should you rest, Georgie. You do not sound like yourself."

Adopting my sweetest smile, I patted Fitzwilliam's arm. "I assure you, I am well. I find sleep evades me at this time and I would rather attempt to be useful here."

"Very well," he responded reluctantly, "since you insist." He held out an arm to Elizabeth and smiled. "Shall we?"

A soft, weary giggle escaped her. "You sound as though you are asking me to dance, sir, not escorting me from the room." A blush covered her cheeks as their eyes met.

All about them were witness to the flash of fire which blazed in Fitzwilliam's eyes as he looked upon the lady before him. Taking her hand and placing it upon his arm, he turned toward the door and spoke softly to her. "I suppose it is because I had every intention of requesting your final dance last evening."

"But, Mr. Darcy, we had already danced the supper dance. What would people say?"

They left the room before he could respond, but a few moments later Elizabeth's light laughter was heard flowing down the stairs. I looked longingly toward the door, wishing I were with them so I could hear what was said. A soft chuckle at my side drew my attention and I turned to glare at Captain Jacobs, certain he had been able to read my thoughts.

"Well, Colonel," Mr. Bennet sighed. "It appears we must have this business done with as quickly as possible in order for my elder daughters to secure their futures."

"Indeed, sir." Richard leaned forward. "I will reassure you, my cousin is the best of men. I believe they will be happy together. Miss Elizabeth appears to be just what he requires to make him more jovial." He turned his attention toward me. "Poppet, why do I feel you know more of this than any in the room? Perhaps, in future, I should enlist you as one of my spies. What brought you to Hertfordshire?"

Shrugging my shoulders, I took a seat near his desk. "I missed Fitzwilliam and decided to accept Mr. Bingley's invitation to visit Netherfield."

"After initially refusing? Were you aware Mr. Wickham would be here?"

My eyes grew large. *Does he believe I intended to follow the lout about?* Drawing my shoulders back and raising my head, I gave him my most wilting Darcy look. "I most certainly was not. I know not whether being aware of his presence would have changed my decision, but I have no desire to see *that man* again."

Richard struggled to maintain his cool expression and finally succumbed to another hearty laugh. "Good God, Georgie, you are beginning to look like Darcy at his fiercest. Stop it this instant. I believe you."

"You should not say such things, Richard." I glanced about.

"Forgive me, Poppet." He stood and rounded the desk, stopping just beside me where he knelt and took my hand. "Darcy assures me Mr. Bennet is trustworthy, and Captain Jacobs is aware of your prior encounter with Mr. Wickham. He is my most trusted officer. He has been following Wickham for some time; keeping an eye on the man and making certain he had no contact with you."

My jaw fell open. "You had no faith in me?"

"No, I believe the worst of him! I feared he may attempt to kidnap you and then say you ran away with him." His eyes drifted away from me. "I will admit to fearing he could use his silver tongue to convince you of his love and steal yours once more."

"Richard!" I was incensed. "You still see me as that thoughtless child? Fitzwilliam has explained to me what Mr. Wickham is. I would not be fooled again. I know what my family expects of me; what could come of my reputation. I would never ..." Tears burned hot against my eyes, and I turned and fled the room before they spilled down my cheeks.

I could hear the gentlemen calling after me, but I did not stop until I was in the gardens. Even then, I continued until the tears blinded me and I was forced to slow for fear of tripping. As I neared a bench, I dropped down and cradled my head in my arms upon it, releasing my anguish.

When my tears began to slow, I lifted my head in search of my handkerchief. Realizing I had left my reticule inside, I muttered under my breath until I noticed something white dangling at my side.

I turned and found Captain Jacobs standing nearby. His back was toward me, but a handkerchief hung from his hand, just within my reach. Reluctantly, I accepted it and wiped away the tears before blowing my nose. As I began to rise, he turned and took my elbow to assist me.

"My cousin has sent you to look after me?" I asked bitterly.

"I am certain he would have done so, but I followed you on my own volition." Once more, he turned his back toward me as I brushed the dirt from my skirt and righted my appearance.

I opened my mouth to speak, but my voice came out in a barely audible whisper. "Thank you."

"Think nothing of it, miss."

He still faced away from me, and it began to irritate me. "Lord, you may turn around. I suppose I am decent."

"Forgive me, Miss Darcy. I simply wished to provide you with the privacy you may prefer at this time."

"While watching my every move," I muttered as I dropped onto the bench.

At that, he did turn and looked at me condescendingly. "I am not watching you, rather watching *over* you. Can you not see I am here to protect you?" He cleared his throat and nudged a stone with the toe of his boot. "When the Colonel and I were in battle, we would speak of home as a way to keep our spirits high. I have come to think of you as family."

Reticently, I raised my eyes to look at him. Since we met, he had reached out to me; looked after me. Yes, he had reprimanded me at times, but he had been correct regarding my behaviour. Perhaps he was simply acting the way Fitzwilliam or Richard would when in my presence. *So why does it offend me?*

Shaking away my thoughts, I forced a smile. "Captain, I believe we have started ill. Will you forgive my insolence?"

His eyes lit as a smile crept across his countenance, showing him to be much younger than I had originally believed. "Of course, milady," he said as he dropped into an exaggerated bow causing me to giggle. He held out his hand. "Shall we return inside?"

Taking his hand, I stood, brushed the dirt from my skirts once more, and then wrapped my hand about his arm. "Tell me more of how you met my cousin. How old were you?"

His chest rumbled with laughter and I felt it against my arm. "I was but a few years older than you, having not yet reached my majority. As I told you, my father was concerned regarding my tendency to speak openly regarding my beliefs. He feared I would not do well in school and hired tutors instead. I far exceeded his expectations and, I believe, he felt the need to find something else for me." We walked toward the house as the Captain explained how cruel young men could be and his father's hopes to see his son protected.

I nodded. "Young ladies are quite the same. You have not yet met Miss Lydia Bennet, I believe, but she could easily rival the meanest girls in the best finishing schools."

"Oh, I am familiar with Miss Lydia." His frown spoke louder than his words. "She has made a point of speaking to *all* the officers."

"Does she vie for your attention?" I smiled at the thought of Lydia flirting outrageously with the serious man at my side.

"I dare say she attempted it, once. She has since found me to be too disagreeable and gone on to other pastures." He shivered and I fought the urge to laugh.

"You do not appreciate a pretty young lady showing you attention?" I asked innocently.

"If a proper young lady wished to speak on gentle topics, I would not be displeased no matter her appearance. However, I see little of worth in Miss Lydia beyond her looks." Captain Jacobs became thoughtful. "I have often wondered how she came to be so unlike her sisters."

"From what I have gathered, the elder sisters have spent a great deal of time with relatives. Miss Lydia is her mother's favourite and has rarely been from home." I fell silent lost in my thoughts.

It felt wrong to be speaking so calmly regarding this young girl who had fallen victim to Mr. Wickham's charms. I knew only too well how convincing the man could be. Perhaps Lydia was more innocent in this situation than was believed. Worse, what if she was not with Mr. Wickham and Miss King? What tragedy could have befallen her? "Miss Darcy?"

We were no longer walking and the Captain stood at my side, watching me closely. I wondered which of us had stopped first as I lifted my gaze to meet his.

"Are you unwell? You appear quite distressed."

His concern for me resounded in his words and I was forced to look away again. *Why does my heart beat so when he looks at me in that manner?*

Taking a deep breath, I turned back to him. In order to maintain some calm, I stared at a small white scar along his left cheek, just below the bone. I had not seen it before and began to wonder if he had earned it in battle. *Oh, this will not do. I must look a fool.*

Closing my eyes briefly, I hoped my complexion was not as rosy as I feared, then responded. "I was just wondering if Miss Lydia is truly with Mr. Wickham. What if we have all misjudged the situation? Could she have left Longbourn in hopes of coming to the ball and now be lost or injured?"

The Captain's features relaxed and he laid a hand upon mine, which rested on his arm. "You have a caring heart, Miss Darcy. From what I have learned, I believe it is safe to say Miss Lydia had no intention of attending the ball when she left Longbourn." We began walking once more. "Her ball gown remained behind, but she had taken a few belongings. It is true there was no note as to her whereabouts, but Mr. Bennet has given a list of places she may have gone. Colonel Fitzwilliam is arranging search parties as we speak. If she is not with Wickham, she will be found soon enough."

"Though you anticipate she will be found *with* him." I stared at his profile. He had not removed his hand from mine, and I found his touch to be comforting.

We had reached the porch leading to the side entrance and he guided me up the steps, but he paused before entering the house.

"Shall we rejoin the others?" The Captain's voice held a hint of hesitation. "I should see if there is anything the Colonel requires of me."

"Of course." I bowed my head, but neither of us took a step forward. "Thank you for following me. I should not have run out as I did, but the thought of what occurred last summer continues to fill me with guilt and shame. My brother has been exceedingly patient with me, but Richard continues to see me as a small child who requires constant supervision. It is frustrating."

His hand came into my line of vision just before he gently placed a finger beneath my chin and lifted my head to meet his gaze. "Of what are you guilty? Being drawn in by a pair who plotted against you? Why should you be ashamed? For trusting a woman who was charged with guiding you? I am certain the men in your life would rather you relinquish these ideas and move forward."

My pulse rushed as I stared into his hazel eyes, noticing for the first time the flecks of amber, which caught the sun and shimmered. So distracted was I, that I did not notice the door open a few feet away until I heard a gentleman clearing his throat. The

Captain and I both startled and turned toward the sound.

"I suppose you were simply waiting for someone to open the door before entering?" Richard asked, a rare frown gracing his lips.

"Forgive me, sir." Captain Jacobs bowed as he allowed his hand to fall to his side and escorted me inside.

Once we entered the study, he led me to the settee and saw me seated. He then continued toward the desk and viewed the maps of the area. "Where shall we begin?"

I felt my cousin's eyes upon me, but refused to meet his gaze. Instead, I stared resolutely at the Captain's back as I attempted to sort out the emotions that bubbled inside me.

Chapter Nineteen

The search parties had been gone for some time and we ladies who remained behind at Netherfield were anxious for their return. Any manner of enterprise had long ago been abandoned until we all sat staring towards either the windows or the doors; hopeful of seeing some movement.

I glanced about as I stretched my neck, now stiff from remaining in one position too long. Elizabeth's soft laugh drew my attention.

"Forgive me, Georgie, but Miss Bingley assures me a turn about the room is very refreshing after sitting so long in one attitude." She rose and approached me, holding out her hand. "Shall we?"

A sad smile graced my lips as I agreed and joined my friend in walking about the room. Neither of us spoke, though we hesitated in front of each window we passed, gazing longingly across the landscape.

"I just do not understand," the soft whispers began once more and we all sighed in unison.

Mrs. King had been reciting this mantra every few minutes since the gentlemen made her aware of their concerns regarding her daughter. The lady was certain they were mistaken, but could provide no other explanation for her daughter's disappearance.

"He seemed like such an agreeable gentleman."

Mrs. Annesley, who remained at Mrs. King's side, patted her hand but said not a word. What more could be said than what had already been spoken?

Being so near to Elizabeth, I could almost feel the frustration roll from her in waves as she took a deep breath. "Perhaps we could walk in the garden?" she asked no one in particular.

"I believe the gentlemen wished us to remain inside," Jane said firmly as she eyed her sister.

"But if we remain together, it is no different than us being together inside." Elizabeth took another deep breath and released it slowly. "Perhaps I am simply tired of staring at these four walls."

I looked hopefully toward Jane. "I would like a bit of fresh air."

Sighing, Jane turned toward the older ladies. Mrs. King stared off as she had since the gentlemen left while Mrs. Annesley met her eye and nodded.

"I suppose a brief walk about the gardens nearest the house might revive us." Jane turned toward us. "Lizzy, I believe you and Georgiana should play for us when we return inside."

"Certainly," Elizabeth nodded as she glanced toward me for agreeance.

"It would be preferable to sitting in silence," I whispered for only my friend to hear.

Bonnets, pelisses, and shawls were gathered and we stepped out the side door a short time later. Mrs. King followed where Mrs. Annesley led, though she seemed unaware of her surroundings. Jane stayed close by in the event her assistance was required while Elizabeth and I set a faster pace and soon left the others behind.

"Please do not go far," Jane called to her sister.

Slowing slightly, we turned and waved our acknowledgement. Taking a path, which would bring us back around to the others, we began speaking softly.

"Is it possible they have been found?" I asked.

Elizabeth shrugged her shoulders. "I cannot say. If they were at the nearest location, the men would have returned by now. Though I suppose it would be foolish for Mr. Wickham to remain that close. I fear …" She bit her lip and looked about. "I fear the Colonel is underestimating Mr. Wickham. Surely he has left Hertfordshire. He would be foolish to remain."

Sighing, I shook my head. "I fear my cousin is rarely wrong. He and Fitzwilliam are very similar in that regard; they both study things until they understand them thoroughly. Richard has made it his business to understand Mr. Wickham better than that man knows himself." I dropped my head and studied the tips of my shoes, which peeked from under my gown as I walked. "If Richard believes Mr. Wickham will come for me, I am afraid he will do just that."

"Did you not say Mr. Wickham appeared repentant when he spoke to you?"

"Yes," I nodded, "but he is a gifted deceiver. I fear I shall never trust myself to know when he is being truthful."

"If only we could know for certain where they would …" Elizabeth stopped, her eyes growing wide and her jaw falling open.

"What?" I asked. When I received no response, I shook Elizabeth's arm. "What is it, Elizabeth?"

"The Colonel asked the wrong Bennet sister." She continued to stare into space for another minute before taking my hand and leading me back to the others.

"Jane!" Elizabeth called as we approached her sister. "Did Mr. Bingley leave word on how to contact them should we need them?"

Shaking her head, Jane glanced at the older ladies beside her then back to her sister. "He said there would be officers coming and going. I suppose we could pass a message through them."

Elizabeth turned up the path toward the house and hurried inside with me still in tow. As she reached the front hall, she called out causing servants to rush forward.

"Mrs. Nicholls." Elizabeth stopped before the housekeeper, laying a hand upon her chest as she tried to catch her breath.

The housekeeper glanced toward the other servants and they returned to their work before she met Elizabeth's gaze. "Yes, Miss Elizabeth. How may I be of service?"

"We must get word to the gentlemen and have my sister Kitty brought here from Longbourn."

The older woman looked sceptical, but Elizabeth laid a hand upon her arm and looked at her beseechingly.

"I believe my sister, Kitty, may know where they have gone without being aware of it. If so, the gentlemen may be able to limit the number of locations they must search. Please, send someone to Longbourn to bring her here."

"Would it not be better for one of the men to go to her?"

Elizabeth shook her head. "If we send someone to Longbourn and another to the gentlemen, they can both arrive back at Netherfield at the same time."

"I see your logic. Very well, I shall do as you say."

"Thank you, Mrs. Nicholls." Elizabeth relaxed a bit and gave the woman a heartfelt smile.

Turning back, we found the others approaching.

"All will be well." Elizabeth said reassuringly.

I hoped it was true.

****

Elizabeth paced in front of the windows that looked out over the front entrance to Netherfield while I watched from my place at the pianoforte. Having just completed a simple piece I knew from memory, I took a moment to shuffle through the sheet music while I observed my friend.

"Lizzy, will you not play for us?" Jane asked. "Your pacing is exceedingly distracting." She glanced toward Mrs. King who sat on a sofa by Mrs. Annesley wringing her hands.

Releasing a long sigh, Elizabeth moved toward the instrument and began leafing through the music.

"Shall I play another while you look?" I asked timidly.

"Yes, please. I fear my mind is not on music at the moment. Hopefully someone will have arrived by the time you have finished."

Tears shone in her eyes as she spoke and I gave her a reluctant smile before placing my fingers on the keys. The light melody I had chosen, hoping it would dispel the gloom in the room, seemed instead to be overcome by the atmosphere and turned hauntingly sad. Uncertain what to do to correct it, and not wanting to simply stop and draw attention, I was thankful when the door opened and Mr. Bennet entered the room.

"I understand you may have news?" he asked as he crossed to his second daughter.

"Not yet, but I believe Kitty will be here any moment and she may be able to assist." Elizabeth replied hesitantly.

"Mr. Bennet." Mrs. King's voice was soft, but filled the room, stopping him from responding to his daughter. "Have you found my Mary?"

With a gentleness none had ever seen from him, he knelt before her. "Though we have searched several possible locations, we have found no sign of her. The others continued on while I returned to speak to Elizabeth." Taking her hand, he met her gaze. "No stone is being left unturned. We are determined to find her."

"Thank you," she whispered as tears slipped down her cheeks.

The sound of a carriage approaching the house caused all to turn toward the windows. Elizabeth rushed forward and looked out.

"It is Kitty!" she called. A moment later, her countenance darkened as she turned back to the small group. "And Mother."

Mr. Bennet heaved a sigh as he pushed himself upward. Straightening his coat, he stepped into the hallway in an attempt to intercept his wife and daughter. Elizabeth and I followed behind him until we stood in the doorway.

"Mrs. Bennet." Mr. Bennet bowed to his wife as she reached the top step. "I am surprised to see you here."

"I could not allow Kitty to come alone. It is only right that I should be here." The handkerchief, clutched in her left hand as always, began fluttering about as was its wont while tears filled its mistress' eyes. "It is my Lydia who is missing also, Mr. Bennet. Only I can understand what Mrs. King is feeling."

I watched as Mr. Bennet glanced about before releasing a fatigued sigh. "Come, come, get out of the hallway," he groused.

A tug on my arm caused me to follow Elizabeth back into the room so we were out of the way when the others entered. Mr. Bennet escorted his wife to the sofa where the older ladies rested before he looked back at the others.

"I will speak to Kitty in the study. I ask the rest of you wait here and remain calm. Hysterics will not improve the situation." This last was said to his good wife, who appeared properly chastised and dropped her gaze to her lap.

"Papa." Elizabeth stepped forward. "May I come with you? To the study? I may be able to help Kitty remember some detail she would deem unimportant."

After appraising her for a brief moment, Mr. Bennet nodded his approval then turned toward me. "Miss Darcy, will you also accompany us? Your experience may be of assistance."

Happily surprised, I simply nodded and followed the others from the room. As we entered the study, Elizabeth stepped quickly to her father's side.

"Is there truly no sign of them?"

Mr. Bennet ran a weary hand over his face. "None. It is as though they simply vanished." He turned toward Kitty and motioned her forward. "What say you, Kitty? Have you any idea where your sister, Mr. Wickham, and Miss King have gone?"

Looking as though she had been accused of murder, Kitty's eyes grew wide as she shook her head. "I had no idea this would happen. I know nothing of their disappearances."

Elizabeth stepped forward and took her sister's hand. Leading her to an overstuffed leather chair, she urged her to sit before kneeling in front of her. "Kitty, no one has suggested you were involved. I thought, since you and Lydia spent so much time together, you may know where she would go."

"Yes, Kitty." I stepped forward and laid a hand upon my friend's arm. "You told me once Miss Lydia had many secrets only you knew. Could one of them be helpful in finding her and Miss King?"

A crease appeared between Kitty's brows as she appeared to think very hard upon the question. A moment passed, but she said not a word.

"Perhaps the two of you stumbled upon a secluded area during your walks?" Elizabeth suggested.

Kitty shook her head. "We mostly walked to Meryton or Lucas Lodge and home, no farther."

Mr. Bennet released another sigh. "Well, your logic was good, Lizzy, but I fear I must return to the search."

"Wait!" Kitty cried as her father turned toward the door. "There was nothing *we* found, but the soldiers were discussing a place."

"Yes?" the others all urged in unison when she paused.

"I am trying to remember," Kitty snapped. She pushed herself from the chair and walked around the outskirts of the room, to the hearth and back. "That Captain who is always finding things for them to do sent the officers out to an area for ... oh, what did they call it? They were to scout out the area for something."

"Yes, what of it?" Mr. Bennet asked in exasperation.

"Mr. Wickham and Mr. Denny separated from the others. They said they found a place to hide until the drill was finished and they could rejoin their battalion. Wherever it was, they could see the others, but their presence was unknown. No one noticed their absence."

For the first time, a hint of a smile crossed Mr. Bennet's lips as he stepped forward and embraced his daughter. "Well done, Kitty! I shall return and find Captain Jacobs. I am certain he will know the event you described." Grabbing his hat, he rushed out the door and called for his horse.

Elizabeth, Kitty, and I followed at a slower pace, reaching the front door as he mounted his steed.

"Remain inside until you hear from us, but know that your assistance has been invaluable." He winked and waved before urging his mount forward. We stood and watched until he disappeared from sight, leaving only a cloud of dust in his wake.

"I hope they find them soon," Kitty whispered.

We all exchanged an anxious glance before turning back inside and climbing the stairs in silence, but as we drew closer to the drawing room, Mrs. Bennet's voice was heard clearly. Hesitating, we listened as the woman attempted to *encourage* her friend.

"I am certain the gentlemen are looking in the wrong area. Why would they still be here in Hertfordshire? They must be on their way to Scotland. How else can Mr. Wickham marry my Lydia? I just do not understand why they chose to take Miss King with them."

"Mrs. Bennet." Mrs. King's voice sounded much firmer than it had since the disappearance of her daughter. "Mr. Wickham has been paying court to my Mary, not your daughter. They shall be the ones to marry once they are found."

"I suppose we shall see whom the gentleman prefers." Mrs. Bennet's voice was crisp with irritation, though her next statement seemed to drip with honey. "Oh, I have been meaning to give your daughter some of Mrs. Hill's cream. It does wonders for nasty freckles."

"Oh dear," Elizabeth muttered as she quickly entered the room.

I was about to follow when Kitty laid a hand upon my arm. Looking back, I found my friend's eyes wide and unfocused.

"What is it, Kitty?" I asked in great concern.

"I have just thought of something else. There is a log, a hollow log that Lydia found a fortnight ago. She said it would be perfect to place secret messages or to hide things until they were needed." She turned to look at me. "What if she told Mr. Wickham? Maybe there is something there now."

We turned and looked toward the drawing room, but the volume had only increased as the mothers defended their offspring and the eldest Bennet sisters, with Mrs. Annesley's assistance, attempted to calm them. Before we could decide what to do, Jane stuck her head out the door as though searching for us.

"Oh, Kitty, Georgiana. Please have Mrs. Nicholls bring some fresh tea." She glanced back over her shoulder before looking back to us and speaking a bit softer. "And perhaps some sherry or laudanum." With that, she returned inside, closing the door behind her.

Kitty and I exchanged a glance and nodded. Going in search of Mrs. Nicholls, we delivered the request. Then, when no one was looking, we gathered our outerwear and slipped soundlessly out the nearest door.

Chapter Twenty

"Are you certain you know where we are going?" I asked again as I looked about the unfamiliar landscape. It felt as though we had been walking for hours and I knew we had been missed by now. A frustrated sigh was the only response, but Kitty seemed to pick up her pace and I had to walk faster so as not to lose her.

The further we went, the thicker the woods became until branches were a constant obstacle and we were forced to slow down for fear of snagging clothing or tripping over roots. I was about to question the wisdom of our decision once more, when I saw the trees begin to thin as I looked ahead. Moments later, we stepped into a small clearing and Kitty ran toward an old tree that was leaning precariously.

"How did you and Lydia find this place?" I asked as I looked around. It did not appear to be near either Meryton or Longbourn, but I had lost my sense of direction some time ago.

Kitty glanced back over her shoulder as she pointed straight ahead. "Longbourn is just a short distance that way. Papa wanted us to work on our studies one day, but Lydia was determined not to do so. We spent most of the day in these woods." She pointed to the left. "There is a stream and berry bushes that way. The juice spoiled our pelisses. Mama was more upset than Papa when we returned."

"Oh," I muttered as I looked about.

"I think there is something here!" Kitty called out as she reached into the log.

"Is it safe?" I asked, leaning backward. "There aren't any animals in there, are there?"

Kitty yanked her hand back and leaned forward to look inside. "I don't think so," she said hesitantly.

Leaning from one side to the other, she looked into the opening from different angles until she appeared certain the tree was uninhabited, and then she reached inside again. This time when she removed her hand, it held a folded sheet of paper.

I rushed forward and peered over her shoulder as she opened it. We read it together.

My Darling George,
Papa is determined I am not to attend the ball. You must come to Longbourn and rescue me. I have everything you asked for, but I will not leave it here. You must come for me.
All my love,
Lydia

"Oh, what a fool!" Kitty cried.

I took the note and read it through once more. "I do not understand. When did she leave this here? And why is it still here?" I looked about. "Is there an easier way to this place?"

"Yes." Kitty nodded as she pointed to the right. "The road is just through those trees. The path we took is the fastest on foot from Netherfield."

"So if they were in a carriage, they would have taken the road. Perhaps Mr. Wickham arrived after Lydia left the note, but before she returned to Longbourn." I tapped the paper against my other hand as I surveyed the area.

"I wonder what he asked her to bring." Kitty mumbled to herself.

"Probably money. From what Brother has told me, Mr. Wickham is always in need of funds." Taking a deep breath, I looked around once more. "We must get this to the men." I bit my lip. "But I was not to leave Netherfield."

"What? Why not?" Kitty's eyes opened wide in alarm.

"My cousin fears Mr. Wickham did not go to Scotland as he wishes to have me instead of Miss King. She has only ten thousand pounds where my dowry is thirty thousand."

"Oh, dear," Kitty whined as she looked around. "Do you think he might be near? Would he hurt us?"

I shook my head. "Mr. Wickham is only concerned with his own wellbeing and pleasure. If he were to injure someone, it could mean terrible consequences for him."

"And what of Mary and Lydia? Are their reputations not now ruined? And if Lydia is ruined, my sisters and I will also be tainted by association." Kitty's breathing became rapid and her hands flew to her chest as her eyes took on a glazed appearance.

"Kitty!" I moved to her side and took her hand. "Look at me! You must not faint!"

Anxiously, I looked about, still unsure of where we were. *Kitty said Longbourn was straight ahead.* I pulled my friend forward, pushing through the trees and hoping to see something familiar. We walked a short distance when I heard voices and turned toward them. As we broke into another clearing, two gardeners planting shrubs along a newly excavated path leapt to their feet.

"Lordy, Miss Kitty, you did give us quite a start." The closest man took a step closer to them. "'ere now, are you unwell?"

"Please, can you help us to the house?" I asked.

Leaving their tools, the man who had spoken took Kitty by the arm and began leading her while the other ran ahead for assistance. As the house came into sight, I saw Mrs. Hill rushing toward us.

"Miss Darcy! Miss Kitty! I thought you both were to stay at Netherfield." She motioned for Kitty to be taken to the nearest bench and sat down beside her. "Here Miss, just take a deep breath." She waved a bottle of smelling salts under Kitty's nose and the girl shook her head. "Now, deep breath until your head has cleared."

Kitty complied with a grimace before turning away. "I am better now, Hill, I promise."

The normally kindly housekeeper turned back to me with a frown before returning her gaze to my friend. "Tis fortunate for you I always have salts in my apron for your mother or I don't know what would have become of you. What are the two of you doing traipsing over the countryside unescorted? Have you not been told there are unsavoury people about?"

The warmth flooding my cheeks told me I was certainly a deep crimson in colour. "We thought we could be of assistance."

"Oh, did ya now? By causing everyone concern and making the men go looking for you?"

"How ...?"

"They've been here, that's how." Mrs. Hill took Kitty's arm and helped her to rise, then turned us toward the house. "Samuel stayed behind in the event you might show up here. I'll send him after the men."

"Oh, please, have him take this note to my cousin, Colonel Fitzwilliam," I pleaded. "It is why we left Netherfield."

"What's that you've got?" Hill took the note and read it before shaking her head and continuing on her way. "That child has certainly burned her bridges this time," she muttered under her breath. She shook her head once more and spoke a bit louder. "I dare say this weren't worth risking yourselves over. Where did you find it?"

"There's a hollow log in the woods," I responded softly. I had hoped we would find something to lead the men to Mr. Wickham. Perhaps Mrs. Hill was right and it was all for naught.

"In the woods, you say?" She glanced back over her shoulder. "So that's where she went. I thought the little minx was asleep and went downstairs to be about my chores. When I returned she was gone."

"We think Mr. Wickham must have found her after she left the note, but before she returned home." Kitty said softly.

Clucking her tongue, Mrs. Hill continued to mutter about us not thinking of our own safety until we came at last to the house and she reached to open the door leading to the kitchen. "Inside now. Go on with you."

As we entered the house, the smell of sweet bread filled the air and I realized I had eaten very little that day. When my stomach rumbled its annoyance, Mrs. Hill motioned toward the table.

"Cook, fetch some of the freshly made butter and that warm loaf. The girls have just come from a long walk and need nourishment. Did Samuel return to the stables?"

"Yes 'm," Cook responded as she took down two plates and moved the kettle over the fire. "Sit down. I'll put the tea on to steep then cut the bread."

Though both of us felt the sting of Mrs. Hill referring to us as 'girls', I recognized our actions had been exceedingly immature and unwise. I looked at Kitty and realized she was as thankful as I that no ill had come to us.

A moment later the door leading to the hall banged open and Mary stood before us. "I do not suppose the two of you are familiar with the scripture 'Honour thy father and thy mother'?" She placed her hands on her hips as she shook her head. "Georgiana, your brother was beside himself with worry; as was my sister. They have taken a few men from the search parties and are out looking for you this very moment."

I was about to respond, but Mary continued. "And you, Kitty! Is it not bad enough that Lydia has run away, and now you find it necessary to follow in her footsteps?"

"I did not run away, Mary." Kitty raised her eyes to the ceiling. "After Papa left I thought of something else that might be helpful. Georgiana and I decided to investigate it ourselves instead of forcing the men to return to Netherfield once more."

"And yet your leaving Netherfield did cause the men to return there." Mary shook her head, a scowl upon her face. "I simply cannot understand you. Is it not bad enough that Lydia has acted so foolishly? Mr. Collins is speaking of returning to Kent so as to distance himself from this scandal. I fear he will never propose now. No one will, and we will be forced to remain at Longbourn until Papa is gone and Mr. Collins returns to toss us all out into the hedgerows."

I had never seen Mary so angry. There was no fear, like when Kitty had realized the consequences of Lydia's actions. This was righteous indignation if I had ever seen it.

"Now, Miss Mary." Cook stepped in front of the middle Bennet daughter. "The girls know they were wrong. I've put on tea. Would you like a cup? I have freshly made butter and warm bread as well"

"No thank you, Cook," Mary said abruptly while continuing to stare at Kitty and myself. "I will be in the front parlour trying to convince Mr. Collins that we are not *all* wanton sinners." Finally, she glanced at the servant. "Please have Mrs. Hill bring us tea and Mr. Collins' favourite biscuits as well as some of the sweet bread."

Throwing one more glare in our direction, she turned and stomped from the room. The silence that descended after her departure was only broken by the sound of Cook's preparations. Kitty and I kept our eyes lowered until plates were set before us. Reluctantly, we began to nibble at the treat, though it was now sour to our stomachs. Uncertain what was expected of us, we both remained seated until Mrs. Hill returned with Samuel close behind her.

"... should remain here," Mrs. Hill was saying as they entered.

"I believe Mr. Darcy thought it best the ladies return to Netherfield. With the officers coming and going ..."

"That Wickham could slip in a side door without being suspected," Mrs. Hill finished. "No, I think the less they move about the better."

Samuel frowned as he looked at us. "Well, I best ride out to find him and tell him what you've said."

"Is Miss Lizzy still with him?" Mrs. Hill had lowered her voice as they walked to the door, but I was still able to catch her words.

"Yes'm." Samuel smiled broadly. "When she found them missing, she ordered one of Mr. Bingley's horses saddled and rode out herself to find Mr. Darcy. He was a sight sore at her, but she told him Mr. Wickham wouldn't give her a second glance without a dowry. And she refused to go back to Netherfield, so he demanded she stay with him so he could protect her if need be."

Mrs. Hill's grin matched his. "He did, eh? Perhaps some good will come of this dreadful business after all."

"Only if the others are found without a scandal. I can't imagine the gentleman being able to overlook such a family disgrace, no matter his inclination."

As their smiles faded, the servants nodded and separated. I caught Mrs. Hill's eye as she turned back toward the kitchen table. The sadness there was unmistakable, causing me to shiver.

Please, Lord, do not let everyone's hopes be in vain, I prayed silently as I followed Kitty and Mrs. Hill out of the kitchen.

****

The door to the back parlour flew open as Fitzwilliam burst through it. I was immediately wrapped in his arms, barely able to see Elizabeth embracing Kitty just behind him. As fast as the hug had begun, I was released and held at arm's length.

"Just what were you thinking?" he demanded.

"Forgive me, Fitzwilliam," I whispered as I stared at the buttons of his waistcoat. "I believed we could be of assistance."

"By frightening me out of my wits?" He led me to the sofa and took the seat beside me, holding my hands in his. "Georgie, what possessed you to go off without saying anything to anyone?"

Elizabeth stepped forward, her arms still about Kitty. "I believe I can answer for her. It is dreadfully frustrating sitting at Netherfield waiting for word of what is occurring elsewhere."

Fitzwilliam gave Elizabeth an exasperated look before turning back to me. "You have said as much before, Miss Bennet, but I am asking Georgiana."

"Elizabeth is correct, Brother." My voice was forceful in protection of my friend. "When Kitty thought of the hollow log, we knew it was possible there would be nothing there. We did not want to take someone away from the search in vain. We were together the entire time. Nothing happened to us." Though I had started strong, my voice ended in barely a whisper under the weight of his obvious disapproval.

He released one of my hands and reached into a pocket to retrieve the note we had found. With a heavy sigh, he responded. "It appears you were correct. All this proves is that Miss Lydia knew what she was about."

Kitty took a step forward. "But it says nothing of Miss King. Do you think Lydia knew Mr. Wickham had Miss King?"

"It is difficult to say," Elizabeth answered as her eyes searched Fitzwilliam's.

"One thing it does tell us, your sister was not as trusting of Wickham as he thought she would be." He looked to the note once more. "It appears he wanted her to leave whatever he requested, but she would not do so."

The weariness in Fitzwilliam's voice tugged at my heart. Once more my brother was beset by Mr. Wickham. How many more times would it be so?

"What will you do now, Brother?" I asked softly, not meeting his gaze.

Taking a deep breath, he looked to Elizabeth then back at me. "I believe it best that you and Miss Bennet return to Netherfield. The constant activity there with the soldiers should keep Wickham away."

"But what of Kitty?" I asked as I glanced toward my friend.

"Miss Catherine may accompany you, if she so desires. I shall ask Samuel to escort you."

He stood, but paused when Elizabeth cleared her throat. Hearing him take a deep breath, I looked up. It appeared my brother was bracing himself for battle.

"Yes, Miss Bennet?"

"Mr. Darcy, I believe we have already spoken of this."

"And *I* believe you understand my feelings on the subject."

"Can you not see I would be helpful …?"

"No, I cannot! Elizabeth, you are a distraction!"

"I beg your pardon? How do I distract?" Fire shot from Elizabeth's eyes as she glared at him.

"I cannot think clearly when you are about!" he shouted. "Blast it, woman, do you not see I would be completely useless for fear of you being injured in some manner." He took a deep breath and looked at her beseechingly. "Will you not respect my wishes in this?"

The look of confusion which settled upon Elizabeth's features nearly caused me to laugh. Before another word could be said, Fitzwilliam stepped forward and took Elizabeth's hand in both of his. Slowly, he raised it to his lips and kissed it reverently.

"Please," he whispered.

Elizabeth's nod was barely perceivable, but Fitzwilliam smiled. "I shall have Samuel escort you to Netherfield, and I will return to you as soon as we find our quarry." He kissed her hand once more before releasing it and rushing from the room.

When he was gone, Elizabeth stood staring at the door through which he had passed. Kitty and I exchanged knowing glances, barely able to suppress the giggles which bubbled within us.

"Insufferable man," Elizabeth mumbled as a smile tugged at her lips.

Chapter Twenty-One

Several minutes after Fitzwilliam's departure, Elizabeth appeared to regain her composure. She then proceeded to scold us for leaving her behind with no idea where we had gone.

"I knew not what to tell your brother." She paced before us as she waved her hands about. "I knew he would be beside himself, which he was; and I could give him no possible reason for your disappearance."

Both of us begged for her forgiveness, which was reluctantly given just before Mrs. Hill announced Samuel was waiting for us. Once we were inside the carriage, a silence descended which threatened to suffocate us. Kitty took it upon herself to lift our spirits by chattering about anything which entered her mind. The most difficult task became avoiding mention of Lydia and Miss King.

Halfway to our destination, I was lost in my own thoughts and it took a moment before I realized my friend had fallen silent. I turned and found Kitty with a small smile playing about the corner of her lips as she stared at her sister. Following her gaze, I learned the reason for her amusement. Elizabeth was turned toward the window, a dreamy expression on her countenance as she caressed the hand Fitzwilliam had kissed.

As we exchanged a knowing glance, the carriage jerked to a halt. It rocked when the driver dismounted and we all leaned toward the door in anticipation of some explanation since we had not reached Netherfield and were, in fact, out of sight of any structures.

When the door was yanked open, it thoroughly startled us even though we had anticipated it. Samuel stuck his head inside and urged us all to remain in place until he returned. The door closed as abruptly as it had opened and he was gone.

Elizabeth, Kitty and I exchanged worried glances before we gathered around the window to see what had drawn his attention. A soft whimper escaped from Kitty, and Elizabeth reached out to take her hand.

"Samuel would not leave us if he thought it was unsafe. Besides, the footman is still with us." She pointed toward the young man standing just a few feet away.

Biting the inside of my cheek, I surveyed the area before looking out the opposite window. "Have you any suspicion of why he would stop here?"

Kitty shook her head, but Elizabeth hesitated. After a moment, her eyes widened. "I had not thought of it."

"What?" we asked in unison.

"The Schmitt's home." Opening the door, she stepped out and surveyed the trees before them.

"Of course!" Kitty followed Elizabeth, taking hold of her hand.

"Who are the Schmitts?" I asked, choosing to remain in the carriage.

Elizabeth turned back to look at me before explaining. "Tenants of Longbourn. They left immediately following the harvest to visit family and are not expected back for several weeks."

Kitty nodded and added, "Lydia has been caring for their animals." Both Elizabeth and I stared at her in surprise until she blushed. "I had not thought of it before. It was the only time she wished to be alone and I enjoyed that time by myself."

A frown overtook Elizabeth's countenance as she released her sister's hand and began to pace. "Did you not find it suspicious that Lydia would do something for another person? She dislikes work of any nature."

Kitty dropped her eyes to her fingers, which twisted in front of her, and whispered, "I was pleased to be away from her. I thought no more of it."

"Oh, what has she been doing there?" Elizabeth muttered under her breath and made to move toward the woods.

The footman stepped forward hesitantly. "Miss Lizzy, Sam said you weren't to follow."

Placing a sweet smile upon her lips, Elizabeth turned her attention toward the young man. I could see it was done simply to placate the youth, and I wondered if it would succeed.

"Jeremy, I know your brother said we should remain, but I believe I can be of assistance to him. Please stay and keep an eye on the other ladies." Her smile brightened a bit as she stepped closer to him. "I am certain you will not allow any harm to come to them. You have grown into a fine young man."

The lad blushed as he glanced toward Kitty and me. By the time he turned back to respond, Elizabeth was already entering the woods.

"Miss Lizzy!" he called after her, but it was too late. "Blast!" Jeremy muttered as he turned back toward the carriage. "Well, get inside. I'll not have Sam thinking I can't keep you two in order," he grumbled.

Kitty nodded sheepishly and climbed in beside me. We both sat staring out the window, hoping for some sign of what might be occurring.

****

I had begun to think the sun would set before we returned to Netherfield. Jeremy stood directly in front of the carriage door, facing the woods. There had been no sign of Elizabeth or Samuel; to be precise, there had been no sign of any movement at all.

A soft sigh issued from Kitty, breaking through my contemplation. I looked to my friend who appeared exceedingly remorseful.

"Kitty, what is the matter?"

"I should have known something was suspicious. Why did I not think of the Schmitts when Papa asked me?"

Slipping an arm about her, I began to rock in a comforting manner. "But Elizabeth did not think of them either. Do not blame yourself. You gave them other suggestions."

"Yes, but that might have drawn them further away." A tear slipped from the corner of her eye and made a slow track down her cheek. "What might have happened to them in the meanwhile?"

"I am certain all will be well. We must not lose hope."

I had barely finished speaking when the sound of horses' hooves pounding the ground could be heard. "Listen! It sounds like a battalion is descending upon us."

We both moved toward the windows, but were unable to see what was approaching when Jeremy stepped away from the carriage and then ran for the front. Within seconds, the coach rocked and began to move slowly forward and to the side. I grabbed the overhead strap as we lurched forward when the equipage left the road.

Before Kitty or I could react, we heard the screams of horses and shouts of men attempting to rein in the beasts. Our carriage swayed as the other raced past, barely missing us. When the other coach had drawn to a halt, a new sound assaulted our ears.

"Why have we stopped?"

The high-pitched scream was all too familiar to me and I cowered into the corner of the seat. Kitty looked at me with great concern before glancing toward the window.

"If we have not arrived at our destination, there is no excuse for this inconvenience!"

The sound of men's voices were followed by another loud shout. "What care I for a wayward carriage? It should not have been in the roadway. Let them tend to their own. I must speak to my nephew immediately!"

The door opened and Jeremy glanced inside. "Forgive me, ladies. I wasn't expectin' a coach to be travellin' this road at that speed. We barely made it outta their path in time." He looked at us with concern. "You weren't injured, were you? Miss Darcy, you look mighty pale."

"Miss Darcy?" The woman's voice sounded from just outside the door and Jeremy was pushed roughly aside. "Georgiana! What are you doing in this unknown carriage? Why are you not with your brother?"

"Aunt C-catherine," I stuttered. "We were not expecting you."

"No," the lady's eyes narrowed. "I am certain you were not, but I am here and all shall be made right at once. Where is your brother?"

I hesitated, knowing I must not say anything regarding Mr. Wickham and the missing ladies. "He and Richard are out riding with the gentlemen of the area and some officers from the militia."

"A hunt? Well at least there are no ladies present." Aunt Catherine screwed up her face and reached forward to take hold of my arm. "Come along. You will ride with me to Netherfield."

Instinctively drawing away, I shook my head. "But what of Kitty?"

A curious expression crossed my aunt's countenance as her gaze fell to the ground. "What kitty?"

It took all of my power to withhold the laugh threatening to escape. "My friend, Miss Catherine Bennet." I raised my hand to indicate the young lady at my side.

"Bennet?" Aunt Catherine's eyes narrowed further as she stared at the Kitty, who was making every attempt to disappear into the squabs. "You cannot be the grasping nobody who has imposed herself on my nephew. Are you one of the Bennets of Longbourn?"

"Y-y-yes, ma'am." Kitty quaked in her seat and I took her hand.

"You are nothing to my niece and nephew. Release her hand, Georgiana, and come with me."

"No." I sat straighter and met my aunt's gaze directly. Though I was unable to fully summon the Darcy glare, I held my head high and refused to flinch. "Brother instructed Kitty, that is Miss Catherine, and I to return to Netherfield together."

Aunt Catherine's eyes widened in surprise before narrowing in suspicion. "Then why were you stopped on the road?"

Feeling my false bravado slipping away, I was grateful when I heard another voice from outside the carriage.

"Our driver saw something in the woods and we went to investigate it. Forgive us for not moving our coach out of the way; we thought we would be but a moment."

Aunt Catherine stepped back revealing Elizabeth just behind her. "And who are you?"

"Aunt, this is Miss Elizabeth Bennet of Longbourn, Kitty's older sister. Elizabeth, this is my aunt, Lady Catherine de Burgh of Rosings Park in Kent."

"Ah, Mr. Collins' patroness," Elizabeth's eyes sparkled with mirth as she curtseyed. "We have heard much of you, madam."

With a grunt, Aunt Catherine looked Elizabeth over from head to toe and back again. "I might say the same. You are also travelling to Netherfield under my nephew's orders?"

A blush crept across Elizabeth's countenance as she nodded. "Yes, he was quite insistent we remain there until he returned."

Kitty and I glanced at each other and back at Elizabeth as she again lightly caressed the hand which had been kissed. I could see Kitty also fought the smile which threatened to overtake her, obviously knowing Aunt Catherine would not be amused.

Once more Aunt Catherine took Elizabeth's measure before stepping back from the doorway. Holding Elizabeth's gaze, she spoke. "Miss Elizabeth shall ride with her sister. Georgiana, you will accompany me. We shall *all* proceed to Netherfield and await Darcy there."

I began to protest once more as I wanted to know if they had found the runaways, but Elizabeth smiled. "Of course, Lady Catherine, I am certain you miss your niece and wish time with her. Shall we lead the way?"

The great lady inhaled through her nose as she stood taller. "My coachman is perfectly capable of finding the estate." She glanced into the carriage. "Come, Georgiana," she commanded before turning and moving away.

Elizabeth nodded and I quickly embraced Kitty before slipping from the coach and following my aunt. I was no sooner seated than Aunt Catherine knocked on the roof with her cane and the equipage lurched forward, nearly sending me into her lap.

"Tell me what you know of this Miss Elizabeth Bennet." Aunt Catherine demanded.

"She is the second daughter of Mr. and Mrs. Bennet of Longbourn, and a kind and giving person." I wondered what else was expected of me; what my aunt might wish to know.

"What are her intentions toward your brother?"

"Her intentions?"

Releasing an exasperated sigh, Aunt Catherine leaned forward. "Yes, her intentions. She expects to be the next Mistress of Pemberley, does she not? She sees Darcy as a means to raise her family from their lowly status and rescue her mother and sisters from poverty should her father pass."

"No!" I raised my head as my posture stiffened. "Why until I arrived, she disliked Brother. She cares not for what he has, only who he is."

"The nephew of an earl!"

"No! A good man." I was angry; something that rarely occurred. I knew I should not speak so to my aunt, but I was unable to stop myself. "Why are you here, Aunt? What brings you to this place?"

"Mr. Collins informed me that Miss Elizabeth was to marry him, but she saw the larger prize in my nephew and has been using her arts and allurements upon your brother."

"Elizabeth has done no such thing. Brother fell in love with her without any encouragement." As soon as the words had left my mouth, I knew I should not have said them. The look of astonishment on my aunt's face, gave me but a moment to attempt to right my mistake. "They are formed for each other. Elizabeth eases Fitzwilliam's discomfort in public. She makes him smile; something he has rarely done since Father passed."

"Formed for each other? Anne and Darcy are formed for each other! They are descended on the maternal side from the same noble line; and on the father's, from respectable, honourable, and ancient, though untitled families. Their fortune on both sides is splendid. They are destined for each other by the voice of every member of their respective houses ..."

"Not every member," I muttered.

"Every member who should have a say. It was the favourite wish of your parents. While in their cradles, your mother and I planned the union. Your father supported it, as does my brother."

"I have never heard Uncle support a marriage between Anne and Fitzwilliam."

"Why would he discuss such things with you? These are matters beyond your scope. I am here to see that the upstart pretensions of a young woman without family, connections, or fortune, and the romantic falderal of a child, do not distract your brother from what he knows is expected of him."

I crossed my arms across my chest and glared at my aunt as the carriage made its final turn into Netherfield Park. Aunt Catherine returned the glare as she stared down her nose at me. We held this pose until the carriage rocked to a stop at the front steps of the manor. The door was opened and the steps lowered before the footman reached inside to assist Aunt Catherine from the coach and I followed her.

The Bennet carriage drew to a stop just behind us and Elizabeth and Kitty quickly climbed out and approached me. Aunt Catherine ignored them as she climbed the stairs. Looking up, I realized Jane stood at the door, her eyes wide as she glanced between us and the woman quickly approaching her. Curtseying, she welcomed Aunt Catherine to Netherfield.

"I assume you are Miss Bingley, the mistress of this estate. I shall require a room and a maid to wait upon me until my nephew returns. When he does, have him sent to me immediately."

Jane's eyes grew larger as she stared at Lady Catherine and then glanced toward me and her sister. "I … I am not Miss Bingley."

"Aunt, this is Miss Jane Bennet, Miss Elizabeth's older sister. Miss Bingley has returned to London with Mr. Bingley. Jane, this is my aunt, Lady Catherine de Burgh of Rosings Park in Kent."

"Am I to understand that Mr. Bingley and his sister have left their home and allowed the neighbourhood reign of it?"

"There was an unusual situation …" Jane tried to explain, but was interrupted.

"Will someone have a room prepared?" Lady Catherine bellowed and Jane stepped backward into the entryway.

Mrs. Nicholls stepped forward quickly and offered to escort Lady Catherine to a room. As they climbed the stairs, I could hear my aunt's disgruntled mutterings.

Once the grand lady was out of sight, all remaining in the hall released a collective breath.

"Wherever did she come from?" Jane whispered.

"Mr. Collins sent for her." I sighed before turning toward Elizabeth. "Did you find them? Were they at the house?"

Elizabeth glanced about and motioned us all toward the study. Once we were inside and the doors closed, she walked toward the window and looked out as though she were watching for something. A moment later, she nodded and turned back to us.

"Samuel and I found tracks indicating someone had been at the house. Before we could get close enough to see if they were there, we heard Lady Catherine's carriage approaching. We were afraid you were still in the road."

"No, Jeremy reacted quickly and moved us out of the way." I bit the inside of my cheek. "So we are still uncertain if they are there?"

Nodding, Elizabeth motioned toward the window. "Samuel has just ridden out to inspect the house while Jeremy has gone for the men."

"What house?" Jane asked.

"The Schmitts." Elizabeth glanced toward Kitty. "Apparently Lydia has been tending their animals while they are away."

"Lydia?" Jane asked clearly confused. "But Mrs. Schmitt told me the Jacksons were taking in their animals until they return."

The entire room fell silent as what we had feared was confirmed. Lydia had lied. The question was, what *had* she been doing? I shuddered as I considered the consequences to my friends.

Chapter Twenty-Two

A hesitant knock, cracking like thunder in the silent room, brought us from our thoughts. "Enter," Jane called as we all turned toward the door.

One of the maids stepped inside, her head down and hands clasping her apron. "Begging your pardon, Miss Bennet. Lady Catherine de Bourgh is asking for her niece to attend her."

I sighed as I crossed the room. Stopping in the doorway, I looked back at the sisters. "I am certain Fitzwilliam will return as soon as he hears Lady Catherine is here. Until then, I will attempt to keep her in her room."

The Bennets gave me a sympathetic look as I left. I followed the maid up the stairs, but paused before my aunt's door. Laying a hand upon the maid's shoulder, I indicated she need not announce me. The look of relief upon the servant's countenance was nearly comical. After the girl had walked quickly away, I remained staring at the door. Finally, I took a deep breath and knocked.

"It is about time! Enter!"

Drawing my shoulders back and holding my head high, I opened the door and entered the room.

"Has word been sent to Darcy demanding he return?" Lady Catherine asked without turning around.

"One of the footmen rode out to locate him," I replied sedately. I refused to allow my aunt to see anything more than a calm exterior.

Lady Catherine turned around, eyes narrowed as she studied me. We stood in this manner for a few minutes until she finally pointed toward a chair. "Well sit. I asked that woman to bring tea."

"Mrs. Nicholls?" I asked as innocently as I could manage.

"If that is her name." Lady Catherine took the seat opposite me, and continued to study me. Just as I felt the urge to squirm under her demanding gaze, she spoke. "It has been too long since we have been together, Georgiana. You have changed."

"I am grown, Lady Catherine," I said in a factual manner.

"Unlikely. You are only sixteen." The older woman leaned forward and peered closer. "But there is something in your manner that reflects a certain impertinence. Your brother is obviously negligent in his care of you. He has allowed you to be influenced by those inferior to ..."

"No, Aunt, I fear I must disagree. Brother has simply encouraged me to ask questions and speak out when I feel a situation is improper." I could feel the heat suffusing my cheeks, but I would not allow my aunt to berate my brother who had done so much for me. "It is in keeping young girls ignorant of the evils of the world around them that they fall victim to the first scoundrel who crosses their path."

Lady Catherine sat back in her chair, her eyes wide. "Upon my word, you give your opinion very decidedly for so young a person."

"Indeed?" I drew up an innocent air once more. "When you were my age, did you speak your mind any less openly?" Knowing from stories my uncle had told that my aunt had always been very demanding and opinionated, I waited to see how the grand Lady would respond.

Lady Catherine's jaw dropped and hung in a most unbecoming manner for a minute before the lady finally closed her mouth and the corners of her lips began to twitch. "You are inferring that outspokenness is a Fitzwilliam trait?"

Shrugging my shoulders, I glanced about the room in an attempt to fight the urge to laugh. "Have I any relatives, other than Anne, who do not display it? Even Lady Matlock who is only a Fitzwilliam by marriage has a certain commanding presence."

A strange sound, almost like a humph, issued from Lady Catherine as she sat forward and straightened her skirt. "Do not let her fool you, Georgiana. She was not a soft spoken thing when she wed my brother, she only pretended to be." Her eyes drilled into me once more. "I had always believed you to be like your mother. My sister Anne was the sweetest, most pliable, woman I have ever known."

I tipped my head to the side as I considered my aunt's words. "Truly? I have few memories of Mother, but Brother has told me she could be very determined when she felt passionately about something."

"Ah, but determined and opinionated are quite different things." Lady Catherine smiled and her eyes took on a distant look. Before any more could be said, there was a knock at the door. "Enter!" With that, the grand Dame had returned and the intriguing aunt was gone.

The maid entered with the tea service and set it on the table between us. "Will there be anything else, M'Lady?"

"Has my nephew returned?"

The imperious tone caused the young girl to tremble as she replied. "N-no, Ma'am."

"He is to wait on me the moment he does."

"Y-yes, Ma'am." The girl hastily curtseyed and scurried from the room.

I caught the satisfactory gleam in my aunt's eye as the door closed behind the frightened maid. "I do not understand why you take such delight in intimidating the servants," I said as I began to pour out the tea. "I am certain they would be able to fulfill their duties in a more satisfactory manner without quivering in fear."

Lady Catherine's features set into a well-defined scowl. "Servants must always understand who their superiors are. I have seen far too many ladies become friendly with their ladies' maids only to have them steal from or spread gossip about their mistresses. They must understand they can be let go at any moment for the simplest offense, in order to keep them properly submissive."

As I opened my mouth to speak, another knock was heard. This was much firmer and demanding. I knew immediately my brother had arrived. A glance at my aunt revealed she was also certain of who waited on the other side of the door. I watched as a most discomposing smile crossed my aunt's lips.

"Enter!"

The door swung open and my brother strolled into the room, followed closely by Richard.

"Fitzwilliam, what are you doing here? I was under the impression only Darcy was staying in this forsaken county." Lady Catherine appeared a bit discommoded that her other nephew was in residence. "Do you not have duties to which you must attend?"

"Happily my commander saw fit to grant a day or two of leave so that I might enjoy a hunt with my cousin." Richard stepped forward and bowed over her hand. "It is always a pleasure to see you also, Aunt."

Waving him away, she turned her stabbing gaze on my brother. "And what have you to say for yourself?"

Fitzwilliam Darcy stepped past me and bowed stiffly over our aunt's hand. "To what do we owe this pleasure, Lady Catherine?"

"You know why I am here." Lady Catherine pulled her hand from his and leaned toward him. "I have it on the best authority that you are being importuned by what passes as gentility in this uncivilized society."

Standing fully erect, Fitzwilliam squared his shoulders and glared down at Lady Catherine. "I suppose your authority would be the toad of a clergyman you sent to Hertfordshire in order to obtain a wife from amongst his cousins?"

"Mr. Collins notified me he was all but engaged when the object of his affections became captivated by your wealth and position in society. She then began making such advances upon you as to make you forget your duty to your family."

"Ridiculous! Miss Elizabeth did not even like me at the time Mr. Collins entered the area." Fitzwilliam sneered. "She cares not for wealth nor position."

"Yet her feelings toward you changed? However do you explain her reversal?"

A quick, nearly imperceptible glance passed between Fitzwilliam and myself, but it was not fast enough to be missed by the woman. She turned her indignation upon me.

"You promoted a relationship between your brother and a country nobody?"

I was struck dumb by the vehemence in her voice, but Fitzwilliam came to my rescue. "You will not address my sister in such a manner. I believe it best you return home, Lady Catherine, for you shall accomplish nothing here."

"You are quite mistaken, Darcy." Lady Catherine rose from her seat and stood toe to toe with him. "If I return to Rosings, you shall accompany me in order to announce your engagement to your cousin Anne. I shall not leave you here to be worked upon by these ..."

"I would not complete that sentence, *Aunt*." Fitzwilliam's teeth were clenched and his voice was barely audible. "My business in this area is incomplete. I shall remain until I have accomplished all I set out to do." He took a deep breath and his shoulders relaxed a bit. "In regards to my cousin, though I care deeply for Anne's well-being, I have proof that the supposed engagement you insistently mention is of your own fabrication. My mother was against the marriage you support."

"That is not so. While you were in your cradles ..."

"Lady Catherine, have you forgotten I am a full three years older than my cousin? I was well out of the cradle when she was born. I no longer wish to hear your claims and demands regarding my family's expectations of my wife. The only obligation

I feel is towards the happiness of myself and the woman I choose. *That* was my mother's wish."

I sat quietly, my eyes moving quickly between my brother and my aunt with an occasional glance at my cousin. Richard had taken on a soldier's stance, masking his emotions, though his eyes sparkled with amusement. Fitzwilliam and Lady Catherine stared fiercely at one another, neither showing any sign of relenting.

A soft knock followed by a woman's voice finally broke the tension in the room. "Forgive me." Elizabeth stepped through the doorway. "The door was open," she assured. Her eyes fell on Fitzwilliam, holding such emotion that she appeared as though she would rush into his arms. "Samuel has returned and wished to speak to the gentlemen."

The smile which lit my brother's face as he gazed at the woman he loved took my breath away. "I shall be with him momentarily." He glanced at our cousin and nodded toward the hallway.

Richard's lips twitched as he bowed again to our aunt. "If you will excuse me, Aunt." Without awaiting her response, he turned, offered Elizabeth his arm, and left the room with her at his side.

Fitzwilliam's eyes fell on me and he winked before turning back to our aunt. His voice took on a softer tone, but lost none of the determination. "My decision is made, Lady Catherine, and nothing you say or do will change it. I ask that you respect my wishes. If not, then you must return to Rosings Park. Know that I shall not be visiting this Easter nor any future years until you have come to accept my choices."

A look of complete disbelief settled upon Lady Catherine's features. "You are then resolved to have her?"

"I am only resolved to act in that manner which will, in my own opinion, constitute my happiness, without reference to *you*, or to any other person."

"She will ruin you in the opinion of all your friends, and make you the contempt of the world," she spat at him.

"Were my friends excited by my marrying her, it would not give me one moment's concern — and the world in general would have too much sense to join in the scorn." Fitzwilliam's posture had relaxed, but his countenance continued to hold an implacable resoluteness.

"And this is your real opinion! This is your final resolve! Very well. I shall now know how to act." She stepped forward until she was once again toe to toe with him. "Depend upon it, Darcy, I will carry my point."

Slowly releasing a fatigued sigh, Fitzwilliam stepped back and bowed. "I am certain you shall try, but you shall not succeed. Good day, Lady Catherine." He turned and took my hand in his to assist me to my feet. Laying my hand upon his arm, he escorted me from the room and closed the door behind him.

Once in the hallway, he glanced about. Seeing the maid nearby, he motioned her forward. "My aunt will be leaving as soon as her coach is readied. Please see to her things and have Mrs. Nicholls notify the stables."

"Yes, sir." The young girl gave a quick curtsey. I was certain a relieved smile lit her face as she turned away to see to her duties.

"Shall we see what Samuel has learned?" Fitzwilliam whispered as he guided me toward the stairs.

"Oh, yes." I bit my lip. "Fitzwilliam, do you believe Lady Catherine will leave so easily?"

"She will leave on her own, or I will bundle her into the carriage myself." His voice was bitter and I felt his arm stiffen under my hand.

"Will you truly cut ties with her? And with Anne?" Though I was not close with my aunt or my cousin, my compassionate side felt for Anne who had no influence on her mother's actions and less freedom of her own.

"I will speak to Uncle about aiding Anne, but I will not subject Elizabeth to Lady Catherine's tirades."

He led me down the steps and toward the study. Upon entering, he motioned toward Jeremy who stood just inside the door. The lad approached, showing his eagerness to be of assistance.

"I want you to stand outside this door and keep any who approach away. I want no one to enter or even get near enough to hear what is being said inside. Do you understand?"

Jeremy nodded and Fitzwilliam smiled as he patted the boy's shoulder. The lad slipped into the hall and drew the door closed behind him.

Fitzwilliam looked back toward the desk where Richard and Elizabeth stood, speaking softly with Samuel. Still holding my arm, he moved toward them.

"So Lady Catherine has succumbed to the Darcy glare?" Richard asked, his eyes flashing in amusement.

"She will be gone as soon as her carriage is readied." Fitzwilliam's jaw was set.

I glanced at Elizabeth, but she was looking down at the handkerchief she twisted in front of her. The look of overpowering emotions which had suffused her countenance earlier was gone and she appeared almost remorseful.

Before I could address my friend, Fitzwilliam led us closer so he was standing beside the lady. She raised her gaze as we approached and Fitzwilliam smiled reassuringly at her. A light blush covered her cheeks as he took her hand, raising it to brush a kiss across her fingers. I could not suppress my grin as I watched the couple.

"Ahem." Richard cleared his throat to draw everyone's attention back to the crisis at hand. "I have sent Miss Bennet and Miss Kitty to see to Mrs. King." He turned his gaze upon me. "Georgie, perhaps you should join them."

My eyes widened in disbelief. "No, I shall remain." I turned to my brother, seeking his support, but saw only doubt. "Fitzwilliam, six months ago it could have been me. Please allow me to be of some assistance."

Our gaze held for a moment longer. Finally, he nodded before looking to our cousin. "She may at least hear what has been learned and what plan we devise." He turned back to me once more. "But you will remain at Netherfield, Georgie. I will not have you anywhere near Wickham."

Nodding, I released his arm and focused on Samuel as he gave his report.

"I was able to get near enough to hear voices. It appears there be one gent and two ladies within the Schmitt home. One of them is most definitely Miss Lydia, and she were not pleased."

"What was said?" Elizabeth asked.

The servant's countenance reddened and he glanced at the Colonel. "I don't rightly like to say in front of ladies."

"Samuel, it is my sister. I doubt I would be surprised."

Again, the man looked to the officer, refusing to meet the ladies' gazes. "I can say that Miss Lydia were not expecting the other lady to be present. She demanded the man, George she called him, send the other lady away so they could be on their way."

Richard leaned forward. "On their way? To where?"

With a shrug and shake of the head, Samuel replied, "I know not. The door opened and I had to hide before I was seen. The gent stepped outside and slammed the door behind him. The ladies' voices grew loud quickly and he ran back inside, demandin' they be quiet. I decided to leave while they were being loud enough to cover any sound I might make."

"Wise decision," Richard said as he placed a hand on the man's shoulder. "Well, at least we know where they are. Now, we must decide what is to be done with them."

"Done?" Elizabeth asked. "Can they not be returned to their families and the matter addressed privately?"

The men exchanged knowing glances before Samuel turned toward Elizabeth. "Beggin' your pardon, Miss Lizzy. I do not believe Miss Lydia will return home willingly. I suspect she will make quite a to-do."

"Well, Papa will have to be firm." Though her words sounded strong, by the time Elizabeth ended it was clear she understood the folly of such hope. Her eyes fell to her hand which still rested in Fitzwilliam's, and she began to withdraw it.

I saw Fitzwilliam clasp her fingers tighter as he placed a finger from his other hand under her chin and forced her to look at him. "Do not fear. I shall make it all well. If need be, we will find a school or companion for Miss Lydia. This will not affect you or your other sisters, I swear it. We will find a way."

A knock on the door kept Elizabeth from responding. Everyone looked confused as Fitzwilliam had issued strict orders for them not to be disturbed. Before any could respond, the door opened and young Jeremy poked his head inside.

"I beg your pardon, sir. I know none was to interrupt, but the young lady's uncle has arrived. I thought you might want to know."

Fitzwilliam nodded. "You did right, Jeremy. Please show him in."

As the door opened wider, a loud voice was heard from the stairs. "I will not be treated in this manner! I will leave when I decide to do so!"

A groan escaped Fitzwilliam as he released Elizabeth and moved toward the door. "I shall see to Lady Catherine. Richard, you continue and I will return as quickly as possible."

I watched my brother leave and an older gentleman enter the room. He was dirty from the road, but what struck me was the look of anger and disgust which was clearly displayed on his countenance and in his very stance. Stealing my aunt's favourite sentiment, I decided Miss King's uncle was "most displeased".

Chapter Twenty-Three

I stood quietly to the side and watched the gentleman look about anxiously as he entered the room. "I received a letter from a Mr. Bennet regarding my niece."

Richard stepped forward, offering his hand. "I am Colonel Richard Fitzwilliam. Mr. Bennet is currently searching for Miss King. My cousin, Mr. Darcy, attended the ball which was held here last night and enlisted my assistance when he was made aware of Miss King's disappearance. I fear our family has a history with the man who was behind it."

The man's eyes narrowed as he reluctantly accepted the outstretched hand. "Mr. Arlen Singleton. Where are my sister and her daughter?"

"Your sister is in the drawing room with a few other ladies who are keeping her company." Richard glanced toward Samuel and back to Mr. Singleton. "We believe we have just learned the whereabouts of your niece and were in the process of devising a plan for returning her to her home."

Mr. Singleton's countenance became flushed as he glanced about the room. "And how many people are aware of my niece's shame? She will be ruined if she returns home."

"Please be assured, we have taken every precaution to avoid such a thing, sir." Richard took a deep breath as though considering the man before him. "I fear the man who absconded with your niece is not the sort you would want her to wed. He is a profligate waste of good space." His normally jovial appearance hardened as he spoke until I could well imagine him frightening any enemy in the field.

"That well may be, but what can be done to keep the knowledge of my niece's foolishness a secret from her neighbours?" Mr. Singleton appeared to relax somewhat, but his concern was still great.

"We have kept your sister sequestered with only a handful of trustworthy ladies who also have a concern in the manner. You see, Mr. Wickham disappeared not just with your niece, but with another young lady as well." Richard returned to the desk.

"There are two such foolish young girls in this neighbourhood? Do they breed them here?" The bitterness dripped from Mr. Singleton's words, but a look of tired repentance quickly suffused his features. "Forgive me, I am more displeased with myself. I knew my sister should not be left alone, but I dallied in coming to Hertfordshire."

Richard gave a brief nod. "Do you wish to see Mrs. King?"

Taking a deep breath, Mr. Singleton ran his fingers over his eyes. "I suppose I should, but I do not wish to delay the return of my niece."

"We are capable of …"

"No, Colonel, I shall be present when she is found. If so much as a hair on her head has been harmed, the man will answer for it."

I was unable to suppress the shiver which ran through me as I observed the man's determined mien. Taking a deep breath, I stepped forward. "Richard, since Fitzwilliam has not yet returned, perhaps I could escort Mr. Singleton to the drawing room to see his sister."

My cousin met my gaze, but did not immediately respond. I looked at him quizzically as he took a deep breath. Before he could actually speak, Elizabeth stepped between us.

"Perhaps, Colonel, you could introduce us and Miss Darcy and I could both accompany Mr. Singleton to the drawing room."

Suddenly I realized my cousin's hesitation was due to his reluctance for me to be alone with a strange man. Though I realized I should be grateful for his concern for my well-being, I was actually quite disconcerted. Would he forever see me as a helpless child?

"Thank you, Miss Bennet." Richard bowed his head in the lady's direction before turning toward the gentleman. "Mr. Singleton, may I present Miss Elizabeth Bennet of," he turned toward the lady to be certain he was correct, "Longbourn." Elizabeth nodded. "It was her father who wrote to you and her youngest sister who is also missing."

Elizabeth curtseyed as Mr. Singleton acknowledged the introduction with a brief bow.

"And this is my cousin, Miss Georgiana Darcy of Pemberley in Derbyshire. Ladies, may I present Mr. Singleton of …?"

"Sizemore Abbey in Liverpool, sir," The gentleman replied as he acknowledged my curtsey. "It was estate business there which kept me from collecting my sister and niece before now." He ran a hand across the back of his neck.

"Well you have come and I am certain your sister will be pleased to see you," Elizabeth said as she approached him. "If you will step this way." She motioned toward the door and I followed her and Mr. Singleton from the room.

As we entered the hallway, the man gave a soft harrumph. "Pleased is not the word I would use," he muttered under his breath, just loud enough that I could hear.

Before I could consider the reason for his comment, we had reached the drawing room door. Elizabeth was about to open it, when a voice was heard from the other side.

"Enough! Mama, if you are unable to remain respectful or quiet, you must return to Longbourn. Mrs. King, I believe we are all agreed that the most important thing is the safe return of *both* Lydia and Miss King. Any speculation on who shall be married and who shall not is fully indefensible!"

"Oh dear," Elizabeth whispered. "I fear they have pushed even sweet Jane to her breaking point." She pushed open the door and rushed inside, quite forgetting her companions.

I followed Elizabeth and Mr. Singleton into the room, though none of the inhabitants noticed our entry. Mrs. Bennet sat with her back stiff, indignation radiating from her being, while Mrs. King stared in shock at the normally quiet young lady. Kitty and Mrs. Annesley sat, eyes wide, observing the scene.

"I did not raise my daughter to speak to me in this manner!" Mrs. Bennet began fanning herself violently.

Quietly, Elizabeth stepped up to her sister before anything more could be said, and slipped an arm about her waist. "Oh Jane, please have a seat and take some tea to calm yourself. I will see to things."

As Jane glanced at her sister, I saw a look of gratitude and relief pass over her features. When she moved toward the nearest chair, it became clear she was shaking. I wondered if Jane had ever spoken so harshly to anyone in her life.

Elizabeth made certain her sister was well settled and asked Mrs. Annesley to pour out a fresh cup of tea for her before turning her attention to the matrons. Her lips pursed in disappointment as she looked from one to the other. Mrs. King had the decency to lower her eyes to her lap.

"Mrs. King, your brother has arrived." Elizabeth announced coldly.

The older lady's hands flew to her face as her eyes grew wide and she looked about. The moment her gaze fell upon her brother, a look of fear crossed her features. "Arlen!"

"Abigail," he replied, looking more like a disappointed father than a concerned brother.

"Oh," Mrs. King began to whimper as she twisted her handkerchief. It was clear she was uncertain what to do. Neither sibling moved.

The brother continued to stare at his sister, as though he had forgotten the others were in the room. Finally, he took a deep breath and broke the tense silence. "It appears you have ignored all my directives. If you had remained at home, mindful of your mourning, this would not have happened."

"But the officers were so thoughtful, speaking their condolences and not wanting us to be alone. They were so attentive to Mary and me. I thought it the perfect opportunity for Mary to find a husband ..."

"From a group of penniless men who only saw her dowry?" Mr. Singleton shouted. "How long was Father dead before you announced the amount of her inheritance? I have always known you were foolish, but this is by far the most imprudent thing you have ever done!" He ran a hand over the back of his neck and took a deep breath. "I am going to ride out with the others and retrieve Mary. When we return, we shall be leaving for Liverpool at once. Send word to your home to have what is needed for the journey packed. The rest will be handled once we are away from here."

With that said, he turned abruptly and marched from the room. All eyes remained upon Mrs. King who stared disbelieving for but a few seconds before she collapsed in sobs upon the cushions of the sofa where she sat.

Mrs. Annesley quickly moved to the lady's side and began reassuring her, while Elizabeth moved to the tea service and poured a fresh cup for her.

While all bustled about Mrs. King, I watched Mrs. Bennet. A cruel smile slowly spread across her lips as she stared at the woman she had called a friend. *Is she truly seeing this as a victory? That her daughter has won the prize in Mr. Wickham?*

I shivered in disgust and backed toward the doorway, but I was brought up short when I collided with a firm but warm obstacle. Glancing over my shoulder, I realized Fitzwilliam was standing behind me. He slipped an arm about my shoulders and led me from the room.

"I heard raised voices and thought I would investigate." He spoke softly as we stopped just outside the doorway and he let his arm fall to his side. "Are the ladies well?"

"Mr. Singleton, Mrs. King's brother, just announced he will be taking his sister and niece back to Liverpool as soon as Miss King is found. I believe he has returned to the study to speak to Richard." I bit my lip and glanced back toward the room. "Prior to then, Mrs. King and Mrs. Bennet were arguing over which of their daughters would marry Mr. Wickham." I looked back to see my brother's reaction.

His lips formed a thin line as he also looked back into the room. "I suppose Mrs. Bennet sees this as a victory for her daughter."

I nodded solemnly.

Fitzwilliam frowned. "If I did not believe Wickham would abandon the girl at his earliest opportunity, I might consider it a lesson well taught." He shook his head as his gaze fell upon Elizabeth and Jane, and the fierceness of his expression fell away; replaced by sadness.

"It is amazing they are part of the same family," I whispered. "What can be done to save the girls' reputations?"

My brother sighed and met my gaze. "We shall have to see what we learn once we find them. I am hopeful, but the afternoon visiting hours have come. If Miss Elizabeth is correct, there will be much activity as ladies move from house to house to discuss the ball. It might appear odd that the Bennets and Kings are not available to visitors, but perhaps people will think they are out visiting."

"Until they are unable to confirm whom they were visiting." My brow drew together. "At least

Miss King will be leaving the area and the story may not follow her. What about Miss Lydia?"

Fitzwilliam slipped an arm about my shoulders again and squeezed as he kissed my forehead. "We shall see. Now, I must return to the study. Lady Catherine has been bundled into her carriage and should be on the road to Kent. Will you remain here with the ladies?"

I nodded, but grabbed his arm before he could leave. "However did you get her to go?"

The twinkle in his eye shone as the corner of his mouth turned upward. "I simply escorted her in that direction while speaking to her in a calm, rational manner. Before she knew what had occurred, I was closing the door and motioning for the coachman to drive on."

"Surely it was not that easy," I giggled.

He shrugged and winked. "More or less. I believe I heard her promising she *would* carry her point and this would *not* be the last we heard on the subject as the coach pulled away."

"Oh dear," I moaned. A part of me had hoped our aunt would simply cease speaking to us.

Fitzwilliam drew me into another embrace. "Hush, dearest. There is nothing Lady Catherine can do to interfere with our lives. She is but a nuisance, not a true threat."

I nodded against his chest, then pushed him away. "Go, see to the plans to retrieve Miss King and Miss Lydia." I turned back toward the drawing room. "I shall care for the ladies."

My brother placed another kiss upon my head then disappeared down the hall. Taking a deep breath, I sallied forth into the fray. As I entered the room I realized Mrs. King was still sobbing uncontrollably and I saw Elizabeth look longingly at the laudanum bottle on the sideboard.

"Well," Mrs. Bennet said in a haughty voice, "it appears my Lydia shall be the one to marry after all."

Elizabeth and Jane both looked at their mother incredulously as Mrs. King sobbed louder.

Taking a deep breath, I moved toward Mrs. Annesley and whispered in her ear. "Perhaps you could take Mrs. King upstairs to gather her things and help her write the letter to her staff."

My companion nodded and slipped an arm about Mrs. King. "Come, Abigail. Let us retire to my room so you can write the directions per your brother's instructions."

"Oh, oh yes, Florence. It will not do to make him angrier than he is." Mrs. King clutched Mrs. Annesley's hand and the ladies rose from the sofa and left the room.

Elizabeth and I exchanged a perplexed look, wondering when the ladies had come to use their Christian names. We looked to Jane who shrugged and sat back on the sofa, obviously glad the responsibility of Mrs. King no longer rested upon her shoulders.

Mrs. Bennet sat forward and appropriated a lemon biscuit from the tea tray. "Have the gentlemen gone yet? When shall we expect Lydia and Mr. Wickham?" She smiled in a self-satisfied manner as she looked at the biscuit. "Surely they will have to obtain a special license in order to be wed immediately. Oh, to think of it!" She took a bite of cookie and savoured it.

"Mama, you cannot be serious!" Kitty stepped toward her mother. "You wish to have a man like Mr. Wickham in our family?"

The older woman looked at her daughter, obviously not fully comprehending the source of her ire. "Oh hold your tongue, Kitty. Mr. Wickham is everything a gentleman should be ..."

"No, Mama, he is not. A gentleman does not abduct *two* young ladies from their families and hide them away. A gentleman speaks to the father and asks permission to call, or court, or propose. Have you no idea what is proper? Did Papa not do these things?"

Kitty flung an arm in her sisters' direction. "Look at your daughters, Mama. Jane and Elizabeth both have proper gentlemen showing interest in them, but what will come of it now? After what Lydia has done, will Mr. Bingley and Mr. Darcy still wish to be connected to our family? Even Mr. Collins is attempting to distance himself from us. Can you not see that Lydia has ruined us?"

With those words, Kitty rushed from the room. I hesitated but a second before running after her. As I left the room I heard Mrs. Bennet crowing, "I knew Mr. Darcy had taken a fancy to you, Lizzy! Ten thousand a year!"

A door slamming down the hall allowed me to find Kitty in the breakfast parlour. It was deserted at this hour, so I closed the door quietly behind me and approached my friend. Since the room was on the east side of the house, it was mostly in shadow now, so I was unable to make out Kitty's features.

A soft whisper, broken by sniffling, reached me in the dimness of the room. "Forgive me, I should not have spoken so against my mother. I am certain she is quite displeased with me."

"Actually, she did not appear so when I left the room." I kept my voice soft in the quiet of the room.

Kitty turned toward me, a look of incredulity barely recognizable in the shadows. "Did she hear nothing I said?"

Reluctantly, I shrugged my shoulders. "Only the fact that my brother is interested in your sister."

"Oh, that woman!" Kitty growled. "She did not hear me say it will amount to nothing due to Lydia's shame?"

"I fear not."

"Any man would be a fool to marry into my family." Kitty kicked the chair in front of her, then lowered her head. "Forgive me again, Georgie. I did not mean to insinuate your brother is a fool. Of course, now he will never offer for Lizzy, so he will prove he is not."

Her hands flew to her face and she began to weep. I stepped closer and drew her into an embrace. "Hush. Fitzwilliam cares deeply for Lizzy. I am certain he will find a way for them to wed. He defied my aunt for her. He would be loath to admit defeat and not follow through on his intentions."

"Do you think so?" Kitty asked between sniffles.

"Of course." I slipped my handkerchief into her hand and smiled. "Come, let us go …"

I hesitated. Where could we go? Mrs. Bennet was in the drawing room with Jane and Elizabeth. The men were in the study planning the rescue and would not want us underfoot. Mrs. Annesley and Mrs. King were upstairs. Where else would we be both safe and quiet? And wherever it was, we must tell someone where we went.

I led Kitty toward the door, opened it, and looked about the hall. The only footman on duty was a short distance away. I drew Kitty into the light and looked at her countenance. Her eyes were red and her lashes wet, but at least her complexion was not blotchy. Smiling, I linked arms with Kitty and moved toward the footman.

"Are the gentlemen still in the study?" I asked as we approached.

"Yes, miss."

"Please tell Mr. Darcy that Miss Kitty and Miss Darcy will be sketching in the garden once we gather our things." I turned toward my friend. "I have a sketchpad in my room."

We walked up the stairs feeling much brighter than before. After gathering our outerwear and sketching materials, we returned back downstairs to find Captain Jacobs waiting by the garden door.

"Ladies." He bowed formally.

"Captain Jacobs." I curtseyed. "Have you met Miss Catherine Bennet?"

"Yes, I have had the pleasure." He tipped his head in her direction and she curtseyed.

With my head high, I forced a smile. "We were just going outside to sketch."

"Colonel Fitzwilliam has asked that you remain inside." He met my gaze in an unflinching manner.

"And what does my brother say?" My smile slipped slightly.

"I do not believe he was consulted. The gentlemen were leaving when the footman passed on your message. Mr. Darcy was already on his way out of the house."

"And you are not joining them?" I challenged.

"I am to follow, once I am certain you are safe *within* Netherfield." He held my gaze, as though questioning whether this would be quickly and easily accomplished.

I folded my arms before me. "Is no one remaining behind?"

Captain Jacobs took a deep breath. "A few soldiers have been placed about Netherfield in the event Mr. Wickham would come this way. It is highly unlikely, but we wish to err on the side of caution."

"And would they not keep us safe should we be sitting quietly in the side garden sketching?"

Kitty tugged at my sleeve. "I am certain there is someplace in Netherfield that is well lit where we could sketch."

Refusing to acknowledge her statement, I held the Captain's gaze. The man's lips began to slowly curl upwards before he turned to my companion and gave her a full smile.

"Thank you, Miss Catherine. Your wisdom and cooperation at this trying time are greatly appreciated." He bowed to her, glanced momentarily toward me, and then offered Kitty his arm. "May I escort you to the sitting room? It is just off the ballroom and has a lovely view of the gardens. The light should be perfect for sketching at this time of day."

Kitty giggled as she slipped her hand into the crook of the Captain's arm. "Thank you, sir. Do you draw?"

Allowing his smile to grow, he nodded as he led her away. "I have been known to carry a bit of charcoal and scraps of paper with me."

"I would love to see your work." Kitty fluttered her eyes and I groaned under my breath.

"Are you unwell, Miss Darcy?" Captain Jacobs called over his shoulder as he continued on his way toward the sitting room.

"I believe I would feel better if I were able to take a bit of fresh air." I said as sweetly as I was able to manage.

"I shall open a window for your comfort," the Captain replied without looking my way. "Ah, here we are." He opened a door and motioned us inside. Once we acquiesced, he crossed to the window and did indeed open it, even though the room was already chilled from want of a fire. "I shall send a maid in to start the fire and order a tray for you ladies." He glanced about. "The lighting should do very nicely; do you not agree Miss Catherine?"

Kitty giggled again as she glanced at the Captain. "Yes, it should."

After bowing without looking toward me, Captain Jacobs left the room. Feeling the growing chill from the air coming in through the window, I rubbed my arms as I crossed the room to close the offending aperture.

"Captain Jacobs is quite handsome. Lydia refused to speak to him because she said he was too high and mighty, but I think he is quite a gentleman. Do you not agree?" Kitty took up a chair and moved it closer to the window.

"You certainly made it obvious that you like him," I muttered.

"Whatever do you mean?" Kitty asked as she sat and began arranging the pencils.

"I would love to see your work." I said in a sugary, singsong voice as I batted my eyes.

Kitty laughed, drawing out a sheet of paper. "I believe you are jealous. Should I draw you in green?"

"I am not jealous!" I stomped my foot. "I am upset that we were not allowed to go where we wish. Captain Jacobs and my cousin always think they know what is best for me. I dislike not being able to decide where I shall go and when. It is not fair!"

"They are only thinking of your welfare." Kitty turned her attention to the page before her. "One would think I was talking to Lydia," she said under her breath.

I heard the comment, but refused to respond. The door opened and a footman entered with supplies to build the fire. A maid followed close behind with a tea tray.

"Oh, if I have one more cup of tea, I shall float away!" I cried. "Is this all we are allowed? To sit about, drink tea, and draw while the gentlemen ride out and have adventures? I wish I had been born a man." I dropped into the window seat and stared out the window, determined to be displeased with all I saw.

The maid glanced nervously toward Kitty who shrugged before motioning for the tray to be removed. The footman started the fire as quickly as possible and followed shortly behind the maid.

As the door closed behind him, Kitty rounded on me. "Why are you so irritable? Did you expect Captain Jacobs to invite us along with the men?"

"No," I replied tersely.

"Then what?" Kitty stared at me a moment before her eyes grew wide. "You like him."

"I do not," I snapped as I continued to survey the gardens.

Kitty giggled. "Yes, you do."

I watched my friend's reflection as Kitty stepped directly behind me.

"The Captain is handsome. Perhaps not as handsome as Mr. Wickham or Mr. Darcy, but I believe he is younger. When he frowns he appears to be closer to their age, but when he smiles, he seems closer to Mr. Bingley's. Of course he is much more worldly than that gentleman though that probably comes from his time at war. I believe I heard he is the younger son of an earl ..."

"Kitty! Will you desist if I admit that Captain Jacobs is handsome?" I asked in frustration.

Kitty shook her head. "Only if you admit you admire him."

"I barely know the man. I met him at the ball which, may I remind you, was only last evening." I frowned. It had been less than a day since I had met the Captain, yet it seemed as though it had been so much longer. Surely that was not long enough for me to have feelings for the man. Was it?

Taking a deep breath, I turned to face my friend. "I apologize, Kitty. I am frustrated that we must remain here, though I know there is nothing we could do there. I simply wish I knew what was happening."

Kitty sat down beside me and took my hand. She appeared about to speak, but the door flew open and Elizabeth rushed inside.

"Have the gentlemen left?" Her voice was raised and anxious.

"Yes," the girls replied in union.

"Blast!" Elizabeth muttered, shocking us both.

"Why? What has occurred?" we asked as we rushed to her side.

"Mrs. King has worked herself into an attack of some sort and the apothecary accompanied the men in order to see to Lydia or Miss King, should they be injured. Mrs. Annesley and Mrs. Nicholls are seeing to Mrs. King, but they are both highly concerned." She bit her lip, obviously weighing the options.

"Captain Jacobs said he was leaving officers here." Kitty offered.

"But will they know where the Schmitt house is?" Elizabeth asked worriedly.

I eyed her suspiciously. "You wish to ride out after them."

Frowning, Elizabeth nodded. "I know your brother would be displeased, but ..."

"I shall go with you," I said as I grabbed Elizabeth's hand and headed for the door.

Chapter Twenty-Four

I looked around the stable. The boys who normally worked there were running errands, but there were a few horses saddled and ready to ride. This must have been an order from my cousin so messages could be passed quickly to the men searching for the missing ladies. If Elizabeth and I were going to leave Netherfield, we had to go now, before the stable lads returned.

I walked over to a gentle grey and held out my hand for the mare to take my scent. Once the horse had tossed her head in a welcoming manner, I ran a hand down her side.

"Are you ready, Elizabeth?" I asked as I walked the horse toward the mounting block.

"Georgiana, that horse has a gentleman's saddle," my friend responded, not moving from her spot by the door.

Laughing I stepped onto the block. "And you have never ridden astride? I thought you more adventurous."

"I did not say I had not done so, but we should not." Elizabeth stepped forward reluctantly.

"Lizzy, if we are going to go after the men … to find the apothecary, we must leave now. If we wait for another horse to be saddled, one of the soldiers will be sent in our place." I threw one leg over the horse and pulled myself into position. "Come, we can ride together."

Elizabeth released her breath slowly, but followed me onto the mounting block and then onto the animal.

Once we were both settled, I kicked the mare into motion and we rode out over the fields. There may have been a few voices raised behind us, but we ignored the calls and continued on. Elizabeth pointed in the direction we were to go and I directed the mount.

Before long, we entered the woods separating Netherfield and Longbourn. Not knowing where the men may be, we decided to dismount and walk the remaining distance. I found an area with a patch of grass for the mare to graze while we went in search of the others.

We had not walked far when a rustling sound gave away the location of the men. As we approached, we heard whispering.

"I never did trust that Wickham. Though I'm not surprised to hear Miss Lydia went with him, tis a shame Miss King was brought into it," one faceless voice said.

I glanced in Elizabeth's direction and noted the reddish hue which covered her cheeks. I clasped Elizabeth's hand and squeezed it tightly.

"I hope they are well. Did ya see the look on the faces of Mr. Bennet and Miss King's uncle? They'll want blood if the ladies are injured in any way," the man's companion replied.

Not recognizing either voice, I motioned for Elizabeth to lead us away from there, hoping we would find the apothecary soon. I realized it would not be wise to stumble over my brother or Richard as they would be highly upset I was there.

"I doubt Mr. Jones would be with the military men," Elizabeth whispered.

Nodding, I glanced around. I could roughly see the outline of the house. Richard probably had the apothecary a short distance away so he could be brought in after they secured the area. Richard, Fitzwilliam, Mr. Bennet, and Mr. Singleton were most likely at the front of the home.

"Perhaps we should circle around to the front of the house, but a little distance away," I suggested.

Elizabeth nodded and pointed in the direction we should go. I followed behind her, trying desperately to be quiet while holding my skirts close to me so they would not be snagged on the passing branches. My companion seemed to move effortlessly through the woods, though her appearance was becoming a bit wild as twigs and leaves caught and held onto hair and clothing.

It became difficult for me to suppress my amusement when Elizabeth snatched her skirt back from a branch which had clung stubbornly to the material. The small tear was not given a moment's notice as we continued onward. My mind ran wild with what members of the *ton* would say if they saw the woman before me.

Elizabeth stopped abruptly, clearing my mind. Laying a finger to her lips, Elizabeth motioned for me to remain where I was. I did as I was told, and watched as Elizabeth moved soundlessly through a grove of trees and disappeared.

Standing motionless, I listened to the sounds of the woods about me, trying to determine what was occurring. Leaves rustled in the wind above my head and the soft chirping of birds could be heard. A very distant neigh caused me to hope it was not our grey giving away our presence. A rustling came from behind me, but I was suddenly too afraid to turn around and see what was there.

The snapping of a branch finally made me move. I began running in the direction Elizabeth had gone, but had only taken a few steps when I was drawn up short by a hand grasping my arm. I pulled, attempting to pry the fingers loose, but was unable to break the grip. In a moment of panic, I opened my mouth to scream, but a gloved hand clamped over it.

"Miss Darcy, please stop struggling!" a man's whisper in my ear caused me pause. I relaxed and the hand fell away from my mouth. "Thank you. Now what are you doing here? Did I not tell you to remain at Netherfield?" Anxiety could clearly be heard in Captain Jacob's voice.

I bit my lip as I turned to look at him. "Mrs. King has suffered an attack. Elizabeth and I rode out to find the apothecary."

"Knowing he was with us. How could you be so foolish?" His face reddened as he looked at me and then glanced around. "Where is Miss Elizabeth?"

"She told me to stay here and then she went that direction," I pointed toward the trees in front of us.

His head dropped forward as he released an exasperated breath. "She is heading straight toward the trap we have set for Wickham." Muttering an oath, he shook his head. He still had not released my arm, and now he pulled me with him as he moved toward the left.

"Where are we going?" I asked softly.

"I am attempting to think of a way to keep you safe and out of sight, without your brother or cousin knowing you were here."

"Oh." I followed him a few more feet before he suddenly stopped and turned on me. Unable to stop quickly enough, my hand came up to rest on his chest as I bumped into him. I am uncertain how long we stood in this manner, but I wondered if he could feel my heart pounding in my chest. Reluctantly, I stepped back.

"How did you get here?" he asked, appearing unaffected by our closeness.

"We took one of the horses that had been saddled." I pointed in the general direction where I believed the grey stood.

"You rode astride?"

I blushed as I lowered my gaze. "My brother believes ladies should know how to ride astride in case there is some emergency and it is the only option available."

"Mr. Darcy is a wise man." The Captain's voice held a hint of admiration and he tugged a little less forcefully on my arm as he turned and began walking again.

I drew a deep breath. "You will not tell him I was here?"

This time, the Captain slowed before stopping and we did not collide. He met my eye, his brow drawn down in a frown. "Miss Darcy, do you not understand? By separating from your companion, you have placed yourself in a compromising position … with me." He glanced about, then back to me. "If anyone were to see us together …"

"They would believe you were escorting me," I replied, my eyes wide with innocence.

"Possibly, but neither your brother nor your cousin would allow you to be escorted *alone* by an unrelated gentleman."

His eyes plumbed the depths of mine, seeming to search for my understanding. I knew I should be concerned by his words, but I was lost in the intensity of his gaze. The feelings from our earlier conversation in the garden resurfaced and I felt myself leaning toward him. His eyes grew darker as they dropped to my lips, but then he turned away and began moving once more. I stumbled after him, aware I was making too much noise, but unable to regain control of my traitorous limbs.

Suddenly, the trees gave way and we stepped into a clearing. Elizabeth was standing to one side, speaking to an older gentleman. Captain Jacobs released my arm and made his way toward the others.

As the warmth of his touch left my skin, I ran my hand over the spot where his had been. Uncertain what to do, I remained where I was and awaited instructions.

Mr. Jones gave Elizabeth a slip of paper and laid a reassuring hand upon her shoulder. "I shall return to Netherfield once we are finished here. This should help Mrs. King until that time."

Nodding, Elizabeth glanced up as Captain Jacobs approached. She quickly shifted her concerned gaze in my direction then back to the Captain before swallowing hard. "Mr. Jones has been able to give me some direction. I shall take Miss Darcy back to Netherfield."

"Do you know where your horse is tied?" the Captain asked.

Elizabeth nodded and moved toward me, but the Captain stopped her. "I believe it best if I escort you ladies back to the animal." He fought the urge to smile. "Had you considered how you would mount again?"

Eyes opened wide, Elizabeth and I exchanged a glance. Clearly neither of us had thought of such a mundane necessity.

Captain Jacobs chuckled softly as he asked us to lead the way. Elizabeth went first as she was more familiar with the area. I followed, with the Captain just behind me.

We had not gone far when we heard shouts and sounds of a skirmish. The Captain hesitated. All three of us turned toward the sound.

"I do not hear the ladies," I whispered.

"The plan was to lure Wickham out of the house and capture him." Captain Jacobs responded.

The sounds quieted and we began walking once more. After taking only a few steps, the shouts began anew along with the sounds of someone crashing through the trees, moving in our direction. The Captain drew his sword as he motioned for us to continue on ahead of him.

Before Elizabeth and I could take a step, Mr. Wickham burst through the trees and came face to face with us. The frantic look in his eyes became focused as he saw me and moved in my direction. I took a step back, but Mr. Wickham had suddenly stopped moving. Looking about, I realized the tip of Captain Jacob's sword was resting just under Mr. Wickham's chin. Wickham swallowed nervously, but the Captain did not move.

"On your knees," Captain Jacobs said slowly and clearly.

"He went this way!" Shouts came from behind Wickham and the trees separated again as more men entered the area.

Wickham looked about desperately. Clearly hoping the arrival of the others had distracted the Captain, he grabbed the tip of the sword and pushed it away from himself as he moved toward me with his left arm extended. Unfortunately for Wickham, the Captain's focus was strong and his mission clear: keep Wickham from me.

Reaching out with his left hand, the Captain grabbed Wickham's shoulder while he swung the sword down upon the arm that reached for me. Wickham screamed in pain as blood spurted from the wound. The other soldiers surrounded the man who had fallen to his knees cradling his injured arm.

I remained frozen in place, unable to look away from the scene. I had felt the warm spray of blood but thought nothing of the small droplets running down my face and covering my pelisse. Emotionless, I watched as the men half carried Wickham away in the direction they had come.

"Miss Darcy."

The voice reached me from what seemed a great distance so I was surprised when I turned to find Captain Jacobs standing directly beside me.

"Miss Darcy, are you unwell? Are you uninjured?"

The look of fear in his eyes brought me back to myself and I slowly nodded.

"Thank God!" he declared as he drew a handkerchief from his pocket and began wiping my face. "I was uncertain if he had reached you, and feared I had accidentally hit you."

I shook my head slightly from side to side as I swallowed.

The look of concern returned to his face as he slipped an arm about me. "Come, sit over here. There is a fallen log you might rest upon."

He led me to the log and I sat as he instructed. Slowly I became aware there were others around us. Fitzwilliam was holding Elizabeth where we had been standing, and she appeared to be weeping. I turned to my right and found Richard staring at me with fear in his eyes. I had never seen him afraid before. The reality of that brought me back to myself and I reached out to take his hand.

Clutching my hand, Richard dropped down to his knee before me. "Georgie, what the devil are you doing here?" he demanded as he drew me into an embrace.

"We came for Mr. Jones," I whispered against his chest as tears began to fill my eyes. "Mrs. King had an attack."

Richard pushed me away from him, a hand on each shoulder as his eyes met mine. It appeared as though he would scold me, but he must have seen the fright and shock in my eyes. Slowly he released his breath and drew me to him once more.

"Sir, I believe it best if the ladies be taken into the house to wash before they return to Netherfield." Captain Jacobs' voice was soft. "I fear their current appearance would only cause upset."

"Yes, you are correct Jacobs."

I felt Richard nod, but he did not release me. In the reassuring strength of his embrace, I allowed the tears to slide quietly down my cheeks. I had never seen a battle, nor seen anyone wounded before in such a manner. I knew I had no feelings for Mr. Wickham, but neither did I wish physical harm upon him.

The sound of footsteps caused me to draw back and I looked up to see my brother approach, his arm still about Elizabeth. I looked her over, seeing the same emotions warring in her. Standing, I fell into Elizabeth's arms and we cried.

"I shall fetch the ladies' horse, Colonel, and meet you at the house."

I saw Captain Jacobs bow in my direction before he turned and walked away. I buried my face in Elizabeth's shoulder and allowed my tears to continue.

Richard allowed us a few minutes in this stance, before he laid a hand on my arm and gently urged me away from Elizabeth. Placing an arm about my waist, he led me down the way the men had gone with Wickham. Fitzwilliam and Elizabeth followed closely behind us. The newly made path opened to a clearing a short distance from what I assumed was the Schmitt's home.

There were raised voices coming from inside, and I was able to make out Mr. Bennet and Lydia as well as Mr. Singleton. The only other female voice was wailing. This, I assumed, was Miss King.

Richard led me to the front of the house and inside. The scene before me seemed designed for the stage. Lydia Bennet stared toward a closed door, her fingers twisting a dry handkerchief as she demanded to know who had injured her George. Mr. Bennet stood in front of her, berating her foolishness. Mr.

Singleton stood with his back to them, arms crossed, as he admonished his niece. Mary King appeared little more than a heap upon a bench, her cries growing louder as though she were trying to drown out the sound of the others.

Placing fingers to his lips and taking a deep breath, Richard issued an ear-piercing whistle which drew silence from those assembled. "Now that I have your attention," he motioned for me to take a seat at the kitchen table before he turned his attention to the others. "Is anyone injured?"

"My George ..." Lydia began.

"Anyone other than Wickham?" Richard clarified forcefully.

The ladies silently shook their heads.

"Good. Now, we must learn what occurred here. I will hear your stories, but only one at a time." He met their gazes directly, making it clear he would brook no bickering. When he was certain they understood, he nodded once. "Miss King, why did you leave the Netherfield ball?"

While Richard spoke, Fitzwilliam and Elizabeth approached me. Elizabeth found a bucket of water and ladled some into a bowl, then opened cabinets until she found some cloths. Dipping one in the water, she began wiping the blood droplets from my face and neck. All of us watched and listened to the others, eager to hear what was said.

Miss King sniffled into her sodden handkerchief as she eyed Richard fearfully. "Mr. Wickham ... he ... he said it would be fun. Since we were already in our best clothing, we would elope and ... everyone would be so surprised."

"Foolish girl," Mr. Singleton growled.

"Sir! I will not allow any interruptions or we shall be here all night." Richard commanded.

Miss King's uncle looked as though he wanted to argue, but grudgingly nodded.

"Very well," Richard turned his attention back to the young girl. "And how did you and Wickham leave Netherfield? By coach?"

"Yes, the one in which we arrived." Miss King nodded.

"Where did you go from there?"

"George …" Mr. Singleton growled and Miss King swallowed hard before continuing. "Mr. Wickham said we had to make a stop. He said he was going to collect something he needed before we left."

"Do you know where he stopped?" Richard asked as he paced the length of the small room.

She shook her head and he motioned for her to continue. "He left the carriage and when he returned Lydia was with him." She glared at the young girl who returned the look with equal loathing.

Stepping between the ladies, Richard turned his back upon Miss King. "Miss Lydia, what have you to say?"

"*She* wasn't supposed to be there!"

"Allow me to clarify," Richard said loudly as he took a step closer to her until he towered over her. "How did you come to meet Mr. Wickham and enter the carriage with him and Miss King?"

"George and *I* were planning to elope. He asked me to bring twenty pounds with me when I came to the ball, as he was owed a debt of honour and the officer had not yet paid him." She met only Richard's gaze and would not be intimidated to speak properly. "When Papa would not allow me to attend the ball, I knew George would come for me. I slipped away from Hill and left a note for him at our secret spot. As I was returning home, I heard the carriage and hurried back. George asked me for the money, but I told him I would not give it to him until we were in the carriage."

Exchanging a weary glance with Fitzwilliam, Richard took a deep breath and turned back to Miss Lydia. "What happened when you entered the carriage?"

"When George opened the door, I saw *her* and I refused to enter. I demanded to know why she was there." She crossed her arms and glared at Miss King again. "He told me to get inside the carriage and he would explain everything, so I did. Once the carriage started moving, he asked for the money again. I told him I wouldn't give it to him until he put her out."

For a moment, I felt a hint of pity for Mr. Wickham. Clearly he had not realized how obstinate Miss Lydia could be. He had found himself in a carriage bound for Scotland with two brides. I shook my head.

Suddenly Miss King stood up. "Mr. Wickham would not put me out, as I was the one he planned to marry, not you!"

"Only because your grandfather left you money! Who could want a nasty little freckled thing like you?" Lydia shouted back.

"Ladies!" Richard's voice boomed in the small house shocking them both into silence. He turned to Miss Lydia once more. "Did you give Wickham the money?"

Her eyes fell to the floor and she twisted her lip into a sneer. "I did not have it with me."

"I beg your pardon?" Richard said, a smile tugging at his lips.

Miss Lydia looked at him directly. "I had left it at Longbourn thinking George would come for me there."

Raising a hand to his chin, Richard turned away from Miss Lydia and paced the room. I watched him, seeing the glee in his eyes. I looked at my brother who also appeared to be hiding his amusement.

"So," Richard finally said in a voice not quite as harsh. "When Wickham discovered you had no funds, what happened?"

A look of anger stole over Miss Lydia's countenance and she turned her glare on Richard. "He was upset and said we could not go to Gretna Green."

"How did you come to be here?"

"George said he needed to think. He was going to leave us in the carriage and take a walk, but I suggested we come here instead. I wasn't going to sit in a carriage with *her* while he went who knows where." Miss Lydia sniffed disdainfully.

Fitzwilliam leaned closer to Elizabeth. "Well at least your sister knew she could not *fully* trust him," he whispered.

Elizabeth nodded sadly as she finished bathing my face. "Take off your pelisse, Georgie. Let me see if I can get some of those spots out before we return to Netherfield. We must not cause the others any additional distress."

I did as she said, but continued watching the story unfolding before me. From what we had heard, it was clear Miss Lydia knew Mr. Wickham was not trustworthy, but she seemed determined to attach herself to him. I could not fathom this. I was certain Miss King at least believed herself in love. I could not say such of Miss Lydia.

Richard had begun to pace again, but he stopped near Mr. Singleton this time. "Miss King, would you please tell us what occurred when you arrived here?"

A faint blush covered her cheeks as she looked at Richard and then toward Miss Lydia. "Mr. Wickham and the coachman argued. Mr. Wickham came inside and then returned to the coach. The coachman finally departed, but he was using the most reprehensible language." The dismayed expression on the young girl's countenance would have drawn laughter in any other circumstance.

Elizabeth leaned toward Fitzwilliam. "I suppose Papa will have to ask the Schmitts to determine what is missing so we can replace it."

"Miss King," Richard said in a firm voice, clearly ready to be done with this tale. "You and Miss Lydia were alone with Mr. Wickham for several hours." He paused and allowed his words to have an effect upon her. "What happened during that time?"

Miss King's eyes grew large as saucers as she finally took in the Colonel's meaning. Her mouth fell open and her cheeks took on a blotchy red appearance. "Nothing."

"Are you trying to tell me that rake brought two silly girls to this deserted home and nothing inauspicious occurred?" Mr. Singleton leaned toward her, disbelief written upon his expression.

"Truly, Uncle. Lydia and Mr. Wickham fought the entire time. I was not even able to sleep; they were so loud." As if to prove her weariness, Miss King yawned.

"But she would take the bedroom so George and I could not," Lydia muttered.

"That is enough!" Mr. Bennet erupted. He had waited quietly while the story unfolded, but by this time he knew what was required. "Colonel, am I to understand Mr. Wickham will be facing charges?"

Richard glanced about, but returned his gaze to the man before him. "Yes sir. He has been involved in activities unbecoming an officer. In addition, he has debts which he cannot pay."

"If that officer who owes him money …" Lydia began, but Richard interrupted her.

"There is no such officer. The one who owes the debts of honour is your precious Mr. Wickham."

Mr. Bennet turned toward Mr. Singleton. "You have said you will be taking the Kings from Hertfordshire, am I correct sir?"

"Absolutely!" Mr. Singleton replied as Miss King began to weep again. "Unfortunately it is too late to leave today."

"Then all that remains," Mr. Bennet said as he turned toward his youngest daughter, "is the disposal of Lydia."

"Disposal?" she asked, fear creeping into her voice.

"Mr. Darcy," Mr. Bennet called without turning his gaze. "Where precisely is the school you mentioned?"

"Edinburgh, sir." Fitzwilliam's voice was cool, but his expression held a hint of sympathy for Miss Lydia.

"School?" she cried. "I don't want to go to school!"

"I no longer care what you want." Mr. Bennet stepped closer to her. Though he was not near the height of Richard, he was able to maintain an intimidating stance. "You shall be enrolled immediately and will have contact with no one before you leave. You will remain at the school until you have proven you can behave as a gentleman's daughter. If that does not occur, then when you graduate a position will be found for you. You will *not* return to my house until you have learned your lesson."

For the first time, I saw Miss Lydia cower. Any sign of defiance was gone and for a brief moment, she understood she had pushed her father too far. Unfortunately, it lasted but a minute.

"Mama will never allow it." She began softly, but slowly her confidence began to grow. "I shall run away!"

Mr. Bennet's countenance grew so red as to worry me. He reached out and took hold of Miss Lydia's arm and marched her out the door.

Everyone stood still, uncertain what to do or how to react. A scream broke our trance-like state and we all rushed to the doorway. Outside, near the woodpile, Miss Lydia was bent over Mr. Bennet's knee. Her skirts were laid over her back and he was applying a switch forcefully to her backside.

"Ahem," a voice came from behind and we turned as a group to see what strange revelation would occur next.

Mr. Jones stood wiping his hands. "Mr.

Wickham is ready for transport. His arm has been stitched and I doubt there will be any infection unless it is not looked after. The cut was deeper than I originally thought. It appears, given little effort, the Captain could have removed the hand altogether. It must have taken great restraint to only wound the man."

Richard nodded and turned toward the bedroom where Mr. Wickham remained with a few other officers guarding him. As the door closed behind him, Mr. Jones turned toward Elizabeth.

"Were you able to see to Mrs. King?"

Elizabeth and I turned toward each other. I was certain her look of horror matched my own. "Mrs. King!"

Chapter Twenty-Five

The Darcy carriage rolled toward Netherfield Park with we four ladies inside. Miss Lydia and Miss King sat in opposite corners so there could be no contact between them. The trip had begun with Miss King sniffling and Miss Lydia making snide comments under her breath. We had not gone far before Elizabeth ordered them both to cease. Since that time, a deafening silence had filled the coach.

When we stopped at last in front of the manor home, the door opened to reveal Mr. Bennet and Mr. Singleton.

"Elizabeth," Mr. Bennet said in a firm voice. "I have asked our carriage to be readied. Go inside and collect your mother. We shall return directly to Longbourn."

With wide eyes, Elizabeth nodded and left the carriage. She glanced back once toward me and shrugged her shoulders in answer to my questioning look.

Mr. Singleton reached into the carriage and took Miss King's hand to assist her. Once outside, they turned and walked up the stairs to the front door.

Uncertain what was expected, I sat and waited to see what Mr. Bennet would do next. Lydia began to move forward, but he motioned her to remain in place. Instead, he held out his hand for me.

"Miss Darcy," he said softly as he assisted me from the coach. "I believe your brother and cousin are anxious to speak with you." He nodded toward the gentlemen standing a few feet away wearing matching frowns.

I bit down upon the inside of my cheek as I slowly approached them, unable to meet their eyes. I realized I had been wrong to leave Netherfield, and there was no justification for my actions. As I took the last step before stopping in front of them, I straightened my back and raised my head.

"Fitzwilliam," I met his eye before turning to look at my cousin. "Richard, I owe you both a most sincere apology. I disobeyed your orders and for no better reason than it was what I wanted at the time. You are justified in your disapprobation, and I accept whatever punishment you believe is appropriate."

My gaze fell back to my hands as I finished, being unable to observe the displeasure I saw in their countenances any longer. The silence stretched out between us until I feared it was part of my penance. Finally, I heard my brother sigh.

"Let us go inside to discuss this further," Fitzwilliam said as he took my hand and laid it upon his arm.

I looked up into his eyes, pleased to see his love for me had not diminished. I glanced to Richard who shook his head, but his stern expression appeared to have softened. Before anything could be said, he turned and walked up the stairs with my brother and me just behind him.

Inside, we could hear women's voices coming from the drawing room, but we turned in the opposite direction and entered the study a minute later. The fire was burning brightly and Fitzwilliam led me to the couch nearest the hearth. I took my seat, but he began to pace the room.

Richard dropped wearily into the chair across from me and rubbed his hands over his face. "What were you thinking, Poppet?" he asked in a shaky voice. He let his hands fall to the arms of the chair. "I do not think I have ever been so frightened as I was when I saw you with blood splattered across you. If Jacobs had not reassured me you were uninjured, Wickham would be dead right now and I would be the one on my way to gaol."

"I never meant to upset you. I was not thinking, I simply wished to know what was happening. I felt … I know I was foolish for allowing Mrs. Younge and Mr. Wickham to lead me astray last summer, but I thought it was colouring your decisions regarding me. I felt as though you were treating me like a child." My voice died away, realizing I had only given them more reason to consider me as such.

Fitzwilliam spoke, his voice soft and sorrowful, "Did we treat any of the other ladies in a different manner? Were you singled out in our actions?"

Unable to meet his gaze, I stared at a leaf pattern in the rug at my feet. "No. I felt the censure, but there was no evidence of it."

Silence filled the room once more, broken only by my brother's muffled footsteps. I allowed my eyes to trace the lines of the intricate design all the while wondering what my punishment would be. Unexpectedly, the first real sound I heard was the heavy breathing of my cousin. I raised my eyes to find him sleeping soundly, his hands still covering his face.

Fitzwilliam walked forward and took the seat beside me. Reaching out, he took my hand in his and raised it to his lips. After kissing it, he held it there a moment longer before lowering it to his leg and laying his other hand on top of it. He stared at our joined hands as he spoke in barely a whisper.

"Seeing you, in that woods and in that manner, nearly ended us today, Georgie. Richard and I would give our lives for you. The thought of you injured in any manner is devastating to us."

A tear slipped from the corner of my eye and made a slow trek down my cheek, but I would not move and disturb my brother further. "Can you ever forgive me?" I asked in a raspy voice.

"You were forgiven immediately, Georgie. What you should ask is whether we will have faith in you to make the right decision in the future?"

He fell back against the cushions, leaning his head back as far as it would go. One hand slipped away, but the other still held mine tightly. We sat in this manner for some time before his grip loosened and I realized he too had fallen into an exhausted sleep.

Uncertain what to do, I continued to sit there watching over them; afraid to leave in the event they awoke and feared for me again. A soft rap on the door drew my attention, but I did not want to call out for fear of disturbing my guardians. Thankfully, the door opened slowly a moment later and Captain Jacobs poked his head into the room.

A wave of relief washed over me and I smiled before placing a finger upon my lips and pointing to the sleeping gentlemen. Soundlessly, the Captain entered the room and crossed to my side before kneeling in front of me.

"Are you well?" he whispered.

I nodded, my eyes returning to the leaves at my feet. "Can you forgive me?"

Captain Jacobs sat back on his heels, as though contemplating my question. "I can imagine, with your curiosity, the waiting was a form of torture."

Glancing up, I saw the light of amusement dancing in his eyes as he fought the urge to smile. I attempted a glare, but failed miserably. "Am I nothing more than an amusing child to you?"

The humour left his countenance and he appeared about to reach out to me, but allowed his hand to fall to his side. "You are a blossoming young woman who will become a grand lady one day. I look forward to knowing her."

"But now?"

He glanced toward Richard and frowned. "It is best if I continue on the path before me."

I followed his gaze and then turned to look at my brother. Both appeared to be sleeping deeply so I leaned closer to the Captain. "But you compromised me, sir." I allowed my smile to slowly creep across my lips.

"So I did," he replied as he met my gaze with a matching smile. "Should any ever learn of it; I will perform my duty to you." He took my free hand, kissed it lightly, and released it as he quickly stood. With a bow, he turned to leave the room.

"One moment, Jacobs." Fitzwilliam's voice caused both of us to jump.

"Yes, Mr. Darcy?" The Captain stood still before him.

"I wish to thank and commend you for your quick thinking today. You kept my sister safe." He fully opened his eyes and levelled a stern gaze upon the young soldier. "Now what is this I hear of a compromise?"

Captain Jacobs swallowed hard, but held his stiff stance. "I came upon your sister alone in the woods, sir. I escorted her in the direction she indicated Miss Elizabeth had taken to find the apothecary. We were alone until we found them."

"And did anything untoward occur?"

I stared at the Captain, thinking of the moment when we had been so close and how I had wished he would take me in his arms. His eyes met mine and for a moment, I thought he might have shared my thoughts; but as quickly as it happened, the moment passed.

"No, sir."

"Richard, do you believe him?"

I turned toward my cousin, but everything about his posture showed he remained asleep, until he took a deep breath. Slowly he opened his eyes, looked first at me, and then turned toward his adjunct. "I have never had reason to doubt him … before now."

"Nothing happened!" I cried out.

Richard and Fitzwilliam both turned toward me suspiciously. Richard's brow rose. "The lady doth protest too much, methinks."

"It would appear to be true." My brother nodded as he studied us closely.

I was about to speak again when Captain Jacobs cleared his throat, drawing everyone's attention.

"I am certain it is no secret from either of you that I have certain feelings for Miss Darcy. Until this time, they have been quite innocent as I saw her through Colonel Fitzwilliam's eyes, as a younger cousin." He swallowed before continuing. "Upon meeting her, I realized she is not the child of which he speaks, but a young lady. It has been my pleasure coming to know her during this time, and I would be pleased to be often in her presence." As he finished, he met my gaze and gave me a shy smile.

The heat which rushed through me, surprised me and I lowered my head to hide my flushed countenance.

"Georgiana?" My brother's voice was soft and reassuring. "Have you anything to say regarding the Captain?"

I raised my head and turned toward my brother. Was he truly asking my opinion? Had I not completely lost his respect by leaving Netherfield against his wishes? Did he really want to know my feelings? I paused, and glanced toward the Captain. He suddenly appeared so young and vulnerable, and I realized he must be younger even than Mr. Bingley as I had once supposed.

I took a deep breath and spoke, never looking away from him. "Captain Jacobs has been nothing but a gentleman in all our encounters. I believe he is a good man and I would want to know more of him."

The party lapsed into silence once more; the Captain and I continued to gaze upon each other, while Richard and Fitzwilliam glanced about at all within the room. Finally, Richard broke the trance which had fallen upon us when he stood and crossed to the officer.

"Georgiana is not yet out." He turned and looked at Fitzwilliam who nodded. "But her brother and I would be pleased if you were amongst her suitors when that day came."

Captain Jacobs smiled and grasped the hand Richard held out to him. Fitzwilliam stood, pulling me with him and also shook the Captain's hand.

"Well, Richard, it appears all has been righted and we have earned our rest." Fitzwilliam motioned toward the door. "Shall we retire for the night?"

"I am practically asleep where I stand, Darcy, but my stomach demands sustenance before I can sleep through the night." Richard ran his hand over his midsection and gave his cousin a lopsided grin.

I was about to ring the bell and request food be served to the gentlemen in their rooms, when a knock sounded at the door. Richard, Fitzwilliam and I all called enter at once before laughing.

Jane opened the door and stepped into the room, a look of concern gracing her features. "I beg your pardon; I was unaware you were here until I heard voices just now. Dinner has been announced, will you be joining us?"

As if in response, Richard's stomach growled loudly and he took Jane's arm to escort her from the room. Fitzwilliam and the Captain exchanged a brief glance before the latter bowed and motioned for the prior to follow. Fitzwilliam placed my hand upon his arm and led me from the room with the Captain close behind. When we entered the dining room, we found the Bennets in attendance, including Miss Lydia.

"It simply does not make sense for us to return to Longbourne at this time," Mrs. Bennet declared. "Hill will not be expecting us and dinner will not be prepared. It is better that we remain here until after we have eaten."

"Madam!" Mr. Bennet's voice was harsh and his displeasure clearly written on his countenance. "You have carried your point, please desist."

I glanced at my brother than back at the table. Servants were quickly adding place settings to accommodate the additional guests. Jane stood at the head of the table, the place normally held by the mistress of the home. Elizabeth sat to her left and Mrs. Bennet to her right. Beside her was Mr. Bennet with Lydia to his right and Kitty across from him. Seeing the empty place beside Kitty, I pulled Fitzwilliam forward to that side of the table.

As we all took our seats, Fitzwilliam nodded toward Jane and smiled. "You look well this evening Miss Bennet."

Jane blushed prettily. "Thank you, Mr. Darcy."

I looked between the two, realizing there was some secret communication, but not understanding what it was. I glanced toward Kitty, but she appeared not to have seen the interaction.

Richard took the seat beside Miss Lydia with the Captain on his other side. Miss Lydia smiled flirtatiously at the Colonel until his frown sufficiently discouraged her. For the most part, the table was quiet, but for Mrs. Bennet's effusions over the soup.

Finally, Richard interrupted her silliness. "Have you received a report regarding Mrs. King?" he asked Jane.

Laying her spoon aside, Jane blotted her lips with her serviette as she nodded. "Just before he left, Mr. Jones said Mrs. King was resting peacefully and should be able to travel tomorrow. Mr. Singleton indicated he would join us, but asked us not to wait for him. He is seeing to Miss King who will take a tray in her room." She glanced in my direction. "Mrs. Annesley indicated she was fatigued after caring for Mrs. King, and also asked for a tray to be delivered."

Feeling suddenly guilty for not realizing my companion was missing, I blushed. "Thank you for seeing to her needs, Jane. You are a wonderful hostess."

Jane blushed, allowing the momentary displeasure she had felt fall away. "Thank you, Georgiana. Mrs. Annesley asked that you not worry for her this evening. She will break her fast with you in the morning, just before your lessons."

Jane's brow raised in a manner similar to Elizabeth's and I stifled a giggle as I nodded my understanding. Tomorrow my life would return to the normal routine. I doubted I would ever grumble over my lessons again after experiencing a full day of unease and excitement.

"My Jane shall make a fine hostess once she is wed," Mrs. Bennet gushed. "Oh, if only Mr. Bingley had not been called away, he could have seen how well you have done."

"Mrs. Bennet." Mr. Bennet's low growl was barely audible.

"I am simply speaking the truth. How shall he know how well she has cared for his home while he was gone?" A sob escaped her as her handkerchief magically appeared and began its normal fluttering. "Oh, what if he does not return?"

"I believe I can assure you, Madam," Fitzwilliam said succinctly, "that my friend has no intention of remaining long in London."

Mrs. Bennet glanced his direction, but continued her mutterings as her distress grew. A glance passed rapidly between Fitzwilliam, Jane, and Mr. Bennet until finally the last gentleman sighed and took up his serviette, waving it much like a white flag.

"Be still, woman!" Mr. Bennet looked about the table once more before taking a deep breath. "I had not planned upon announcing this until the man's return, but if we are to enjoy a somewhat peaceful dinner, I fear I must. Mr. Bingley requested Jane's hand before his departure."

Looks of surprise flew between the parties, though Fitzwilliam and Richard continued calmly eating their soup. Mrs. Bennet's exclamations of joy far exceeded her misery, but quieted into an inane rambling which was easily ignored. Declarations of "I knew how it would be" and "you could not be so beautiful for nothing" flowed amongst the list of items which must be purchased and her one-person discussion of the menu for the wedding breakfast. The others said little until Miss Lydia found it necessary to take part in the discussion.

"Shall I stand up with you, Jane? I shall need a new dress."

"Oh, yes, yes," Mrs. Bennet gushed. "You must have a new dress indeed."

"Mrs. Bennet!" Mr. Bennet's exclamation finally silenced the lady. He turned toward his youngest daughter. "Have you heard nothing I have said? You shall not be present at your sister's wedding. You shall not have a new dress. You are going away to school."

"Oh," Mrs. Bennet sniffled. "Can she not stay until Jane's wedding?"

"No. I have been lenient far too long. My mind is decided, an express has been sent, and the school is expecting Lydia's arrival one week from now."

"So soon?" Mrs. Bennet whined.

"Not soon enough," Mr. Bennet replied.

Before anything else could be said, the door opened and Mr. Singleton entered looking as weary as the others. He took the vacant seat by Fitzwilliam and motioned the servant to fill his bowl. Once all was settled, he looked about, suddenly realizing the room had fallen silent upon his entrance.

"Forgive me, have I interrupted?"

"No," Fitzwilliam glanced toward Mr. Bennet. "I believe all had been said."

The table fell silent once more as everyone finished their soup and the dishes were cleared away. The second course was set before us and the normal dinner chatter began as the servants moved away.

When we were nearly finished, Mr. Singleton glanced across the table and spoke quietly. "I say, Captain, I understand you were the man who brought the blackguard down. I must say I envy you the opportunity, but am grateful to you."

The Captain looked toward me before meeting Mr. Singleton's gaze. "You can be assured, sir, Mr. Wickham would not have escaped, but I am pleased I was able to be of service."

A sudden lament from the far end of the table reached them. "Oh, Mr. Wickham! Such a waste. I still do not understand why he is unable to marry my Lydia."

"Enough!" Mr. Bennet tossed his serviette upon the table and stood. "I have finished my meal,

Madam, and we are now leaving." He glanced at his daughters. "Lizzy, Kitty, order our outerwear. Jane, I fear your time as hostess has come to an end for now." He bowed toward the far end of the table. "I beg your pardon if my wife's absurdity has ruined your meal. We shall remove to Longbourn so you may finish in peace."

"But we are not finished," Mrs. Bennet carped, her eyes wide in surprise. "We cannot pull Jane from the duties Mr. Bingley entrusted to her. What will his friends tell him? He may desert her."

"His friends will advise him to marry his bride and take her far away so as not to be subjected to her mother." Mr. Bennet glared at the woman by his side. "For years I have heard you speak of your fear of being tossed into the hedgerows at the time of my demise, but you are unable to see that your actions have nearly fulfilled your prophesy. The choices you have made for your daughters based on your own need for preservation have led to this," he waved his hand toward their youngest child. "We still teeter on the edge of destruction, should any of the individuals involved in the search speak of what they heard or saw."

"More the reason she should marry Mr. Wickham!" Mrs. Bennet exclaimed as she jumped from her seat and stood toe to toe with her husband.

The look of dismay which suffused Mr. Bennet's countenance would have been comical in any other situation. As it was, the older Bennet sisters collectively sighed as their eyes fell to their half-eaten dinners. Kitty was the first to turn away, clearly losing her appetite.

Slowly, Mr. Bennet turned and surveyed the assembled individuals. "I must beg your forgiveness once again," he said with a defeated tone. "It is clear I have allowed silliness to reign in my home far too long. I am pleased that at least two of my daughters," his gaze fell on Kitty and a faint smile tugged at his lips, "perhaps three, were able to escape its grip."

His gaze returned to the woman before him. "Madam, I believe this discussion will be finished in the morning in my study. Lydia and I shall be leaving at dawn. You and I shall speak before then. If you do not appear on your own, I shall drag you from your bed." Taking her arm, he bowed to the others and escorted her from the room ignoring her protests.

The remaining sisters glanced amongst themselves before rising, saying their farewells, and quickly following their parents from the room. Fitzwilliam followed them into the hallway while I remained, uncertain what was expected of me.

"Well, Poppet," Richard drawled as he rose his glass in my direction. "It appears you are now our hostess."

"Seems the man was a bit late in taking charge of his clan," Mr. Singleton muttered as he cut into the slice of roast before him.

My eyes fell upon the door, desperately wishing to know what was occurring in the hall. I felt a warmth upon my cheeks and turned to find Captain Jacobs watching me closely. The look in his eyes held hope, a belief that I was the ideal lady he knew I could be. I found myself unable to disappoint him, and instead motioned for the servants to refill our glasses as I put thoughts of my brother and Elizabeth from my mind. The Captain's approving smile filled me with an unexpected calm.

Epilogue

I stood before my vanity holding my hand mirror at an angle above me as I turned my head slowly from side to side. Hannah had truly outdone herself on the extravagant coiffure. *If I appear as royalty for my bridal ball, must I be done up as an empress for my wedding?*

A soft knock broke through my thoughts and I called "Enter," knowing it would be my brother.

The door opened, revealing Fitzwilliam with his eyes downcast and his appearance grave. He had been this way for several days, placing an unwelcome impediment upon my final week as a Darcy in my family home.

Taking a deep breath, I stood and held my arms out to each side as I turned slowly in a circle. "Will he be pleased; do you think?"

I stopped in time to see the tears glisten in his eyes. "How could he be anything but? If he fails to recognize the treasure before him, I shall rescind my blessing."

Laughing, I moved to stand directly before him. "I hate to see you in this manner. I demand you be cheerful tonight." I laid a hand upon his arm. "Be happy for me. It is not as though we shall not see each other. I shall be living at Darcy House upon my return from our wedding trip, at least until we settle on the property in Derbyshire. Even then, I will be but a few hours away."

"But you will no longer be under my care," he whispered as he took my hand in his and stroked his fingers over the back of it.

I chewed lightly on the inside of my cheek as I glanced toward the doorway. "Where is Elizabeth?" I asked softly.

"She is in the nursery. Bennet refused to eat his vegetables again." A grin tugged at the corner of his lips.

Laughing, I linked my arm with his and turned toward the doorway. "It is good you have had only sons, if you are this unsettled on the eve of *my* wedding, you shall be inconsolable when you have to give away a daughter."

Fitzwilliam laid his hand upon mine as we walked the short distance to the nursery. Standing in the doorway, we watched as Elizabeth rocked an infant in one arm while hopping a spoonful of squash toward her eldest son's open mouth. The toddler ate happily, pleased to have his mother's attention.

The contentment of the moment stole over me and I remembered my time at Netherfield Park nearly four years prior. Once Mr. Bennet had left the area to deliver Lydia to Edinburgh, Fitzwilliam had insisted we visit Longbourn daily. As it turned out, he had promised Mr. Bennet he would assure order would rule in his absence. Unfortunately for my brother, it was not as easy as he anticipated.

Upon the first day, we arrived to find Mrs. Bennet bemoaning the restrictions her husband had placed upon her before he left. Apparently, Mrs. Hill had been ordered to admit only visitors on his approved list. She finally had wonderful news to share, and she was not allowed to do so.

Mrs. Annesley had taken the seat beside the mistress of the house and seemed to bring her a much needed calm. I later learned my companion was following Mr. Bennet's request to "educate his silly wife". That gentleman was pleased to return home to a wife with a clearer understanding of what would be expected of her in the future. Gossip was to come to an end, replaced by tenant visits and productive activities.

During the visits, I spent most of my time with Kitty, but witnessed my brother and Elizabeth steal glances or brush hands whenever they thought no one was watching. I hoped they would become engaged once Mr. Bennet returned.

To everyone's great surprise, when that man did return, it was announced that Fitzwilliam and Elizabeth had been engaged since the day of Mr. Wickham's arrest. Apparently my brother had seized the time alone with Elizabeth's father while they waited for the scoundrel to reveal himself. When he comforted Elizabeth after the attempted escape, they had already received her father's blessing.

Fitzwilliam stepped into the nursery, breaking through my memories. "Be careful, Ben." He wiped a bit of the brightly coloured mush from his son's chin. "We must not get Mama dirty. Does she not look lovely?" He turned a longing gaze upon his wife.

"Mama pretty!" Ben clapped his hands and laughed.

"Thank you, Ben." Elizabeth smiled as she filled another spoon and began the journey toward the happy toddler once again, but the boy turned his head to the side and pinched his lips together. "Are we finished?"

He turned forward and nodded his head emphatically before holding his arms toward his father. "Up!"

I covered my mouth as my brother carefully inspected his son before lifting him into an embrace. It would not do for the brother of the bride to be covered in squash this evening. My eye met Elizabeth's and we both lost our battle to hide our mirth.

"I am pleased we are able to amuse you," Fitzwilliam said in a cool tone as he turned toward Ben. "Mama and Aunt Georgie think us comedic."

The boy paid little attention to his father's words as he had discovered the pin upon Fitzwilliam's cravat. With a speed that still amazed his father, Ben was tugging upon the sapphire, completely eschewing the once pristine knot.

"Oh Ben," Elizabeth cried. "Look what you have done." She tsked the lad while attempting to smooth her husband's neck cloth with one hand.

Fitzwilliam laughed as he placed a kiss first on Ben's forehead and then on Elizabeth's. He turned to see the nursery maid standing to the side and motioned her forward. "Sophia, if you would take Masters Bennet and Edward. I believe I shall return to my rooms before we go below."

He handed the toddler to his nurse before slipping from the room, but Elizabeth waved the young girl away as she carried her sleeping son to his cradle and laid him down. Placing a kiss upon his spattering of curls, she straightened and smiled.

"Mama, mama!" Ben called from his bed.

She gently shushed him before leaning over and kissing him also. "Now listen to Sophia, Ben, and go

to sleep when she says. Be a good boy for Mama."
She tipped her head to one side and gave him a
serious look.

Reluctantly he nodded his head as he turned
toward his nurse. "Story?" Sophia held up a book in
response and Ben clapped excitedly.

Elizabeth joined me in the doorway and looked
back over the scene, a contented smile gracing her
countenance. I slipped an arm about my sister's waist
and we turned to leave the room.

Once in the hall, Elizabeth handed me a
handkerchief and I looked at it questioningly. Before
I could ask, I became aware of the tear making slow
progress down my cheek.

"How silly of me," I said as I applied the
handkerchief. "I cannot understand why I am so
emotional. I told Fitzwilliam not thirty minutes ago
that I am not going far."

"Ah, but when you return to this house, you will
no longer be Miss Darcy. Instead, you will be Mrs.
Jacobs and a very handsome, accomplished officer
will be escorting you." She slipped an arm through
mine and began walking toward the stairs. "It has
been difficult for your brother to watch you mature
and ready yourself to become a wife. He is
exceedingly proud of you; we both are."

We had just reached the top step when Richard
bounded up before us. "Ah, I am not too late." He
stepped forward and offered me his arm. "May I
have the honour of escorting you to your ball,
Poppet?"

A displeased voice sounded from behind us.
"Richard, how the devil did you get here so quickly?

I thought you would not arrive until later this evening."

"And allow you to escort our darling girl to her ball *and* down the aisle? I think not. I am *also* her guardian, Darcy." Richard stood to his full height, knowing he was still a few inches shorter than my brother, and laid his hand upon the sword at his side.

I laughed as I took my cousin's arm. "You would wound my brother for the honour of escorting me, Richard? And on the evening before my wedding?"

Richard shrugged good-naturedly. "I could then escort you to both." He turned toward Elizabeth and smiled. "It is not as though he will be lonely. He must escort his beautiful wife." He leaned forward and placed a kiss upon her cheek. "You look lovelier each time I see you, Elizabeth."

A feminine voice called from below. "Will you not come down? I see carriages approaching!"

We turned to see Kitty, or Catherine as she was now called, standing in the foyer below. I had been so pleased when Fitzwilliam invited Elizabeth's sister to live with us most of the year. We had taken lessons together, including time with an art master. Catherine's talent with sketching had far exceeded my own, so I quickly returned to my pianoforte and left the drawing to my friend.

We had shared our coming out and so many other experiences through the years, but tomorrow I would marry and Catherine would take up residence with the Bingley's. Tears filled my eyes once more as Richard led me down the stairs. I silently scolded myself for behaving so foolishly.

As we reached the bottom, a mischievous spark entered Catherine's eye and she glanced over her shoulder. There, out of sight from the steps, stood my fiancé. Colonel John Jacobs stepped forward, his gaze never leaving mine, until he stood before me. The warmth I had felt so often when he looked at me was intensified. *Tomorrow I will be his wife.*

He took my hand in his and reverently raised it to his lips. "How have I been so blessed?"

Arching my brow, I smiled. "As you compromised me nearly four years ago, I am pleased you finally saw fit to do the gentlemanly thing."

John threw his head back and laughed heartily. "You are correct, of course, my love."

"What is the raucous? Have the guests begun to arrive?"" Lydia Bennet stepped from the ballroom and looked about. "Oh, it is just Captain Jacobs." She sniffed and returned from whence she had come.

Lydia's time in Edinburgh may not have completely dampened her enthusiasm, but it had given her clearer expectations of her behaviour when out in society. She had improved to the extent Fitzwilliam was willing to include her in some social events. With Mrs. Annesley at her side, her behaviour tonight would decide if the Darcys would host her during the next season.

My thoughts were drawn once more to that November in Hertfordshire. I had become friends with all the Bennet sisters, other than Lydia. The only one who would be missing this evening was Mary.

True to her word, she had secured Mr. Collins, though not in the manner she would have preferred. Indeed, it had been one of Fitzwilliam's trials during the time Mr. Bennet was away.

Upon returning to Longbourn, Mr. and Mrs. Bennet had found the couple alone in the drawing room. This was no scandal as they were cousins; however, when her parents entered the room, they found the couple in what appeared to be a passionate embrace. Mrs. Bennet immediately demanded they marry, while Mr. Collins sputtered "It is not as it appears" repeatedly and Mary stood silently beside him, her countenance redder than any had ever seen.

Following their wedding breakfast, just before the couple left for Kent, Mary admitted to me that she had, in fact, been trying to stop Mr. Collins from leaving the room and he was attempting to move her from his path when her parents came upon them. Though she was not pleased to be married under a scandal, Mary had succeeded in securing her future. As she left Longbourn, I saw her look over her childhood home in a covetous manner. It was clear in my mind Mrs. Bennet would not be pleased should her middle daughter gain possession of their home during her lifetime.

A warm hand upon my back drew me once more from my memories. I turned and gave John a loving smile as he led me to the receiving line. Though we enjoyed dancing, both of us would rather sit quietly in a drawing room or parlour with close friends and family than being the toast of the *ton*. However, John's eldest brother had been experiencing health issues, and the possibility that my soon to be husband might one day be earl loomed before us. With this in mind, John had treated society as the enemy he must conquer; with a single minded determination to gain favour with those who would be beneficial to any platforms he might decide to support.

Elizabeth and Fitzwilliam took their places at the head of the receiving line, followed by John and I, and Richard stepped up behind me. I turned to smile at him, and noticed there was more gray scattered in his dusty blonde hair and the creases about his eyes and mouth were deeper than they had once been. A thought occurred to me as the door opened to reveal our first guests.

Society poured through the doors of Darcy House and I watched each member closely; focusing mainly upon the eligible ladies and my cousin's reaction to each. When I noticed a sudden unusual awkwardness about him, as though he were a young lad thrust into his first social gathering, I turned to see who may have inspired it.

Fitzwilliam had just finished bowing to Elizabeth's best friend, Charlotte Lucas, who was in London with her father. Charlotte had been invited to Darcy House and Pemberley on several occasions and I now called her friend as well. I greeted the lady from Hertfordshire with enthusiasm before turning to see my cousin bow.

"Miss Lucas, it is good to see you again." Richard said softly. "I hope you have an opening for me on your dance card. I would be pleased if you would accept my hand for the dinner set so I might share your company during the meal."

"Of course, General." Charlotte blushed as she curtseyed then moved away and into the growing crowd.

A nudge at my side reminded me there were other guests. I continued to smile and curtsey as expected, while my mind ran over what was needed to bring my reluctant-to-wed cousin and my spinster-friend together. When I heard my fiancé's exasperated sigh, I turned to see what caused him distress. I found his gaze upon me.

"Will it be listening at doors or strong-headed thoughtless actions?"

I sniffed as I smoothed my skirt. "I know not of what you speak, sir."

John leaned closer until his breath caused the loose curls to dance about my neck and a shiver ran through me. "I had thought you relinquished your matchmaking ways after that farce with Miss Catherine during the winter."

A blush passed over my countenance as I straightened my glove. "We agreed not to mention that again."

In November, Fitzwilliam had hosted a gentleman who graduated a year after him from Cambridge. The gentleman was passing through Derbyshire on his way to the lakes and had an eye for art. He was very encouraging toward Catherine, and I had determined they would do well together. I was certain Kitty's extreme dislike of the man must be due to some misunderstanding, as with Fitzwilliam and Elizabeth. I was the only one who held the belief, and the gentleman continued on his way as planned without any hint that he would miss the occupants of Pemberley or my matchmaking schemes.

A few more guests stopped before us to offer their well-wishes, but there was a slight lull a moment later when one of the society matrons took the time to entreat Elizabeth and Fitzwilliam to participate in an upcoming event. As guests backed up behind her, John turned fully toward me.

"I implore you, my darling, to allow love to grow where it may and not put your hand in it." His gaze fell upon Richard who was paying us no mind. "Your cousin will take action, should he see fit."

I turned to find the source of Richard's distraction. He appeared to be searching the crowds longingly. My eyes scoured the room in search of Charlotte, hoping Richard was doing the same.

"Georgie," John whispered once more, a hint of pleading or displeasure in his voice, I was not sure which.

"However can I call myself a matchmaker if I do not seize the moment?" I asked, my eyes dancing merrily as I turned back to him.

"Are you saying your brother and Elizabeth would not have married had you not interfered?"

I turned to look at the loving couple just as Fitzwilliam placed a hand upon his wife's back and Elizabeth leaned against him ever so slightly. The look they exchanged spoke of the depth of their love.

"I do not doubt my brother would have eventually offered for Elizabeth, but I *am* certain he would have botched it up terribly leading to many miserable months of the two of them searching their feelings; followed by an awkward period where they both wished to speak of their affections, but feared the other did not reciprocate them." I looked at the couple once more before smiling at my fiancé. "I believe I protected them from months of angst and misery by travelling to Hertfordshire when I did." My smile grew and I placed a loving hand upon his arm. "Besides, we may not have met otherwise, and I would have continued to wonder if anyone would ever see me for who I was and love me despite it."

John lowered his head until our foreheads nearly met. "How could I do otherwise, Georgiana Darcy, matchmaker?"

The End

About the Author

Bronwen Chisholm grew up in Central Pennsylvania, the youngest of four sisters. Though she was not introduced to Jane Austen's work until later in life, she grew up reading the Bronte sisters, Gone With the Wind, and other classics as well as watching vintage Hollywood movies. Her love of books and literature could have led her to a career as a librarian. Instead, life and love carried her to Virginia where she took a position as a state employee and began raising her family.

As her children grew and became involved in their own interests, Bronwen returned to her love of the written word. No longer content to simply read it, she began writing. Though the first attempts ended up on a shelf, she would not be discouraged. Finally confident enough to take the step to publish, Bronwen was thrilled with the acceptance of her first offering, The Ball At Meryton: A Pride and Prejudice Alternative Novella.

Her love of writing has led her to several writing groups, including The Virginia Writer's Club, Lake Authors, and James River Writers. She is currently serving as the Vice President of The Riverside Writers.

Bronwen will be working on her women's fiction next, but hopes to return to Regency romance in the near future. For more information, visit her website at www.bronwenchisholm.wordpress.com.